The Left Side Of The Stairs

Julie Egert

Aberdeen Bay

Albion - Beijing - Topeka - Washington, D.C.

Aberdeen Bay
Published by Aberdeen Bay, an imprint of Champion Writers.
www.aberdeenbay.com

PUBLISHER'S NOTE

This is a book of fiction. Names, characters, places, and
incidents are either the product of author's imagination or are
used fictitiously. Any resemblance to actual persons, living or
dead, business establishments, government agencies, events,
or locales is entirely coincidental.

AUTHOR'S NOTE

Many of the settings in this book, such as the Varsity and
Stone Mountain, are real, but used in a fictional context to
capture Atlanta's unique flavor in this story. Some settings,
such as Halloran Park and Club 404, are entirely fictional.

International Standard Book Number
ISBN-13: 978-1-60830-038-9
ISBN-10: 1-60830-038-2

Printed in the United States of America.

Thanks so
much for coming!
Julie Egert

"Always walk in
the middle"

Acknowledgments

So many to mention, so little space, but I'm going to take as much as I want anyway…

First and foremost to God. I can do anything with His help. Things like finally finishing a manuscript.

To my husband Rick, who's my "Paul" and my "Eric" and everything else in between. For all of the formatting… for all of the "is that how you pronounce it…?" moments. For listening to my whining. For crying with me when I accidentally deleted the first forty-nine pages. And for just being wonderful you.

To Claudette Fisher, my "Momma Extraordinaire," who helped inspire the idea in the first place and who has a sharp editorial eye. (Yes, Mom, I will finish the other one…) She's seen her share of "kerfuffles" in life but always manages to come out on the other side.

To my "seester" Jennifer Snare, who in true sister fashion even took pictures of stairs for me. She's the only one who can quote "Some Kind of Wonderful" and "My Cousin Vinny" all the way through with me…also to my nephews Cole Michael and Jonah…thanks for the names kiddos… Love ya too Chad, Mr. Ring Tone…

To Diane and Rick, "Ma and Pa" Egert. You two are incomparable. The lengths you go to for family amazes and inspires me. To the sibs…love ya Jeremy and Jenny… Jeff too...To my Godson Ben, who's got something new and hilarious to do every time I see him, which isn't often enough.

To my Dad, Dale Brasel, just because…

To Aunt Fi Fi and Uncle Joe Cool...WHEN ARE WE CRUISING AGAIN???

To Ellen "Ethel" Northam, my five o'clock gal...There's no way to measure the worth of picking up the phone most every weekday and hearing a fiercely loyal friend's voice.

To my "roomie" Diane Faber, who went through this with me every step of the way...and I mean every step...what else needs to be said except TEAM OF TWO???????

To Miss Sarah, who read the thing on her phone no less. Now that, my friends, is a friend.

To Anne Arthurs, my own personal "literary sniper" and friend who helped shape the story with her input. I'll never forget the day you "saved" me in college...Hey Jim, I gave you your aliens, though in a slightly different context than I think you meant...

To the wonderful Andrea Douglas at Colborne Communications, one of my early cheerleaders and faith-givers. You do indeed write a kickin' evaluation.

To the Empowerment crew. Love ya all, both staff and clients.

To Cecille Mondragon, who lent her own wonderful, unique presence to this book.

Many thanks to Andy Zhang, Jill Cline and Marjorie Schafer for welcoming me into the Aberdeen family and helping to bring this to fruition.

To the ones I've lost. My Gram, Ruth Leverenz...there's no way to sum up such an amazing spirit so I'm not going to try...Grandpa Leverenz, the sweetest man who ever lived. Period. No contest...Grandma Rieches, the original Skip-Bo Queen...Grandpa Rieches and Grandpa Clyde...and my father Joe Bury. We'll have that picnic someday.

And finally, to the "AA's"...you kept me going and re-instilled in me a "never say die" attitude.

The Left Side Of The Stairs

CHAPTER ONE

The reporter watched the cursor blink away on the empty computer screen. It had been taunting her for hours. Finally her fingers started to click out a staccato rhythm on the ancient but willing keyboard. She didn't want to write this story, but she was out of options.

Paragraph one…"Joe Norris died Tuesday, January 10…" *You turned out to be a selfish coward, Joe Norris. At least you died famous, just like you said you would…*

Paragraph two…"Norris was a local contractor and member of various community organizations in Layton…" *Damn you, Joe.*

Paragraph three…"Memorial Services were held…"

She tapped out a few more sentences and printed the document. Finished. Now his entire existence was boiled down to thirteen inches of newsprint, the reality of it all neatly wrapped up.

The reporter shrugged on her coat and bolted out of the newspaper office into the kind of cold that paralyzes. A sense of propriety called for her to stop and lock up, and her shaking hands fumbled to turn the key in the tiny gray building's door. She shivered and yanked the black scarf tightly around her neck, mist from her quick gasps shooting out of her mouth and curling upward into the darkness. Her eyes darted to the bank clock up the street. 1:22 am. The only sound besides the soft swish of the heavy coat against her legs was the chink of the clock as it switched over to display the temperature. *Chink*, Six degrees. *Chink*, 1:23 am.

Each click echoed in the silence, marking time, reminding

her there were decisions to be made. *Chink, what next? Chink, what now?* Damn him.

She crunched through the snow, her kid-sized feet leaving icy imprints as she went. She only made it a few steps before she whirled around and made a beeline back towards the office. Back to the scene of the crime.

Just outside of the door she slid on a patch of ice and wiped out like a failed Olympic skater. Well, maybe she'd just stay here and let the cold and ice seep through her jeans. Someone would find her here in the morning, frostbitten with a dislocated shoulder. The whole town had been asking themselves the question for the past two weeks, anyway: Would she crack? Would she *lose* it?

Bingo, she thought as she glanced up at the star-shot sky. *Lose it would be the correct answer.*

After hauling herself to her feet and making sure all body parts were in working order, she limped to the small bathroom inside and was sick.

The paper's faithful readers would get *the facts.* Everyone in Layton, Indiana knew most of them, anyway: Joe's age, profession, what he liked to do in his spare time. That he had killed himself. But they didn't know him like she did, the way he'd flip three times before he rolled over and fell asleep in bed, or the shape of the scar on his inner thigh. She thought about that as she stretched out on the bathroom floor and stared up at the small water stain on the ceiling.

Things like that jumped out at her now: signs of trouble you had to squint at to see first. The stain was so subtle a person might wonder if they were seeing what they thought they were seeing, or just mistaking a harmless shadow cast on the ceiling for something more ominous. Right now it was a miniscule hole and a tiny leak, little droplets of water letting themselves through. But it could turn into a hell of a mess later on, major water damage over time. After awhile the stain would spread outward and morph into a misshapen brown blob against the white tile and fluorescent lights. Must and rot in a years' time.

The leak had started with a tiny hole in the roof. Joe's problem had started with a hammer.

On a Thursday months ago she'd found Joe toppled over on shards of broken glass, cursing in pain. The hammer had slipped out of his weakened hand. When he'd bent to pick it up, his leg had given out on him and he'd fallen right on top of the picture he was preparing to hang.

The failure of his hand and leg was a subtle sign of the disease taking root in his body, the start of what had led to all of this. *Must and rot...*

Now you understand, Shelby Norris, the reporter told herself. *You ignored subtle warnings of trouble and it led to sitting in an abandoned office and writing your husband out of existence.*

CHAPTER TWO

Miranda Linn was on hour twenty-six of no sleep when she bent low, flipped her hair, and methodically gathered it into a ponytail with her trusty scrunchy hair band. Music from the seedy Atlanta bar known as Club 404 pulsed on the other side of the dingy bathroom door, causing her to pause for a minute and consider hitting a new low point in a dump like this. But she just couldn't wait any longer.

With her hair out of the way she fished for the spoon and package of syringes in her purse, more necessary pieces to an unlikely survival kit. After pulling off the top of the syringe with a small *Pop!* she ran water into it and carefully replaced the plunger. The water she shot onto the spoon slowly seeped outward and transformed the powder into a tiny amber pool.

Her tool of choice for tying off was a thin latex glove. With shaking hands she stretched it around her small arm and pulled it tight enough to make a vein appear. After she flexed her hand a few times one popped up cooperatively, like a blue electrical wire running up her arm. Once she was done pushing the needle in she slumped back and waited for the feeling of calm to roll straight through to her toes.

Miranda remembered watching a kid on one of her favorite shows, *Intervention,* talk about his addiction. She was a big fan of irony. He had explained how drugs had been just like a lover with the way they broke his heart and disappointed him. She'd been surprised at how eloquent he was. He was missing half of his teeth and his cheeks were sunken in, but he spoke like a poet.

Miranda knew all about going back to the bad lover time and again, disappointment and heartbreak or not.

If anybody ever cared to interview Miranda the junkie, she would tell them what used to be about chasing that first high was now about shooting up so she wouldn't feel like shit. It was like staying with a person who was completely wrong for you because you were trying to recapture those first-date butterflies.

She pulled a worn journal out of her purse and put the thought on paper. Like her scrunchy, the journal went with her everywhere. At work, in the car, in a dirty bathroom stall, it didn't matter; if the thought was worth saving she wrote it down.

It had been habit ever since her Mom had given her the very first journal, a way to keep her focused and "channel" herself. Her Mom had always worried about her ending up just like this. The pocket-sized dictionary she pulled out along with it was also a trusty aid in helping her preserve her thoughts, find new words.

Miranda treasured words. They lasted. The journals also served that purpose as of late, a way to get back time lost when she was high. Such an eerie feeling to go back and read about feelings and situations that were lost to her: like experiencing the uneasy sensation a newly-legal twenty-one-year-old gets when they see the pictures of their birthday and note themselves smiling drunkenly into the camera. The moment is frozen in time, right there for them to see, but they can't recall it.

It was only a matter of time before her Mom, Dad and possibly even her ex, Clint, lured her into the room where they would read their letters, cry, and deliver their ultimatums. The way her Mom and Dad would stop talking when she came into the room was a not-so-subtle clue. She'd probably interrupted their rehearsing: *"Miranda, should you choose not to accept treatment today, you will no longer be welcome in my home. I will no longer give you money…I will no longer accept your calls. Please accept this gift of treatment, the opportunity we are offering you today..."*

She didn't know if she'd just walk out or if the sight of them all together would be powerful enough to make her jump on a plane to God knows where for the requisite ninety days of treatment. Her parents and Clint together, holding hands and praying that the intervention would work? Now *that* would be a trip. Her Mom, a new-age type, would probably go in beforehand to make sure the "energy" of the room was right. Would the no-nonsense Jeff VanVonderen, her favorite interventionist on the show, help her Mom burn sage and incense to disperse any lingering negativity?
They would need all of the positive vibes they could get for this one. She pictured her Mom chanting over Clint, trying to cleanse his aura, and let out a mirthful snort.

She scrubbed her hands vigorously before she stepped out of the bathroom. Club 404 was pulsing with people and music. The harsh, edgy notes of the song, sharp barks of laughter and multicolored graffiti on the walls and tables melded together in a discordant, dizzying mix of light and sound.

It was a psychedelic cocktail that would manifest itself in slow motion thanks to the drugs if she didn't get out of here soon. But Miranda ignored her surroundings and they ignored her back. On the street or in a mall her acres of tan skin set off by the white tank top might have drawn appreciative stares, but not here, where everyone was too high or too drunk to notice. She fanned herself, already feeling the humidity generated by the bar, and played with the tiny crystal cross she always wore around her neck. It was a contrast to the oversized hoops in her ears. The glass in the center of the cross magnified the words of the entire Lord's Prayer written inside. The prayer was an interesting detail missed unless you knew to look for it.

He wasn't here yet. The only person who mattered to her right now was Jon, who was always reliably late. *He can't even make an effort when it means money for him.* If he didn't show up what was she going to do about tomorrow?

She despised the dealer but she needed him. As she had

the thought, she spotted his greasy, curly mop of hair and the ratty ten-year-old Garth Brooks T-shirt he always wore.

Jon sauntered up to her and playfully yanked at her mass of blond curls, a familiar gesture she didn't appreciate. "I can always find you by your ponytail," he told her.

She batted his hand away from her hair. "And I can always find you by the nasty T-shirt you never take off."

His genial smile evaporated. "You're becoming a real super-queen bitch, you know that, Miranda? You should be nice to me. I'm the one with your drugs."

"No Jon, you should be nice to me. I'm the one with your money."

She was distracted from insulting him further when she caught a glimpse of trouble barreling through the crowd at Mach speed.

Here come the fireworks, she thought wearily. Trouble wore Doc Martens and a faded red T-shirt and looked like he had absolutely no interest in booze, drugs, or fun at the moment. It wasn't so much Trouble's 6'4 frame but the angry expression he usually wore that caused people to give him a wide berth. A red bandana was tied around Trouble's forehead, as if it were part of some third-rate superhero getup as he swirled in to save the day. He was more nuisance than superhero in her eyes, at least when she was doing things he didn't approve of. At just twenty the superhero was aging, a has-been. His powers seemed to diminish each time he took it upon himself to fly to her aid, weaker after every encounter, succumbing to his own twisted, individualized version of Kryptonite. A slow drain.

"I told you to stay away from her, Jon," Clint Mullen told the shorter, pudgy man, flexing his arms unconsciously. Clint's hair was black underneath the strobe lights of the club, the expression on his face even more so. The hair that swept over one eye left the other one free to glare menacingly at the world.

Jon made a pitiful attempt to puff up. "This little meeting is private. And she always comes to me, thanks to you."

"First of all, Jon, look around you. There are hundreds of people here; it's hardly private. Secondly, I don't care if she comes to you or not. *Walk away.*"

Miranda thought he might lunge and send Jon's face smashing into the concrete floor littered with trash, but he opted instead to cuff him hard on the side of the head and left it at that. There was no contest: As drug dealers went, Jon wasn't very intimidating, a fact he used to his advantage with customers. The dealer's persona was all curly-haired sheepishness, the slacker friend of a younger brother who was aimless but harmless. Someone who would smoke pot with you in your basement and then chat with your Mom and eat her cooking afterwards. He would rave about the meal and charm Mom. Mom would never suspect he was devouring her food due to a case of marijuana-induced "munchies." People felt comfortable coming to him.

Clint was another story. Mom would run away screaming from him.

Now Clint clamped his arm on Miranda's shoulder and hustled her toward the door. "*Three, two, one…*" he muttered, a countdown he always started when he knew she was ready to boil over.

"Take your hands off of me, you asshole! Congratulations on coming to Jesus and continuing on with your twelve steps or whatever's working for you at the moment, but we're not together anymore," she hissed. She twisted away from him and attempted to kick him in the shin. "Somebody get him off of me!" she shrieked for good measure.

"*And she blows…*" he finished with a resigned sigh. He picked her up and hoisted her over his shoulder like a duffel bag, leaving Jon shrugging and everyone else around them laughing. She knew he was probably replaying Jon's words in his brain, even as he hauled her out of the bar: *She always comes to me, thanks to you.*

Miranda had taken her first hit a year ago, thanks to him, as Jon had pointed out. Now he was "recovering" and clearly thought she was drowning. Nearly every day he attempted to cast her a clumsy line and pull her back.

She decided to take advantage of the position and sunk her teeth into Clint's broad shoulder. He almost dropped her, which sent everyone coming through the door into fits of laughter.

"Jesus, Miranda, you're just like a kid, except you *understand* that I'm just trying to help you!" he snarled, taking a minute to gingerly rub his shoulder.

Here it was, the conclusion of another tired scene in their merry-go-round of break-ups and make-ups. "Why do you still care?" she demanded, losing some of her steam. "Why do you keep coming back?"

"Sometimes I wonder," he told her as he pushed a long sigh out. "Just call me a sucker for punishment."

"You've got your own multitude of problems to solve. Worry about yourself and stop trying to solve mine," she muttered petulantly.

"If I get you straightened out, that's one problem to check off my list," he answered mildly, and finally set her down. He kept his hand circled around her wrist, one part command and one part plea to listen.

Those words, too, were part of the familiar scene. Even as she stewed at the well-deserved insult she knew she'd probably slink into their workplace tomorrow, contrite and ready to start over with him again, but the near certainty of that didn't make her feel any more certain about things at all. As if to prove that point to herself, she wrenched free from his grip, stomped on his foot, and sprinted toward her own car.

Clint didn't have time to react before she squealed off into the Atlanta night.

CHAPTER THREE

I'm going to move, Shelby decided, wrapping the cocoon of blankets more tightly around herself. *Someplace south and warm.* She yanked the covers over her face when the cold air in the 110-year-old Victorian house ran its icy fingers down her cheeks. The better climate would be a bonus in addition to the whole escaping her grief and demons bit.

She got up and choked some more Pepto-Bismol down. Her stomach was souring again as she relived the betrayal of typing in the short synopsis of Joe's life. She should have deleted the damn thing line by line, watched the cursor on the screen move backwards, as if not having the obituary down on paper would make it not true. Things were only true in her mind after they went to print.

And final: *Joe Norris, thirty-four years old, Layton resident, preceded in death by his father and mother, survived by his wife Shelby Ann, brother Adam, and sister-in-law Trisha...Died after a brief illness...In lieu of flowers donations may be made to the Muscular Dystrophy Association or the American Foundation for Suicide Prevention.*

Shelby grabbed the comforter and let it trail behind her as she shuffled out of the room. No use. She regarded the sign on the wall, half amused and half annoyed by the clear message left by her mother. Embroidered in blue and edged in white lace, it spelled out the house rule of making your own bed and breakfast. That's exactly what the room looked like: the suite in a Bed and Breakfast, one giant blue and white doily complete with a four-poster antique bed.

She didn't belong here, in this temporary oasis from

her grief. She was in purgatory at her mother's house, a stop on the way to God knows where. But she didn't belong in her own home two streets over anymore, either. This was a problem.

She patted down her hair, felt it sticking out in alarming red spikes and standing at attention. She had a terminal case of fish-hair, she noted. Adam, her brother-in-law, had coined the phrase one day when he had crowed, "Shelb, did you even comb the back of your hair this morning? It looks like a fish sucked on it!"

She had a habit of neglecting the part she couldn't see. She was always done in by the things she couldn't see. Her schizophrenic hair was nothing new. The small diamond stud that glinted in her nose was. One week after the funeral she'd marched into a body art shop and had her nose pierced, something she'd always wanted to do. It probably had something to do with not wasting any more time, fulfilling things on her "life list" since Joe's time had run out. Whatever it was, any shrink would *love* the timing and have that one for breakfast, lunch and dinner.

The sudden death of a loved one usually aged a person but seemed to have the reverse effect on her. No gray hairs or new wrinkles that she'd noticed. She always looked younger than her thirty-two years, but now she could pass for seventeen, if that. A few years ago she'd been able to get in half-price at the movies and had been given kids' menus at restaurants. She would just shrug and grab some crayons to draw on the paper menu before ordering her Jr. hamburger and small fries. "Can I have a soda too, Daddy?" she would ask, and Joe would snicker in response. Waiters either missed the wedding ring on her finger or thought she was a child bride.

Now it looked like she was headed that way again, aging in reverse. Eleven years since she'd been educated, graduated, and liberated from the Journalism department at Purdue University. But now she had the uncertain look of a kid who's been up too many nights, pressured with college applications and trying to decide their entire future in a few weeks' time. She even had on her old Purdue sweatshirt to complete the look.

Shelby restlessly shuffled into the kitchen, poured herself a Sam Adams over ice, and propped her feet up at the kitchen table. Her mother had stocked the fridge with them for her. She could almost see Joe's grimace underneath the dim light, the teasing one he would make every time he watched her get a beer. "For God sakes, put it in a glass that's been in the freezer. But don't water it down with *ice*."

She grabbed her purse from the table, reached in and pulled out the note she had carried around for the past few weeks. There was no need to re-read it, but she skimmed the familiar words anyway: *Know you're going to be angry with me for a long time…You taking care of a sick man is not how I'd prefer for you to remember our marriage…Wish I could write something better to last you…*

Her breathing was ragged but she did not cry as she swirled the beer around in the glass and relived the anguished screams tearing from her throat. She'd thought Joe was sleeping until she'd spotted the pill bottle. She'd started shaking him then, as hard as her four-foot-eight, ninety-five pound frame would let her.

There were only about a million and one more moments left for the invisible fist to slam into her stomach. Last week she'd called Land's End to see about returning an extra large coat she'd ordered for Joe's birthday. The customer service operator had asked her the reason for the return and been truly alarmed when she started to cry. *Whoosh,* there it was again, the invisible fist, sending the air rushing out of her lungs.

And now there was the short column dedicated to his life to remind her that Joe had died famous. Joe's favorite song, "Everybody Dies Famous In A Small Town," looped in her head again.

"You and me, we're gonna die famous, Shelb," he'd laughed after hearing the song for the first time. She was famous these days too, so much that she had taken to hiding out until the office was officially closed for the day. She couldn't deal with the genuinely worried but irritating sidelong glances everywhere she went.

At the office, in the grocery store, even when she was paying her water bill, she heard the unspoken questions: *How did he do it? Did he leave a note? How could she not know what he was planning to do?*

She was fourteen again, with everyone staring at the side of her face after she'd been burned. The steaming hot chili had splattered across her face as her little cousin Tia plowed into her and accidentally sent the bowl flying out of her hands. The next day at school Shelby had scrawled a sign on a piece of notebook paper, tired of being plagued with the questions in gym class. Every time her classmates would look at the mottled red skin on the side of her face and start to form the question, she would wearily flash the message spelled out in bold red marker: "I got burned with hot chili. It was an accident. Yes, it hurts, what do you think? No, I haven't seen doctor about it."

She felt like carrying a sign around now: "No, I had no idea Joe would do this, or else I would have stopped him, what do you think? Yes, he did leave a note, by the way."

Aloe Vera had done the trick for the burn, not a sticky green gel from the drug store but the actual plant broken open, its clear juices applied faithfully to the side of her face every night. Her mother had insisted and it had paid off. Not even a trace of a scar there. For a few months afterwards whenever Shelby was flushed or scrubbed her face she'd notice a slight pink discoloration in the uneven pattern the soup had left on her skin. Then she had stopped looking for it and it had just disappeared.

You could never pinpoint the exact moment these things go away; they just do so gradually that human nature can only allow us to focus on them for a certain period of time. Shelby wondered if this would be the same. Would she wake up one day and realize that the instant grief wasn't there, and wonder when it had started to fade?

*   *   *

Elise Waring sat up in her bedroom and glanced at the clock. 3:30 a.m. The familiar scene was playing itself out a little later than usual tonight: the sound of the refrigerator opening and her daughter sitting at the kitchen table, swirling her beer around in a glass. Then she remembered it was the day before the paper went to print. Shelby would have been shut up in the tiny newspaper office, arranging the layout to make everything fit. She hoped the return to that routine, an old one, would nudge this new one out of existence.

It was frightening to watch the deft, quick motion as the amber liquid whirled around faster and faster, picking up momentum and speeding toward some inevitable, frightening conclusion. A maelstrom of Sam Adams Shelby might get lost in. Elise had even had a dream her daughter was drowning in a swimming-pool-sized glass of the stuff. Shelby tried to grab onto the ice she always put in her drink, use it as a raft, but she kept slipping off of the gleaming white cubes. As the liquid churned around faster and faster and her daughter around with it, Elise could not reach the hand she desperately thrust out. She didn't see Joe in the dream, but she heard that deep, unmistakable voice boom, "Let her swim, Elise."

She'd never forget that voice or the first time she had heard it. Here was this big man who looked like a damned grizzly bear with her child-sized daughter, and his loud voice had bounced off of the walls and almost knocked her over like a boomerang. The grizzly and her daughter had turned out to be a good fit. He had taken care of Shelby, and now Shelby would have to take care of herself. Elise had tried but failed in some ways to teach her daughter how to do that.

Elise had lost her own husband thirteen years before, a piece at a time to cancer. There are lots of lessons mothers want to impart to their daughters, Elise thought. How to survive losing a husband isn't one of them.

She set her feet down on the cold hardwood floor and slipped on a robe, her gray hair falling around her shoulders. Determined, she grabbed the pack of Skip-Bo cards she kept ready on her bedside table. The games were a nightly occurrence now. When Elise would hear her daughter get up she'd grab the pack of cards to rescue Shelby with the distraction. They would play under the dim light in the kitchen, have a beer, and then switch to tea in mugs that read "Skip-Bo Queen."

It was time for another battle to be Skip-Bo Queen in an attempt to make Shelby forget the unforgettable for a little while. *Bam,* there's the twelve I need to finish my pile of cards and I win!

They had this terrible thing in common now, she and her daughter; she should be able to help her. But this was the only thing she knew to do for her.

"You're shuffling, I'm dealing," Elise announced as she stepped into the kitchen. Shelby was staring out of the bay window and clutching the piece of paper that was becoming increasingly worn. Elise knew what was on the piece of paper. Her daughter was definitely in trouble.

"You want a Sam's?" Shelby asked as she grabbed the cards and flipped them absentmindedly between her hands.

"You're getting pretty good at that. You used to not be able to shuffle. I'm just going to start with tea tonight." Elise's eyes flicked to the note. "I worry about you when I come out here and find you with that piece of paper."

"I know, Mom."

"He didn't write it for you to keep it like this."

"Probably not. But in the words of the bitter left-behind, he's not around to argue with me about it."

Elise didn't answer, instead took the cards Shelby handed her and began to deal them into two piles.

"You've been a champ, Mom," Shelby murmured. "But I can't stay here forever. Maybe I'll move back home soon, or out of town altogether. I see him everywhere when I step into that house. There's got to be something else for me to do."

Elise set the first card down on the table. "You'll have to think on that one, Shelby," she said carefully. "In the meantime here's a one to get us started. See what you can make of it," she challenged.

"What we have here, Mom, is the mother of all kerfuffles," Shelby told her, and started to swirl the beer around again. "We used to be able to make just about anything go away with a game of cards. Can't this time."

Elise smiled faintly. "Kerfuffle, indeed. I can't make this right, Shelby, but I'm here."

Elise watched her daughter study the bright blue and red cards in her hand. Joe's card game of choice had been poker. His face had been inscrutable most of the time he was sick, never betraying his worst fears. But he had clearly been plotting his next move all along, planning to die but keeping his cards close to his chest. The master poker player. What was Shelby's next move?

"You know, Mom, I'll probably move back home tomorrow. Might even put the house on the market. Here's a two, by the way," Shelby said as she set her card carefully on top of the one.

CHAPTER FOUR

Miranda placed the paper hat on her head and prepared to put on some fake attitude for customers for the next four hours. When you were subject to regular lifestyle and chemically-induced headaches it was probably not wise to stick with employment that required you and countless other coworkers to demand orders at the top of your voice. She worked at The Varsity, a Drive-In whose menu was home to at least one culinary must-have for most Atlantans.

It felt to Miranda like working inside of a very oversized, nostalgic jukebox. She was expected to put up an exasperated façade behind the counter and yodel out "What'll ya have?" in greeting to the customers. In theory this would make people smile at the not-so-subtle reminder to hurry up with their orders and money.

The Varsity's way of treating its customers was a nod to the frisky impatience displayed by the Drive-In employees of yesteryear. She was supposed to be rude but somehow charming. Rude she could handle, so on second thought, maybe this *was* the job for her. She could get away with demanding that people hurry up and order when she came in with her head throbbing and her entire body starting to pulse from lack of sleep.

She glanced over at Clint, who was busy tossing a chili dog, ring one and bag of rags onto a tray. Lingo for the food was part of the gimmick here too. She and Clint had met here a year ago and he had asked her out insistently. She'd relented. Then he'd asked her if she wanted to shoot up with him. She'd relented. Now he was clean and insisted she get clean too. She hadn't relented.

He was still angry with her about last night, and hell-bent on yanking her out of a lifestyle he'd inadvertently helped her create. So it went: He wouldn't stop until she quit and she wouldn't stop, period. An impossible game of chicken was being played and nobody would blink or swerve first.

A woman with a pleasantly creased face and a slightly blue-tinged Grandma perm stepped up to the counter with a serious-looking young girl. "What'll ya have? So Miss Ruth and Miss Chelsea, think old Victor's going to be killed off of *Days*?" Miranda asked gravely. She didn't wait for their order. The two always ordered chili dogs and Cherry Cokes and watched *Days Of Our Lives* in one of the restaurant's TV rooms.

"Darling, it shot my day to read about that in *Soap Opera Tattler*. Won't happen though," the woman sniffed. "Will it, Chels? But even if they do they'll bring him back somehow. If they could bring Bobby back on *Dallas* the way they did with such a weak explanation they won't have any trouble doing it on *Days* with my Victor. They can't *possibly* carry on without him. All of the young ones on there now are too pretty; he and Stephano are the only real male appeal left on the show. Either of them could put their slippers under my bed any time."

She shared a quick, conspiratorial glance with her granddaughter. "As far as your mother's concerned we only watch educational programming. So forget Grandma said that."

"Grandma, I won't forget because you say it all the time," the girl reminded the old woman. "How come you never sit with us any more, Miranda?"

"I'll try to make it in a little early tomorrow," Miranda told her apologetically. She was unprepared for the little girl's question and didn't know how else to answer. Why, indeed. Sometimes when Miranda arrived a few minutes early for her shift she would head for one of the restaurant's TV rooms. If the girl and her grandmother were already there she would slip in beside them and watch ridiculous plots unfold as the afternoon light filtered in and hungry customers devoured their lunches.

She hadn't done that in months, joined them for a deliciously absurd afternoon escape. She hadn't been out to Stone Mountain, either, to sit on top of the huge mass of granite and stare at the city from a distance. She thought vaguely that this was what it was like to lose your life a piece at a time, giving up the comforting little details one by one until you didn't recognize it anymore.

She handed them their chili dogs and Cherry Cokes and turned her attention back to Clint. He would continue tossing orders on trays for a few more hours until he left for job two as an electrician's apprentice. After work she would finish up a paper due for an English Lit class and then head back to Club 404 in search of Jon and more drugs. After job two Clint would probably come and find her and the tired argument would play itself out again.

Someone was going to have to swerve.

Clint came up behind her while she was pouring another drink. She watched it fizz over the top of the cup in an attempt to ignore him and the lecture she knew was coming.

"You're never late, and you never screw up an order," he began. "Even when you've been up half of the night, even when you come in still high. You churn out half of the damn papers for your Lit class when you're cycling up or coming down from something. You think you're making it, that you can keep a step ahead? That you're doing well enough because you somehow get from point A to point B?"

"Wow, you have really learned how to talk the talk in those meetings of yours," Miranda told him dryly. She moved to the fryer and pulled some onion rings out. "You really want to have this conversation *here?* But if you must know, that's exactly what I think: I'm doing well enough. Besides, there's no mortal danger in typing while intoxicated. Ever hear of Lewis Carroll? He clearly wrote *Alice in Wonderland* while he was whacked out on God knows what. I'm just enhancing my creativity."

He didn't laugh at the joke, just stared at her thoughtfully while she hooked another fryer basket in place. "There's no problem since you haven't hurt anybody yet, right? The girl who skipped a grade in school is smart enough to handle it? *You* don't even believe your bullshit."

He had come a little too close to the truth. Clint was more shrewd than most gave him credit for. "That's me, the functioning genius junkie with a one sixty IQ," she agreed brightly.

Clint's only response was to toss an order onto a tray a little too hard, slightly smashing the chili dog.

*   *   *

Six hours later Miranda snagged a seat in the back of the auditorium, the better to beat it out of there to 404 when the lecture was done. One hundred and twenty minutes to go. She was properly medicated for the class; God knew she needed to be high to get through two hours of Professor Montoya's professing his love for himself.

Montoya's groupies were all positioned up front, ready to fawn over his CZ earring and worldly academic experience. Halfway through the lecture his baritone voice faded into something like a tuba playing. She zoned out but jumped up when everyone else did, tossing her paper on the table as she left. Off to 404. Jon had better be there.

On the way out Montoya handed her the last paper she had turned in. "Nice job," he told her.

She had finished it up ten minutes before class, almost loving her usual game of beat the clock. *Tick, tock,* how clever is Miranda? What can she do in this last ten minutes to net herself an A?

Things were still moving in slow motion when she turned the key in the ignition of her white VW Bug. Driving while high was not on her self-imposed list of boundaries. She was a terrible driver. Wasn't there some joke about a klutzy person walking in a straight line when they were drunk?

At least she drove the speed limit when she was high, rather than her unimpaired Kamikaze style of driving that made even her usually serene Mom scream obscenities at critical moments. She continued out of the parking lot at a respectable, law-abiding rate of speed.

It wasn't she who made the mistake. Miranda watched it unfold in slow motion as the state trooper three cars back flipped on his lights and raced up behind the red pickup in the next lane. Obviously startled, the pickup's driver attempted to get out of the trooper's way and let him pass. Unfortunately the pickup swerved right into her lane.

Miranda cursed and yanked her wheel to the right in an attempt to avoid being sideswiped, but still heard the metallic scrape of the vehicles against each other. Then she felt the jerk as her VW jumped over the curb.

She thought the pickup might speed up and continue on, never to be seen again, but it slowed and pulled into the next lot. Amazingly, it was the trooper who disappeared without a backward glance.

Miranda gripped the wheel and fought for air, instantly jarred out of her chemical reverie. She didn't know whether being sideswiped or fear of the trooper stopping her had her gasping. She just stared as the spindly, grandfatherly looking man hurried toward her car. He took off his dirty ball cap, mopped his forehead, and ran his fingers through his sparse white hair as he tried to collect himself. She rolled her window down slowly.

"Damn, Missy, I just didn't see ya," he burst out. "Trying to get out of that trooper's way, just an automatic reaction when he flipped his lights. You okay?"

Miranda nodded mutely and then made her legs work enough to get out of the car. "Are you okay, sir? You remind me of my grandfather," she told him dumbly.

He smiled at this. "I hope your granddad never ran you offa the road. Side of your car got scraped up pretty bad," he noted apologetically, running his fingers along the VW. "I've got insurance. You wanna call the police and have 'em come so we can file an accident report?"

"No, that's okay," she said a little too sharply. "We can just exchange information. You seem like the trustworthy type," she supplied quickly to counteract the sting of her tone. "My car's drivable and I'm fine."

"I think we should, Missy. I'll take responsibility, you know. I shoulda looked into your lane, it all just happened so fast."

"I know. I was so scared..." Miranda didn't finish the thought, how she had been sure that the trooper was coming after her and would know to test her for drugs.

"Well of course you were scared, Missy. I sent you over the curb."

Miranda felt the fear seep through her eyes and fell against the man, sobbing. "Maybe Clint's right," she babbled. "I tell myself I can stay a step ahead, but even I don't believe my bullshit."

Even as she imagined one day smashing into a grandpa type like this one, the accident being her fault next time, she knew she'd still head for 404 after this. "I'll never learn," she told the elderly man now.

"There, now." The old man patted her awkwardly as she burst into a fresh round of tears. "No sense getting upset over a little bump and scrape."

CHAPTER FIVE

It was unseasonably warm for February as Shelby sat on the wraparound porch and pushed the swing back and forth with her feet. She and Joe had bought the Gingerbread Victorian five years ago. Now it was just a house with her carpenter-husband's fingerprints all over it.

She allowed herself to smile as she caught an image of him jumping out of the shower, dripping wet, excited about an idea he had for intersecting oak beams in the living room ceiling. There in the middle of the kitchen, the water pooling onto the floor with nothing but a small white towel wrapped around his huge body, he had exclaimed, "I'm a genius!"

The built-in wooden toilet tissue dispenser in the bathroom: Joe. The tin ceiling in the dining room: Joe. The stripped, refinished pocket doors separating the dining and living rooms, Joe. She'd been back a month but it hadn't taken her that long to realize the house could never be just hers.

She didn't recognize the blue Toyota or the tall, gangly man who stepped out of it in front of the house. A truck pulled up behind the Toyota, and a man as short and squat as the first one was tall and thin hopped out and ambled up the sidewalk.

"Can I help you?" she asked warily.

"Yes you can, if you're Shelby Norris," the tall, thin one responded. "Looks like the address we're supposed to deliver to, 802 Grogan." He had a questioning look on his face, as if he wasn't quite sure he was supposed to be doing this.

"I am Shelby Norris. A delivery?"

"Well, ma'am, I'm Ron Smith and this is Alan. We're with Ewing Toyota over in Reardon. This is unusual for us to say the least, but we're here to drop off a car that was purchased by Joe Norris a few months ago. He made arrangements for us to deliver it here, and asked that we give you several copies of the keys as well." The man held out his hand to her, revealing four gleaming keys.

"But I don't drive," Shelby protested, snatching the keys. "My husband knows I don't drive." She was still having trouble speaking about Joe in past tense.

"Looks like he wants you to start. I'd say a brand new car is some incentive. Here's the title, Mrs. Norris. All paid for. You enjoy your car, and I'd be thanking that husband of yours. Seems like he looks out for you, right down to having those keys made since, as he put it, 'my wife has a tendency to lose things.' " Ron started to shift uncomfortably now.

Shelby nodded mutely. *I have a tendency to lose things.*

"Well, ma'am, enjoy your car," he repeated awkwardly. She watched the two men get in the pickup and drive off without another word.

She inspected the car carefully, inhaled deeply for the prized scent of new upholstery. *That was the smell of freedom,* at least for most people. Would she use the car enough that someday there would be coffee stains on the flawless gray material, food wrappers and tissues shoved in the glove box and side compartments?

She froze when she found the tiny gold earrings, peace symbols, inside the glove box. She had admired them only once and as far as she knew Joe hadn't known a thing about them. He had beaten it out of department store in the mall that day, muttering something about the food court. He'd probably ducked behind a sales rack to see what caught her interest, or come back to ask the sales lady what the small redhead had been looking at.

She drew in a sigh and put the earrings in. That was quintessential Joe: always taking in more than she knew, saving the information for a later date. No note, but the unspoken directive was clear: *I'm not around to get you where you need to go anymore. You'll have to do it yourself.*

Panic gripped her as she sat behind the wheel of the Toyota a few minutes later. Beads of sweat dotted her forehead, and she could feel her heart rate picking up.

"What's wrong with you? It's just around town, you've lived here all of your life," she muttered. She glanced around suspiciously. Was Janet watching? She remembered the day she'd caught the woman wandering around their backyard.

"Just wanted to check on the gazebo Joe was building and see how it was coming along," the short, round Janet had declared cheerfully, waddling back into her own yard unembarrassed.

That was all she needed, to have Janet catch her sitting here and talking to herself. Confirmation of her mental decline would reach Layton's favorite hangout, the local diner, by early evening.

Shelby had grown up understanding the small-town sense of entitlement to knowing neighbors' affairs. It was mostly a comfort to be surrounded by people who knew your history, were interested in your day-to-day comings and goings. Sometimes a little too interested. But she didn't feel that way now. *Everybody dies famous…*

She finally turned the key in the ignition, which officially sent her heart galloping, and put the car in drive. Left on Holland, past the library. Now onto Fay, past the Diner. She thought she could feel the fissures and cracks forming in her teeth from clenching her jaw together.

The Golden Retriever came zipping out of nowhere. Shelby slammed on the brakes and the car screeched to a halt right in front of him. The dog, running at top speed with its tongue lolling out of the side of his mouth, happily continued after the squirrel he was targeting like a yellow, furry missile. She was still panting when she rolled down the window.

"Stupid mutt!" she bellowed after the dog, which was already sprinting past the Little Angels resale shop.

Luckily there were no cars behind her as she sat there

in the middle of the street, her foot pressed down as far as it would go on the brake.

Years of praying she'd never be asked to repeat the driving portion of the test when her license was up for renewal came down to this: sitting in the middle of Fay and fighting off a full-blown panic attack because a dog had run out in front of her. At sixteen she'd suffered a typical teenage mishap, and she could still hear her friend's scream and the squeal of the brakes. Everyone had been fine but not once had she attempted to get back behind the wheel of a car. *If I can't get past that how am I going to get past losing my husband?* She swore and slowly pulled a U-turn, deciding a piece of pie at the Diner was in order.

Shelby blew out a sigh of relief as she pulled up to the nondescript brick building on Layton's main drag, known simply as the Diner by everyone in town. Fliers were plastered in its front window like multicolored Post-It notes: *Layton Old Home Festival...Live music in the park...Layton High School's production of Neil Simon's "Fools."*

The hardwood floor and vintage signs said less about a carefully thought out old-fashioned diner effect than its owner's love for antique swap meets. Early pictures of the town graced the walls. An antique clock, a grinning black cat whose eyes and tail twitched back and forth with the ticking away of each minute, greeted patrons as they walked in. It was positioned next to a chalkboard advertising the specials. "Trish's Killer Key Lime Pie" and the Friday night fish plate were on tap for today.

As she listened to dishes clink and the murmur of conversation, Shelby imagined a large coffee can occupying a space by the cash register with a picture of Joe's face taped on it, donations to help out once his body had failed him completely. The idea would have disgusted him, but that's exactly what Trish, meaning well, would have done if Joe had let things go that far.

Shelby waved down the tall, slim woman with corkscrews of red hair escaping from a loosely tied bun. "Piece of key lime, Trish, and let's plop some extra whipped cream on top of the extra whipped cream if you could." She drew in a deep, appreciative sigh as she ran her fingers along the bright yellow booth's scratchy upholstery. Things she'd had no business taking for granted had been yanked away from her; at least she could still count on the cartoonish clock on the wall to tick away the minutes, and the unfailing combination of sweet and tart in Trish's key lime pie.

Shelby watched the uncertain look spread across Trish Norris' face, and she could almost hear the woman's internal debate happening.

"Trish, just bring me the damn pie, okay? And don't skimp on the whipped cream."

Trish yielded with a sigh. "Do you want some coffee with that?"

"Some coffee with my cream and sweetener, please." Shelby reiterated their tired joke with an equally tired smile. She took a pen out of her purse and doodled some palm trees absentmindedly on the paper place mat, like a child. The Friday night fish fry was just beginning and she decided on a fish plate, warming to the idea of dessert before dinner as the smell of deep-fried things floated over. Why do things in their proper order?

"Trish, might as well make it a meal. I'll have some fish too. By the way, where's Adam?" she asked, in an attempt to sidetrack the woman from any further mothering.

Trish's eyes settled on the last of the pie that Shelby was enthusiastically forking into her mouth. "He's in the back, taking inventory. Honey, have you taken your insulin yet?"

"Going to right now, mother," Shelby muttered. "Want to come in the bathroom with me and make sure?"

"Not your mother, just a concerned sister-in-law," Trish responded mildly, exhaling a stream of smoke from her cigarette. "I want to keep you healthy."

Shelby wanted to point out the obvious hypocrisy but thought better of it. Once she was in the bathroom she resentfully drew up the insulin and watched the clear liquid seep into the syringe. After swabbing her skin with alcohol she let the needle hover for a moment before she reluctantly pushed it in.

"*You're diabetic? I could never push a needle into myself multiple times a day, I just couldn't,*" people were always telling her, horrified, as if she had a choice in the matter.

"Oh, you'd be alright with it in a damn hurry, if it meant the difference between living and dying." Her stock response. These days, though, she had to admit that it seemed like a lot of trouble to go to.

When Shelby slid back into the booth, a plate of fish was waiting for her. She forked in the fish and coleslaw and noticed, with dread, that her boss Leo was there for his usual Friday Night Texas Hold 'Em stint.

Leo McDaniels had assumed various roles throughout the years: boss, savior, surrogate Dad. Now Joe's death had made him a stranger. He seemed to watch her suspiciously these days, waiting for the other shoe to drop, for the impending crack-up. He was tipped back casually in a chair and sported his usual chili pepper tie and hat, his steel-gray curls peeking out underneath. This was the ripple effect of losing Joe: she had lost Leo, too, at least the easy rapport they used to share.

"Shelb!" he called. "Come over here, I gotta run something by you."

Shelby dutifully trotted over to his side. "Where's Jonah?" she asked warily. Jonah was the only other member of the Layton News crew, and Leo and Jonah never missed sitting in on the Friday night tournament. She wasn't ready for a full ambush yet.

Leo waved his hand dismissively. "He'll be along. So, I thought this'd make a great slogan for the paper: *Layton News, the only paper solely devoted to the Layton community.* Whatya think?"

"Leo, what other paper would be?" she asked, the corner of her mouth automatically tipping up. Maybe she'd given Leo too little credit. Maybe still knew how to be himself around her. "Suit yourself, you marketing genius," she told him, and squeezed him with a grateful half-hug. "I'm going to finish my dinner."

When Shelby sat back down, Trish was waiting for her. She had abandoned her crusade for the moment and watched Shelby finish the fish without comment. Adam joined them a few minutes later and snaked his arm Trish's shoulder. He had his brother's height, but otherwise the two men were opposite sides of a coin. Adam was lanky where Joe was bulky, his voice smooth and refined where Joe's had always sounded as if it was catching or snagging on something.

"You're never going to believe this one," Shelby told them. "I had a car delivered today. Seems Joe's full of surprises, even after he's gone. He bought me a little blue Toyota."

Adam stared at her, then shifted his gaze toward the window. "That's your car out front then?"

"That would be my car out front then."

"So—how'd it feel driving it?" Adam asked, an odd mixture of curiosity and concern in his voice.

"Strange."

"Give it time," he told her, his tone neutral now.

"We want you to come over for dinner soon, okay?" Trish finally pressed, already tapping out a new cigarette from her pack.

"Soon, I promise. You know, you should really quit the cigarettes if you guys are serious about trying for a baby." It felt good to turn the tables and lecture Trish. "Finally you'll have someplace to channel those maternal instincts."

Now Shelby started to feel several sets of curious eyes on her. Conversation hadn't stopped when she stepped inside, and no heads had swiveled around to stare at her, but she could still feel them. *How was she holding up?*

Suddenly getting behind the wheel of a car didn't seem so bad. She dropped a hasty kiss on Trish's head and nearly sprinted outside.

Shelby jumped in the Toyota and hit the gas a little too

hard. "Shit!" she swore as the car lurched forward. She eased her foot off of the gas and drove at a crawl for the rest of the two-minute journey home.

The long, drawn-out "beep" of a message was concluding and the eerie glow of the red light blinking on the answering machine when she opened the door. "You...have...one...new...message..." the deep, robotic male voice informed her after she stabbed her finger down on the button.

"Good afternoon, this message is for Shelby Norris," a crisp, brisk female voice said in greeting. "This is Maura Thomas with *Atlanta Minute*. I received your resume and enjoyed some of the clips you sent. You seem to have a knack for capturing the flavor of a place. Atlanta's a different town with a different flavor, to be sure, but maybe it would be a good fit. Let's schedule a time for you to come in and talk about the position."

The voice was confident, commanding her to travel hundreds of miles for an interview. Shelby sank to the floor, drew in a breath, exhaled.

Joe was responsible for this, but how? Newspapers didn't wait weeks before they called someone for an interview. She stayed there, propped up against the wall for a full hour, before she went and poured herself a beer, over ice, and finished half of it.

After swirling the amber liquid around for a minute she reached back and sent the glass smashing against the wall.

"You really thought all of this out, didn't you, you bastard? It must have taken some mighty careful planning. If you wanted to help me, you might have stuck around and fought," she spat out.

A satisfied smile spread across her face as she watched what was left of the beer ooze in rivulets down the lovingly papered wall. After a few minutes she hauled herself to her feet. Smart...she had just broken one of *her* favorite glasses.

"Real original. A glass against the wall," she muttered. Her eyes traveled around for something of Joe's to smash, but she gave up with a sigh. *Typical side effect of petty rage. I wanted to punish Joe but ended up breaking something of mine first.*

She carefully swept up the shards of glass. Why in God's name had he chosen Atlanta? Then she remembered the online quiz they had taken for fun: "Which city are you?"

Fifteen questions later, she'd been Atlanta. Joe had even printed out the quiz for her.

"How in the hell long were you planning all of this, Joe?" she whispered into the darkness, and played message back again.

CHAPTER SIX

Miranda stepped into her parents' living room, resigned. She had, after all, seen this one coming. The man who was sitting there didn't have the fatherly, authoritative look she would have expected. He was young, so freshly scrubbed she could practically see herself in his face; he wore chinos and a baby blue dress shirt. It would be better if he looked more battle-scarred and world-weary.

Someone should definitely be an ex-addict to do a job like this. An ex-addict would really know what they were talking about since they had lived their own version of the life they would ask her leave behind. *Go to treatment.* If it was that simple this stranger wouldn't have a job begging people to do it.

Intervention, she thought. *Noun. The insertion of oneself into the affairs of others, or by one country in the matters of another. Interventionist, noun. One who practices the art of or prefers intervention.*

She felt like a small country no one else knew much about, with secrets and customs that could not be easily understood. She was making trouble for the rest of the world around her. Her ideas did not make sense so an outsider had come to invade, insinuate himself before the situation got worse.

Mr. Chinos looked maybe six, seven years older than she was. She certainly doubted he'd been wrestling with a meth habit for fifteen years. Unless he'd started at twelve.

What would you prefer, Miranda, someone with a pockmarked face and loads of tattoos? Someone who wears his story on his face? Is that what all addicts look like? Is that how you look?

"You're not Jeff VanVonderen," she told him. She did a slow 360, taking in the faces of her parents and her Aunt Viv. Viv was her mother's twin so it was like facing her mother twice, almost. Her cousin Arli, Viv's daughter. They had grown up together but she didn't see much of Arli these days.

And Clint. She was more shocked about her parents letting Clint into the house than anything else about the scene. *A show of solidarity, isn't that the first rule of an intervention? Everybody comes together for the sake of the addict whether they like each other or not.*

"You guys let me down. You didn't call the A&E channel? No camera crews?" she asked, feigning disappointment, not quite pulling off the humor she tried for. Visions she'd conjured up that night in the bar, her Mom chanting over Clint and trying to get him to release his inner demons, returned. She resisted the wild urge to laugh.

"Two things," she addressed Mr. Chinos. "What's your name, and were you an addict?"

She had to hone in on him. If she didn't focus on Chino Boy she would have to look at her parents and Clint. If she did that right now, she wasn't sure she'd stay. And she wanted to see how the scene she'd started in her head would play out in real life. She owed them that, at least.

"David, and yes," he told her neutrally.

"Well, I guess that earns you a point or two there, David." Miranda folded her arms and stared him down.

"Thank you, Miranda. But this isn't about earning points. Or me. It's about you. Are you ready to do this?" No nonsense, just like Jeff would be.

"Mom, I suppose you'll want to read your letter first?" Miranda hated herself for the sarcasm but couldn't let go of it. She was too nervous, this was all wrong, she wasn't ready.

David took control. "Miranda, please let them say what's on their mind, and then you can say what's on your mind."

"Wow," said Miranda. "Spoken just like Jeff. You are a

hard-ass interventionist in training."

Her Mom rose before David had a chance to say anything further and looked her in the eye. "I don't have a letter. I don't need to read from a list of bulletin points to let my daughter know how I feel."

Chilly, the way her Mom had used the phrase "my daughter." There she stood, Mother Earth personified in one of her loose, flowing skirts, but with an uncharacteristic steely edge to her voice. As if Miranda was now a stranger.

Is that how they all saw her? No amount of *Intervention* episodes or mental run-throughs of the scene could have prepared her for the way *that* felt. She already felt the heat of shame creeping up her neck, the urge to run, and they hadn't even started with the "tough love" yet.

"Miranda, you know I think you're a complicated, stubborn, beautiful, astonishing person," her Mom continued. "You have too many gifts to count. The world needs you. We need you. Get help."

"Actually Mom, that does sound like a list of bulletin points," Miranda pointed out.

When David started to speak again, she held up her hand and cut him off. "Don't bother. I'll sit down and listen to the rest without interrupting."

She flopped into a worn, floral chair that had been in the living room forever. Growing up she had slouched down sideways in it almost every day, hooking her legs over the armrest while she read a book or worked on a story of her own. Now she sat up straight, at attention. Silent but on the defensive. Miranda wished she could step outside of herself and watch. Her own expression probably mimicked the sullen one she had seen countless times in the faces of the addicts on TV. Now she was she that selfish, unlikable person with the unrepentant glare.

"...Will not take your calls. You will no longer be welcome in our home." There they were, the conditions. Her Mom was plowing through this part mechanically, forcing the words out.

This was where most of the people in the documentaries got pissed off and left, hurt at what they perceived to be the exact opposite of unconditional love. She'd never seen the guest of honor at an Intervention yet that took well to loved ones admitting that the addict was too much of a problem to deal with in their current state. That the person in question was, in a way, toxic.

Was she toxic?

Her Dad was next. He looked vulnerable with a little more gray in his hair and the lines around his mouth etched in just a little more deeply. She didn't want to think about doing that to him.

"I'm not going to bring up stories and memories from your childhood to try and make you cry," he announced. "You're my daughter, you were there and you know them all. It would be nice to have you back so we can make some new ones." His voice caught in his throat but he managed his piece without tears.

Viv did cry, and did bring up stories from her childhood. She hiccuped out her laughter as she recalled her niece showing up at her door one day with a suitcase bigger than eight-year-old Miranda was. The girl had drug it down the street after a fight with her parents. Clasping the suitcase's handle in one hand and holding a leash attached to a very large Golden Retriever in the other, Miranda had announced grimly, "Flower and I are movin' in, Aunt Viv You won't even know I'm here. Flower, you might notice."

Arli was close on Viv's heels with some cousins-in-trouble stories that evoked more teary laughter. Miranda had hopped on her older cousin's scooter one day and made it exactly six feet before swerving into the side of her uncle's truck. The scooter's side mirror had dangled sadly off of the scooter by the time Miranda managed to stop it, and worse yet, the prized Chevy had a dent in it. Arli had taken the rap.

"You're still a terrible driver, Pseudo-Twin," Arli told her. Her cousin's features and wild hair, curls every which way, closely echoed Miranda's. It was a genetic side effect of their mothers being twins. People were always asking if the girls were twins, and they had long since dubbed each other "Pseudo-Twin". They shared looks, mannerisms, habits.

Not all of the same habits, Miranda thought sourly. Arli hung out with Miranda and Clint on occasion and had even experimented some with them, but she'd never gotten hooked. Was it some genetic flaw or personality defect that separated her from someone so similar, made it possible for her cousin to walk away while she could not? Something just a little more crooked in her DNA strands that were so like Arli's? Miranda wanted to tell her she'd gotten lucky and could easily be the one sitting here, but she decided to skip the rancor.

That left Clint…

"Miranda," he said hoarsely. "You know I'd do anything for you. This is the one thing I should do for you. Get help and I'll hold your hand every step of the way. You know I will. I'm sorry I ever opened up this door for you. I wish I could close it. All I can do is try and help you now."

At that moment a bright yellow and red cuckoo, another staple from her childhood, emerged from the clock on the wall and hooted four times. After it finished she watched the vibrantly painted bird retreat back into its hiding place for another hour. Lucky bird. She thought about the hooting breaking up Clint's monologue and almost laughed again.

"Good tension breaker, don't you think?" Miranda asked.

"What's it going to be, Miranda?" David stared her down. So he was going to take a hard line all the way through and not leave room for discussion. Results-oriented, just say yes or no and we're finished here.

"So where's the treatment center you all have picked out for me?" she asked without emotion.

"Everyone in this room knows you well enough to know that wouldn't be the way to go about this, Miranda," David told her. "I've got a couple of places we can discuss. Once you've found out about them you can choose."

"Well that's good to know," Miranda told him with false warmth. "An interesting strategy, respecting my individuality and all. Kind of like asking an inmate which prison they'd like. Some might be better than others, but in the end there's still no choice. They have to go no matter what."

"It's your decision whether to go or not," David said blandly.

"If you've learned so much about me, David, you know that I'm big into words, definitions. Here's one for you: *Ultimatum.* Noun. A last demand issued by one group of two engaged in negotiations, often done with force from the party issuing the ultimatum. Does that sound like I'm the one making the decision to you?"

"You're way too smart to continue on like this, Miranda. You don't want to choose this kind of life over people who love you. You don't want to be alone with regrets years from now, having accomplished nothing when you can do anything. If you even make it to years from now. I threw my family away for a long time. Don't do it."

David leaned forward intensely with those last three words, as if he were begging her and instructing her at the same time.

"Aren't they throwing me away? 'Make any more bad choices, and you're gone.' A pretty big condition for staying in their lives. How did you feel when the people you love most told you to change yourself or get out?"

She was still having trouble looking at her family and Clint. She especially despised herself now, couldn't believe she would spew out the same argument she had heard a thousand times before from others like her.

"It felt like shit," David told her. "But I know now they were doing what they had to do. Your family's not asking you to be perfect but they're asking you to try. Actually it's the most unconditional love they can show you, because they're willing to risk everything to see you get help."

I know that, she thought, finally taking a long look at each face. She settled on Clint's last and wished she hadn't. An expression like that, devastated, should change your mind. She wanted it to, so why was she still backing out of the room?

"I'd rather disappoint you all now instead of later," Miranda declared.

Three more paces and she was out of the door. An act of mercy, she thought as she closed it. She was tired of infecting everyone around her, having them share in her misery. No more giving them a reason to hope while she tried and backslid; it would be like passing a cold or the flu back and forth for months. Best just to invoke a personal quarantine for awhile, keep them away from the sickness. She ignored Clint's calls after her as she climbed in her VW and sped off.

Once she was out of sight, Miranda drove aimlessly. Where to go now? *My friends will be my family now,* she thought sourly. Maybe she could stay with her friend Cora, who paid extra money for a single dorm room. No roommates to object to Miranda hanging out there. That could last for a few days until some over-vigilant resident counselor caught on.

I've got no right to curse Mom and Dad or Clint for this, she thought wearily. *Wasn't I really the one rejecting them?* She pulled into a gas station and sat there, her hands hovering over the steering wheel.

For the first time in nineteen years she had to think about where she would sleep. It was a lonely feeling that didn't have to be, all she had to do was say *Yes.* If only it was that easy. She started to dial Cora's number, then put her head down on the steering wheel and began to cry. Her hand accidentally tripped the button for the windshield wipers and they began to swish back and forth in earnest, as if to sweep away any self-indulgence on her part.

"Fine," she muttered resolutely, wiping her eyes. She flipped her cell open and dialed up Cora.

*   *   *

Clint paced in the Linns' home, simmering. After the little white car had torn off he was ready to hop in his jeep and speed after it. It was unconscious habit now, running after Miranda. He didn't know how not to do it.

The voice had stopped him. "Let her go, Clint. Remember what we all talked about."

He'd turned around and saw David casually gathering up pamphlets for different treatment centers. They hadn't made it far enough to discuss the details of each place with Miranda. The sight of the man slowly gathering his things, unfazed by what had just happened, infuriated Clint.

"You know, maybe this is all in a day's work to you, but has it escaped your attention that this was pretty much a failure? Why were you even *here*?" he asked derisively.

"She wants to say yes, and I believe she will," David responded calmly.

"Really? How the hell do you know that? That girl that just took off is my best friend, and I sure wasn't getting that from her."

"You asked me why I was here. That's why I'm here. I have experience with this. I feel she is genuinely afraid of letting you all down and therefore afraid to try at all. I know it sounds harsh to say that she needs to be taught that addiction will be a lonely road for her, but that's what you all need to do. Remember, you have to force her to make a choice and trust she'll make the right one."

"Thank you, David. I hope you're right about my daughter," Eileen Linn said softly.

"Thank you for being here, David." Jim Linn rose and finally spoke, the only thing he had said since his short speech to Miranda. He shook hands with the man who certainly looked like something closer to what the Linns wanted for their daughter. Scrubbed and clipped, not some formerly incarcerated kid. And yet David was an Interventionist and former addict, not some suitor there ready to take Miranda out on a date. Jim probably regretted that, Clint thought bitterly. He knew he'd only been welcome as long as it took to finish this little scene and left the house without saying a word. He wanted desperately to find Miranda and wasn't sure yet if he could take David's advice to *let her go.*

CHAPTER SEVEN

"Ding dong, wine's here," Shelby called as she rapped on the screen door of Adam and Trish's house. It was time to follow through with the dreaded dinner invitation.

The uncharacteristic orderliness and perfection was suspicious, and Shelby surveyed the tidiness warily. The porch was freshly painted and swept, a change from the usual disarray, paint peeling off as if it was trying to shed its old skin. Large stucco pots were positioned just so, ready to be filled to overflowing with pink geraniums or some other cheerful flower when the season arrived. New wicker furniture, also perfectly spaced apart, faced the street. Had an "Extreme Home Makeover" crew been alerted to the sorry state of the house and swept in to spruce it up?

Trish materialized in a green dress and took the bottle of Chardonnay from Shelby's hands. "Great!" she declared cheerfully. "Something that's in a bottle instead of a box!" Emerald-colored earrings dangled from her ears, and a thin chain with a single pearl drop accentuated the graceful curve of her neck. Her hair was pulled in and tamed into a smooth chignon rather than tied up in its usual hasty knot.

"Well look who's all gorgeous and domestic," Shelby commented as Trish ushered her into the living room. "When did you do all of that to the porch?"

"Just yesterday. I've been cleaning like crazy. I even double-mopped the kitchen floor." Trish uncorked the wine with a decisive *Pop!* and poured them both a glass. "I'm thinking about hanging ferns up on the porch this summer. What do you think?"

"What do I think? You cleaned your entire house and

redid your porch in two days' time just for me? I'm not buying. I've seen your house in every condition, from reasonably clean to really atrocious, but mostly really…"

"Hey, I cook and clean all day at the Diner. How I keep the kitchen in my own house is my own damn dirty little secret."

Shelby assessed her sister-in-law's ballet-dancer figure and creamy skin. "Somehow I don't think Adam was worried about what kind of housekeeper you'd make when he was chasing after you," she said with a snort.

"Leave my wife alone, Shelb. I'm proud of her. I actually found matching socks to wear tonight. *Clean* ones." The normally rumpled Adam descended the stairs in a neatly pressed blue shirt and starched denim jeans. His face was baby-smooth, the usual stubble gone. Tiny grains of white stuck to his cheeks, probably since he'd had pieces of toilet paper on them where he had cut himself with a razor.

"If you've been yearning for clean socks, you know where the washer is," Trish told him sweetly. She honed in on a small braided rug on the floor and went over to move it. The worn couch she dropped it in front of was newly slip covered.

"What is going on?" Shelby demanded. "You two are scaring me." She sniffed the air. "Wait a minute…I notice the absence of something…no foul odor…no noxious cloud I have to wade through just to see you…no cigarettes! You two are really going to start trying for a kid!" She shared a conspiratorial glance with Adam, who had been begging Trish to quit smoking for years.

Trish pulled up the sleeve of her dress, revealing the flesh-colored nicotine patch. "I had to keep busy. I cleaned the whole house, even organized the silverware drawers. I don't know why I'm bothering with this damned patch. These things don't work for shit."

Shelby engulfed them both in a hug, then said, "Let's celebrate. I'll call Coronelli's. I know this little domestic scene doesn't include you two cooking after spending all day at the Diner."

As she wrapped her arms around Trish and then Adam she wondered how long it would be before everyone else's happiness stopped being a reminder of her own should-have-beens.

"We're grilling out," Adam decreed. "Might as well get used to the whole familial scene. Besides, I want to try a new spice rub out on some chicken. If it works maybe we'll use it at the Diner."

Shelby's mouth twitched. "You two are too damn cute. You know, I'm fairly sure you'll manage to conceive and make good parents whether or not you can eat off of your kitchen floor."

"I'm going to get the chicken started," Adam told them, and disappeared onto the patio to fiddle with the grill. When he came back inside a few minutes later, Shelby thrust a glass of wine into his hand. "Let's toast to fertility."

"Wine to celebrate news of possible impending news. Perfect," Adam said with satisfaction. He flopped down on the couch, hooked his hands behind his head, and put his feet up on the coffee table before letting a long sigh escape.

This was one of the reasons it had taken so long to accept a simple dinner invitation. Joe had done the same thing in their own home thousands of times. She and Trish had even laughed one night when they'd seen the two men, at the same time, do the hook and sigh. The brothers were different but watching Adam's mannerisms, things they shared, were unsettling now. She watched uncomfortably as Trish found a movie on TV.

"We went to go see this one in Loveland," Shelby murmured as they watched Matt McConaughey and Jennifer Lopez feud and fall in love onscreen. "Joe hated it, kept making trips to the concession stand for popcorn. He didn't even see half of the movie, but he knew I wanted to see it. He'd always rib me about Matt McConaughey, tell me that old Matt was so ugly he could scare a dog off a meat truck."

"That is a Joe-ism if I ever heard one," Adam commented with a chortle, then jumped up from the couch as if something had bitten him. "Well, shit!" he swore suddenly.

Shelby started. "Calm down, Adam. I'm fine. You can't walk around forever waiting for me to fall apart over the littlest thing. It's not a tactical error to watch a movie on TV just because Joe and I went to see it—"

"No, the chicken! I forgot all about it!" he muttered as he bolted for the patio.

"It's a good thing he leaves the cooking at the Diner to me," Trish snickered. Adam shuffled back into the room a minute later with a sheepish look and a plate of charred meat.

"Um, plan B? Do you guys want to do Coronelli's?" Shelby suggested mirthfully.

"Can't believe we're now forced to order from our only competition in town," Adam conceded. "I'm not giving up on that spice rub though."

"Better speak up and tell me what you want," Shelby tossed over her shoulder as she made her way into the kitchen for a phone book. "You'd think I'd have Coronelli's number memorized as much as I order from there. Er, sorry, Adam..."

She grabbed the phone book and was still smiling when she watched the small white business card flutter onto the now-spotless linoleum kitchen floor. The familiar logo jumped out at her: Ewing Toyota. Ron Smith's name was scrawled on the back of the card, along with another contact number. The cheerful yellow of the kitchen's wallpaper seemed to flatten in an instant, along with her perception of Adam and Trish.

She walked back into the living room, anger and a strange kind of anxiety at what she was about to find out undulating through her. Adam was sitting on the couch with his arm casually draped around Trish. Shelby thrust the card in his face.

"Adam, what the hell are you doing with this? My God, please don't tell me you knew what Joe was going to do..." She felt a sharp pressure behind her eyes, remembered wondering vaguely how Joe could have been sure the car would be delivered as promised, when promised.

Adam hung his head, unable to face her. When he finally

looked up, his features were rearranged into a contrite, weary look that told her everything. He was suddenly unrecognizable, a stranger. He stood up, put his hands on her shoulders, and eased her onto the couch.

"Shelby, nothing was more important to Joe than making sure you were going to be all right. He felt he'd failed you in certain ways, that he should have made you stand on your own two feet. He always thought that you would on your own time, but then he learned he didn't have a lot of time to do that. He asked me to help make sure you were all right afterwards, see to certain details."

Shelby stared at him, horrified, and felt the ground shift underneath her. Trish sat next to her in stunned silence, tears silently sliding down her face. She tried to reach out but Shelby yanked her hand away, avoiding the contact. Trish got up and left the room, the shocked look gone, her face an unreadable mask.

"You mean you knew your brother was planning to throw his life away and you did nothing?" she whispered, her accusing stare meeting Adam's dejected one. To know what he had done was a betrayal second only to Joe's giving up. How the hell had *that* conversation started? *I need you to do me a little favor, Adam…*

"Shelby, you knew him. He loved to build things. There was going to come a time when he wouldn't even be able to pick up a hammer. He wasn't going to get better, he was going to die," Adam said with an eerie matter-of-factness. "I read his *Patient's Guide to Living With ALS too*. When Joe got to the chapters about wheelchair selection and financial planning, well, I think that's what did it for him. Joe wasn't the kind of guy who knew how to live with ALS. Could you see him being happy like that, having to depend on you and me and Trish just to get through his day? I would have done that for him in a second, helped him live with it if that's what I thought he wanted. But it wasn't. God, I'm sorry you found out like this. I'm sorry, Shelby. I'm just sorry."

Shelby jumped up from the couch. "So did you know when he was going to do it, and how?" she demanded, hysteria creeping into her voice. She wanted to know, like a betrayed wife who needed to hear every detail of an errant husband's sordid affair. "Was it a mistake that I'm the one who found him? Did you two talk about what kind of pills he'd take? There wasn't a word in that pamphlet that convinced me things would be better if he wasn't here."

Then another sickening thought dawned on her.

"It was you," she accused. "Joe told you to send my clips out, get me a new job when you thought I was ready, didn't he? *Didn't* he?" She imagined Joe casually grabbing the stack of resumes she kept to satisfy her "on to bigger and better things" fits. She'd never been serious enough to use one. He'd probably had to blow dust off of them.

"I did," Adam admitted. "I found the *Atlanta Minute* ad online a week and a half ago."

"You *son of a bitch*. Maybe he'd still be here if you had put as much effort into trying to save him as you did into planning all of this! I spent months looking up test trials. I read so much about it I could barely see at the end of the day, trying to figure out the best way to help him. And all the while he gave up, you gave up, everybody gave except for me!"

Shelby paced frantically around the couch. She wanted to rip the ugly beige slip cover off of it and throw it at his feet.

"If he was still here, who would it be better for? Him or us?" Adam asked quietly.

Shelby slapped him hard in response. After she slammed the door on her way out and ran down the freshly swept porch steps, she kept jogging and didn't stop until she was home.

When she made it inside the Gingerbread, she marched over to the answering machine, out of breath, and played Maura Thomas' message again. Adam had applied for this job for her, and she'd give Joe and him both what they wanted. Right now calling about that interview seemed like a damn fine idea.

CHAPTER EIGHT

Shelby stood on the stairwell inside of her mother's house, staring down at the thirteen steps. Thirteen steps down, and four more off of the porch. She could do this.

Minutes before she had smacked her hand down on the alarm and silenced it like an errant bug. A small duffel bag was already stuffed in the trunk of the car, her Holiday Inn reservation confirmation number carefully folded and tucked in her purse. After dragging a comb through her hair and vigorously brushing her teeth, she dressed and grabbed her purse. She tiptoed into her mother's room and dropped a kiss on her forehead. It felt right to leave before the rest of the world woke up. Somehow that made this seem more like an adventure.

As a kid she'd always been instructed to step down the left side of the stairs. The right side of this stairwell creaked and groaned like an old man, and she'd caught hell plenty of times for barreling down the stairs early on a Saturday morning. Now tiptoeing down the left was an automatic response and she was back to being ten, about to catch hell for the sound that some hundred-year-old steps made.

They made the most beautiful sound as she descended down the right side, a deep, complaining groan. She smiled broadly but didn't stop to savor it.

Once she made it to the car, she regarded the gray pinstriped suit hanging in the back. The perfect "dress to impress" interview outfit. It had been another gift from Joe, who had come home one day and set it in her lap. "You never know when you're going to need a good power suit," he'd announced.

Keep going. Don't stop now, he told her through the *ding ding ding* alerting her to an open car door. She slammed it shut and rolled down the window to breathe in the crisp morning air. With her foot on the gas and her hands gripping the wheel in the ten-and-two position, she headed towards Atlanta and the sunrise.

*   *   *

Hours later in the car, Shelby recited her chosen mantra. It wasn't doing a thing to relax her. Her hands were probably going to be permanently frozen around the steering wheel by the time she got to Atlanta; she'd have to call rescue workers to use the Jaws of Life and unpry them.

"As far as U.S. cities go, Atlanta is the ninth largest metro area based on population. The city's count stands close to 500,000..." she murmured, breathing deeply.

A semi barreled past her. He had to be doing eighty. She let out an involuntary half-shriek and started on some facts about *Atlanta Minute*. "The general interest, wide-distribution paper has a circulation of 220,000 and currently employs a staff of fifty..."

Ever since the accident at sixteen she'd taken to reciting useless, random facts in stressful situations. She tried some more deep breathing. *I've taken a week off from my job to go on a road trip to interview for a job I never applied for in a city I've never been to because my dead husband wanted me to...*

She could picture the interview already. *Actually, Ms. Thomas, I never even knew I wanted to work for you until you called me. Didn't even know you were hiring. Why Atlanta? Well, I took a personality quiz. Apparently something about me screams Atlanta...*

Shelby reached into the sack on the passenger seat for some cold fries. She'd also been trying to eat her nerves into submission the entire trip, but that wasn't working either. She screwed up her face after popping a few in her mouth.

"Time to stop," she announced to no one in particular. "Not touching any more of those…"

She was somewhere in Kentucky and her nerve endings were vibrating. She signaled carefully at the next exit and pulled into the gas station. Inside, she loaded up, grabbing Aspirin, Twinkies, Fritos, and several Diet Cokes. No one around to stop her from eating like this. She grabbed some gum at the last minute to combat Frito aftertaste.

"Road trip?" the woman at the register asked, amused. She blew a mammoth bubble of her own gum and snapped it.

"You bet, and this is even more essential than the gas," Shelby told her. "By the way, I want to put twenty on pump two." Sad, how proud she felt of the simple act of pumping fuel into a car. She'd pumped gas maybe twice in her life.

After she went outside and finished pumping, a streak of fur caught her eye, then disappeared behind the building. She couldn't resist investigating and noted vaguely that this probably wasn't a great idea if the streak turned out to be a less-than-friendly dog.

Not a dog, she discovered, but a very large cat with matted gray fur and round yellow eyes, battle-scarred and missing the tip of its right ear. It was frozen like a mini-Sphinx, back legs tucked in, front paws carefully aligned.

Shelby bent down, crooning softly, and the cat started a slow retreat and hissed out a warning. It was a challenge to stop and will herself not to laugh out loud. She could swear the cat's eyes had widened to the size of tennis balls and its mouth had pursed in a silent, terrified "O." The image reminded her of the old "Saturday Night Live" gag, the terrified look on the cat's face as it attempts to drive and crashes the car. The *"Toonces The Driving Cat"* skit. Shelby silently retreated and went back inside.

A minute later she was back with a snack pouch of crackers and tuna. She tore it open, spread some on top of a cracker with a plastic knife, and laid the morsel on the ground. The cat inched forward and thrust a back leg out, stretching languidly in a signature cat move. Shelby hung back as the cat cleaned the tuna off the cracker, its tongue darting eagerly in and out.

"Oh *come on*," she admonished in a soft, exasperated voice once the cat took the cracker carefully in its mouth and began to retreat again. "A little bit of appreciation, some thanks?"

It stopped and Shelby put her hand out, kept it still as the cat moved closer. Finally she felt soft fur brush against her palm. The cat, one that looked like a very large and ugly feather duster with eyes, butted her hand with its head and she laughed, spreading another cracker with tuna as it waited expectantly.

After it gobbled the second cracker down, its head bobbing, Shelby stood up. The sudden movement startled the cat all over again and it streaked away to a convenient dark hiding place. Underneath her car.

"Of course," Shelby muttered as she inched along the concrete and tried to coax the set of yellow eyes out. Was anyone watching her legs stick out from underneath her car and listening to her talk in a baby voice?

The glowing eyes narrowed and an unholy growl escaped from the cat as she slunk further underneath her car after it. Terrific, she was going to get her hand chewed off because she wanted to avoid running over this thing. Just how long did cats have to be on their own before they became feral, anyway?

Against her better judgment, she positioned her hand underneath the furry underbelly. As the cat prepared to take a swipe at her she pulled it out quickly, like the proverbial cane hooking around a performer to jerk them off of the stage. As she panted it settled calmly into her lap. *Now* it just wanted to sit there?

A farmer type who was hauling cattle watched her, amused.

"My first road trip," she told him, as if this explained everything. She dusted her jeans and caught a glance in the

Toyota's mirror at her hair, which was now sticking up in an odd sort of Mohawk. "It was going well up until now."

Shelby thought she heard Joe laughing in her ear, a boisterous sound that had always been so loud it could make a person's eardrums vibrate. The farmer just smiled, shook his head, and spit some Skoal into the nearby trash can in response.

After persuading the clerk to post a note about a lost cat at the gas station, Shelby sighed in the general direction of the passenger seat as she and her new road trip buddy headed onward.

"I think I'm getting crazier with each passing mile. Happen to know where a pet store is so we can get you a carrier and some food? Maura Thomas is going to think it's strange if I bring a cat to an interview. I'll tell her you're a service animal."

Pitiful, the relief she felt talking to this animal. At least now there was another living body to address during the lonely hours in the car. No wild first road trips for her, college-age and headed across the country in search of beaches, beer and boys. She was headed to Georgia at thirty-two with Toonces the cat. Suddenly Shelby burst into tears. Here she was, her two worst nightmares realized: She was without Joe and her only copilot on a long road trip was this ugly mop of fur…

She caught hold of herself, pulled the car over, and stared at the cat. "I'm going to talk, and you're my captive audience. I'm going to tell you about a guy named Joe…"

The cat purred and began to knead the passenger's seat.

Shelby decided to pick up some cat supplies and then passed out of Kentucky. She decided she liked Tennessee, a good thing since she spent five and a half hours driving through it. She stopped several more times even though she didn't need to just to hear the clipped lilt of the cashiers at the gas stations.

The air was different in each state: Kentucky was an old oak barrel; Tennessee was the new-old smell of mountains and earth. She took the oak and mist and earth in with deep breaths at each stop, let them mingle with the smell of the rich Indiana soil that had seeped through her pores for years and was now in her blood.

She made a left at I-24 to pass through Georgia and came into Tennessee again. More mountains and mist. Two hours later she was in Georgia again. The smell of pine everywhere. She felt her fingers drum more insistently on the steering wheel as she pushed through the last hour and a half and exited on Courtland toward Georgia State University. A right at Baker... another left...

And here was Peachtree Street, where she might have a job if she managed to hold it together through a thirty-minute interview and dared to uproot her entire life. As she drove the buildings, some new and some old, winked at her underneath the city lights. She noted the plain gray high-rise that housed the *Atlanta Minute* office. Toonces seemed to be taking it all in too. She had let him out of his carrier for the last part of the trip and he half-stood in the passenger's seat, paws positioned on the dashboard in order to get a better look.

CHAPTER NINE

Miranda strolled around the boutique, running her fingers lightly over the clothes and picking up every third outfit to examine the material of the tiny garments. She had spent enough time in here that the woman's friendly smile would soon start to tighten, her gaze becoming more assessing and suspicious. Any minute now there would probably be another, "Can I help you find something?"

That of course was sales speak for, *If you haven't found something to spend money on by now, you're not going to, so it's time for you to go.*

As if on cue, the saleslady approached her. "Are you finding everything you need, dear?"

"You know, I really have no idea what I'm looking for," Miranda told her with a shrug. *And you have no idea how sincerely I mean that, lady.*

"Well, first of all, are you shopping for someone who might have registered here?" The saleslady's smile was genuine, and that was somehow worse than if she'd been rude. "If so, I can show you their list and help you out. By the way, are we shopping for a boy or a girl?"

"I don't know," Miranda whispered, still clutching the bright yellow baby pajamas printed with tiny giraffes and elephants. The Noah's Ark theme appealed to her. It was a story about taking a few chosen parts from an old life, accepting a lot of new baggage for the trip, and starting over after total destruction. Could she do it? Could she ask Clint to do it with her? "I honestly don't know yet. I'm sorry..." She handed the woman the pajamas and ran out of the store.

Miranda barely reached the bathroom stall in the mall before she was sick. Was morning sickness just a problem in the early stages of being pregnant? She thought so, but wasn't sure. Of course, it was also likely she was heaving on a regular basis because she hadn't used in eight hours. Since right after multiple pregnancy tests had confirmed the suspicions she'd tried to ignore. Eight hours, and she already felt like she was falling apart. *What if I've already hurt him, before he's even born? I knew, part of me knew, and still...*

Maybe she should stop by Barnes and Noble, pick up a few books on pregnancy for expecting mothers. She doubted there would be any chapters containing advice for junkie Moms. *Chapter 15, how to deal with those pesky shakes and sweats...*

"Stop it, Miranda," she said aloud in the empty bathroom. She stood up, went to the sink, and rinsed her mouth out. She splashed her face with cold water and smoothed her miniskirt and leggings. He would be enough. Her baby would be enough to make her change. She had to believe that.

There's nothing like considering the possibility of a new life in a public restroom. She laughed aloud and liked the sound as it echoed off of the tiles and sinks. A little shrill and scared maybe, but still hopeful. On to the baby section at Barnes and Noble. Like reading a book could prepare you for parenthood. Even as she headed for the bookstore, she felt her body start to vibrate and the sweat start to form on her forehead. She bit down on her lip and tried to ignore the need. Eight hours.

*   *   *

"Wow," Clint said in wonder as Miranda stood in front of him a few hours later, clutching the maternity books. She hadn't seen much of him in the past few weeks since she'd chosen to hide out in Cora's dorm room, away from him and her family. Now she was ambushing him with life-altering news as he stood outside of Wally's tiny shop where he was getting ready to go out on a job.

"You know me. I did several tests to make sure," she told him, setting the books down on the hood of his jeep and taking his hand. "Seven Cokes so I could keep using the bathroom and five pregnancy tests later, here we are."

She was feeling worse and worse, partly from nerves and partly from her physical need. Ten hours without anything stronger than whatever chemicals they put in soda. It was getting harder to keep her hands, or any part of her body, still.

Clint actually laughed then, coming out of his stunned trance for a minute. "Wow."

"Wow's the word," she whispered. "This baby is just an hours-old idea and I already feel like I'm a bad mother. Clint, I used right before the first test. I think partly because I needed the courage to take it." She looked down then, her face heating with shame. "Even right now, I'm thinking about how much I want it."

He tilted her chin up. "Hey, remember that you had help creating both of these situations. The drugs and the baby, and both times it was me."

"I've wanted to know for awhile, but we've been too busy fighting since you quit for me to ask. How are you doing it? What stops you from needing it now?"

"You." The statement was simple and matter-of-fact. It undid her.

She buried her face in his battered coat and clutched at it. "Certainly never imagined I'd be one of those girls asking her boyfriend, *'What are we going to do?'* But Clint, what are we going to do?"

"We're going to try. Just try."

CHAPTER TEN

"You are not helping an already stressful situation," Shelby reprimanded. "I have to go in now. This is the moment of reckoning. She's in there waiting."

The cat eyed her and meowed pitifully. He had the damnedest expressions; his terrified "O" at the gas station had only been the beginning of his repertoire.

Here she was, sitting in the parking lot behind the *Atlanta Minute* building, trying to reassure a stray animal it would be okay while she went in for an interview. No hug for Shelby Norris, no "Go get 'em, babe," that was standard for most people when they left their home in search of new employment. Oh, well. At least something that depended on her was sending her off, if against its will.

"I'm cracking the window. It's not hot outside. I won't be more than an hour. You have plenty of food and water in there."

Toonces sent her another doleful expression from behind the door of the cat carrier. The bars cast shadows across his sad eyes and a long, mournful sound escaped.

"I'm going in," she told him firmly. "I'm not going to be any later than fifteen minutes early for this interview. I intend to try very hard for something I'm not even sure I want yet."

Shelby smoothed the pinstriped gray suit. Joe had done a good job. It fit well except for the foot of material that she'd had hacked off of the legs. The only other order of business was a quick swipe with a lint brush to remove the cat hair that settled on her, attaching to the material like a tenacious burr.

"You shed too much. I'll be back. No yowling."

The cat had quickly revealed a nicely developed set of vocal cords when she left him for any amount of time, so stashing him back at the Holiday Inn was out. The occupants of room 212 would call down to the front desk with complaints about strange noises coming from the room next door, or some poor housekeeper would be met with startled hissing when they keyed in.

"You gave me way too much credit, Joe," Shelby muttered, rubbing her temples as she rode the elevator up to the fifth floor where Maura Thomas would be waiting. "I am *so* not ready for this."

The receptionist at the front desk had a steel-gray bun positioned on top of her head, her face strikingly young and childlike in comparison to the gray in her hair. "You're Shelby Norris," she announced. Shelby could see other *Atlanta Minute* employees milling in and out of small rooms on either side of a hallway, but this woman was clearly the one in charge around here.

"You are correct. So what was the first thing that gave it away?" Shelby asked in a low voice. "The time of arrival, the career-woman suit or the look of terror on my face?"

"Mostly the look of terror. I've seen it six times this week," the woman confided. "I call it the pre-interview look. Somewhere between nauseous and constipated."

"Great. Not exactly the look I'm going for. Six other interviews this week, huh? So what does the post-interview expression look like?" Shelby wanted to know.

"She likes your clips, so calm down. You'd better get a drink of cold water before you go in there." The receptionist gestured toward the corner. "There's the cooler. She'll be ready for you in just a minute. We can chat until then but no fishing for any info about what Maura likes or doesn't like. I'm Glenda."

"Wouldn't dream of pumping you for insider secrets, Glenda," Shelby assured her. "Whatever I should do in these types of situations, I always do the opposite. That's why I'll never read *Interviewing For Dummies*. It's like somebody telling you not to think about a certain word or object. Of course that's the first thing you fixate on. I'm going to tell you not to think about something weird, like an ostrich, right now. Bet you think about 'em all day. What do you call that, unconsciously doing the wrong thing?"

"Self-destructive," Glenda supplied helpfully.

"Touché," Shelby told the secretary with a grin, just as a crisp-looking woman swept into the room. All clean lines and angles, all business. Maura Thomas. Some people's appearance didn't match their voice but the brisk, authoritative one she'd heard on her answering machine, not a breath wasted, fit the woman towering over her perfectly. Maura Thomas wore heels but certainly didn't need them. Her brown hair was cut military short, and Shelby suspected she ran her office the same way-- with military precision.

"Come on back, Shelby. I'm Maura." Not a movement or a word in excess of what was necessary. Shelby silently followed her to a tiny, cramped room in the back of the office space.

Once they sat down, Maura pulled out the clips Adam had sent and rifled through them. "So," she murmured as she picked one out and slid it across the black, lacquered desk toward Shelby. "'Breast Cancer Research Is No Joke For Aspiring Comedienne.'"

She stopped for a minute, pulled the article back across the desk, and continued to read. "'Local comedienne Kim Davies spends a lot of time joking around about her trials with breast cancer, but she takes fund-raising and research for the disease very seriously.' You're good with a turn of phrase and I enjoyed the human interest stories. All of them, and there were a lot. But that's a problem. We'd assign you to a specific desk later, but at first we ask our reporters to pull double duty. If we hire you you'll find yourself covering various types of stories until you find your niche. That would require some serious branching out on your part." She tipped back in her chair and folded her arms, a challenging gesture.

"Here's how I look at it, Maura," Shelby returned

easily. She felt like they were beginning a verbal ping-pong match. "I've worked at a small paper for years and that makes me perfect for this. I was the city beat. I was the entertainment desk. I was the photographer, the editor, the receptionist, and the advertising department." *Take that!*

"I like that. So why are there just human interest stories included in the clips you sent me?"

Maura tapped a finger on the desk, studying her. Point for Maura. If they had been playing ping-pong Maura's ball would have whizzed right past her and off of the table.

I didn't send you those clips, my brother-in-law did. And he did that because my husband told him to. But somehow I don't think sharing that piece of information with you is going to help my cause.

"I can share some further clips with you if you'd like. I just felt those stories best reflect my writing style, the type of reporter I am. I like to focus on the human element. People are generally comfortable talking to me, as you can tell from the clips, which is certainly beneficial in any type of story I write."

Guess what my B.S. in Journalism stands for. No way is she going to buy that. Did I actually just break out the phrase "human element"?

Suddenly the smart interview suit felt itchy and ill-fitting. She felt like a kid playing dress-up. What the hell was she *doing*?

"I think I'd like to see some further clips, Shelby," Maura said as she stood up abruptly. "The sooner, the better. You can leave them with Glenda if I'm not around. If I like them we'll talk again. It's been interesting meeting you."

Shelby shook the woman's hand, wondering how they had managed to skip the middle of the interview.

"One more thing," Maura said. "Why the relocation? Atlanta's quite a ways from Layton, Indiana."

"Well, it's like you suggested…I decided I need to do some serious branching out," Shelby told her dryly, and left the office.

"How'd it go?" Glenda demanded under her breath as

Shelby passed her.

"Don't know," Shelby admitted honestly. "You thinking about ostriches yet?"

At that moment Maura Thomas reappeared. "I've changed my mind. Don't bother bringing any more clips by. I'm going to assign you one local story. If I like it, you've got the job. If I don't, I guess *Layton News* readers will be able to enjoy your human interest features for some time to come. I'll call you tomorrow and let you know what to write about. Don't disappoint me." Then she spun gracefully and returned to her office in one fluid motion.

Shelby left the office and pressed the down button of the elevator, ready to hide in her hotel room and wait for instructions on her mystery assignment. The situation sounded exciting on paper, anyway. She'd gone from writing about new park benches in Layton to James Bond assignments in Atlanta. *I don't have the job yet but I've upgraded already.*

When she finally opened the door to her car Toonces was perched on top of the carrier, taking in the surroundings from his new vantage point. He had apparently body-slammed the carrier's metal door open. The backseat was a sea of white. Papers that had been neatly stacked were now strewn around as if a blizzard had hit the inside of the car. The new car smell was long gone, along with the flawlessness of the gray interior. She hadn't picked up anything during her hurried trip through the pet store for removing pet stains. The cat sent her a reproachful meow, his message clear: *Your fault. If you hadn't left me...*

CHAPTER ELEVEN

Things had happened in fast forward with no time to process them: Shelby watched herself walk out of the *Atlanta Minute* offices after the interview and ride the elevator down, each movement comically sped up. In the next scene she was making absurdly fast laps in the hotel swimming pool, slicing through the water faster than Michael Phelps and dripping onto the concrete as she picked up her cell phone by the side of the pool. Maura with her James Bond assignment. Maura's brisk voice had commanded Shelby to head downtown to a city council meeting so she had done as bidden.

The sheer number of complaints at the public safety meeting had intrigued Shelby. There were forty-two claims against the city. Damages due to driving over potholes; numerous trip and fall incidents; money sought for flood damages when a sewer backed up.

Corliss Lay had made his case in a gravelly, rusted-over voice to the council members. It would be filed in the "claims with unfavorable recommendations" section of this meeting's minutes as the city council had opted not to pay the wizened old guy a dime. To Shelby, at least, he'd casually admitted to being a very old and experienced con artist. Atlanta wasn't working out so well for him, and he'd decided to either move or retire. She had to hand it to him. Some if his past schemes were halfway creative.

She'd turned two stories in to Maura the next day: one a straightforward and businesslike synopsis of the meeting and the other a feature on Corliss and his all-time greatest schemes.

"How on earth did you get him to talk to you about

this? And to agree for you to possibly run it?" Maura had asked as she scanned the article.

"Well, Corliss has already done his time for most of them. But getting people to talk is one of my many gifts," Shelby told her. "It's amazing what people will tell you if you're really interested in what they have to say. I'm sorry but I had to write it. I wouldn't be me if I didn't hand you a feature. Don't you love the one he pulled in Texas? I thought Corliss Lay versus San Antonio was pretty great myself."

Maura had also skimmed over the all-business article for a minute and looked up at her with no expression. "Be here by 8:30 a.m. sharp every weekday. Glenda makes the coffee but it sucks so I'd suggest bringing some Starbucks for your own good."

"I heard that," Glenda called casually from the reception area.

"I meant you to," Maura called back just as casually.

As Shelby left the office, numbly making her way through the office humming with reporters and activity, Glenda had crowed happily, "I was rooting for you."

*   *   *

Three Dixie cups filled with Sutter Mill wine were hoisted into the air. There were no decorations in the dusty newspaper office for the going-away party, at least not the typical streamers and signs. Instead fake front pages were posted around the Layton News office. They looked like the real thing and were printed on actual newspaper. Leo and Jonah had tacked them up on the template board where the dummy pages for each issue usually went, like paintings at an art gallery. Shelby lingered over each one in turn. They were arranged in chronological order, proclaiming different milestones in her life.

Her mouth twisted into a smile at the headline that read, "Local Reporter Loses Consciousness, Finds Handyman." Leo and Jonah knew about her first encounter with Joe, no interview necessary for this little faux article or any of the rest. They knew all of her stories.

Local Reporter Loses Consciousness, Finds Handyman
When Layton's own Shelby Norris lost consciousness at a city council meeting, it was undoubtedly the most noteworthy thing to happen that evening--or at any other meeting held locally. Fast-thinking Joe Norris, a new contractor in town, aided her sudden onset of low blood sugar, and she quickly came to. She inexplicably muttered: "Didn't have any peanut butter crackers. Did you start your illicit business out of the back of the restaurant yet?"

Norris has never commented on the statement, and onlookers have wondered ever since: Jumbled thoughts due to hypoglycemia, or something else? Witnesses reported seeing the reporter and the contractor whispering to each other earlier that evening. Whatever the circumstances, Joe Norris placed an ad for his handyman services with the paper the next day, and soon became a permanent fixture at the office. Some suspect he did so with the intention of seeing the reporter again, rather than to actually utilize the paper's excellent classified section to grow his business...

Joe had leaned in that night and caught Shelby in an under-her-breath rant about her wasted education and stories about park benches. "Look out, Christine Amanpour," she'd muttered. "I'm comin' for your job. Today Layton park bench stories, tomorrow CNN international correspondent."

"I'll run an escort service out of the back of my brother's restaurant after we're finished renovating; we'll scandalize the respectable men of this town," he'd whispered, his raspy voice breaking into her thoughts. "You can write about it. I'd love to see that story. In fact, I think I'll stick around and see if you can give Christine Amanpour a run for her money someday."

Shelby felt a stab of regret. He'd stuck around, but not long enough to see her make it.

Now Leo and Jonah were pretending to do other things

to leave her alone with her thoughts. She imagined they had huddled and debated over writing their version of the story, whether or not it would make her laugh or just hurt, and was glad it had not been vetoed.

"I gotta know, Shelb. What exactly did you mean about the illicit business? Come on, not in six years have you ever explained. Spill it." Jonah's voice was relieved as he studied her and knew she was okay with the gesture.

"Not on your life, Jonah Murphy," she said, and sent him a Mona Lisa smile. "Some things will forever remain just between me and Joe." She could have easily shared the rest of the story, but somehow it was important to hold little things like that close.

Shelby scanned the rest of the display. There were pictures of her in a graduation cap on the campus of Purdue; nice candids of she and Joe at their wedding; and their house as it underwent renovations and transformed. She read the article at the end of the row aloud:

Local journalist Shelby Norris recently accepted a job with *Atlanta Minute*, a wide-distribution newspaper based (surprisingly) in Atlanta, Georgia. She will begin her new life in Atlanta in a week's time with a startlingly ugly cat she picked up on the way to the interview for her new job. In her new job and locale, Norris will...?

Nothing else was written after that. The question mark said it all, a dare. In the picture above the last article Shelby held Toonces in front of the Layton News office. He had been startled by the flash from Jonah's camera and was captured mid-twist, trying to claw his way to freedom, eyes like big yellow saucers, his mouth pursed in the trademark "O". Shelby's expression was somewhere between a grimace and a laugh in the photo, her hand stretched out as she reached for him.

"These are getting framed, and they're going up in my new apartment," Shelby declared. That was the best and worst thing Atlanta would offer: the fact that no one there would know her story.

"So," Leo cleared his throat, a signal that one of his famous speeches was coming on. "Remember what I've been telling you since you were sixteen. Rule number one: talk to people, and that means doing a whole lot of listening. Remember that every story…"

"Is a human interest story," Jonah supplied, rolling his eyes upwards.

"Give Leo a break," Shelby told him. "I learned more about reporting from him than I ever did at Purdue. I mean that."

"Shelb, you're leaving next week. You don't have to kiss up any more," Jonah reminded her, his florid features twisted into a look of mock distaste.

"I can only dream of the day she'd kiss up," Leo snorted.

"Time for another toast with something stronger, before Leo imparts any more wisdom and Shelby gets misty," Jonah decreed. He produced a plastic bag and out came a bottle of single malt Scotch.

"This is so wrong," Leo said morosely as he watched him deftly pour the Scotch into Dixie cups. He examined the amber liquid in the cup with a pained expression. "You couldn't bring proper shot glasses? Certain things are sacred and should be treated as such…"

"Quiet, Leo," Jonah commanded in his clipped Irish lilt. "Now let's toast to the rest of Shelby's story, whatever it is!"

"Whatever it is!" they cried out.

Shelby tossed back the Scotch, felt the burn and tasted the faint note of smoke as it went down. *Whatever it is.*

The party broke up after two more rounds of Scotch and some calzone from Coronelli's. The cheese and meat had soaked up some of the wine and Scotch, but Shelby was still weaving slightly as she left, an idiotic grin on her face. Jonah offered to help her home, a bushy eyebrow arched in amusement, but Shelby waved him off.

"You're not that much better off," she accused. She fumbled with the office's smudged screen door and stumbled out onto the sidewalk, her life's story in newsprint tucked firmly beneath her arm. The story up until now, at least.

She shuffled a few more steps and paused in front of the bank clock, glaring at it. 8:58 p.m. *Chink.* 60 degrees. *Chink.* The damned thing was still clicking away at her like before.

She cursed it before weaving down the sidewalk towards the Gingerbread, which was now officially on the market. Bill, the realtor, had assured her that he was "on it." After apartment shopping and arriving back from Atlanta, she had seen to the business of starting over in record time. She'd contacted Bill to sell the house and then Pinkert Brothers to arrange for a furniture auction. She'd made the calls while reciting the pragmatic mantras in her head: *You cannot carry a mortgage and rent an apartment. The furniture you and Joe accumulated during your marriage isn't going to fit in a tiny apartment.*

The Scotch and wine had been an especially bad idea tonight, since the auction was at 9 am sharp tomorrow.

*   *   *

"*I have three hundred and seventy five, do I hear three eighty, three eightyyyyyyyy..*"

Shelby stood on the Gingerbread's wraparound porch and felt laughter bubble in her throat. Dee Pinkert's nasally voice was shooting numbers out of his mouth like an automatic weapon. She knew what would happen next: each time someone would raise their numbered bid card, one of Dee's assistants, a wiry little man in a cowboy hat, would point excitedly at the bidder, dance like he was about ready to pee his pants, and yell out, "*Heeep!*"

What did that stand for? Was it a shortened version of "Right here?" Help? Help with what? Help me find the bathroom?

Four hundred. The bed, dresser and chest of drawers were solid, mission-style design and oak. She had coated each piece with Pledge and run a cloth along the wood until it shone. It would be out of place, take up too much space in the apartment's bedroom. Wasn't there even a George Jones song where he yodeled sadly about watching the bed go at auction? She'd expected to feel more of an indignant sting as she watched people, most known to her, haul the stuff away. Familiar faces in the crowd and familiar hands on her things made the situation better and worse. She heard Joe the whole time, keeping up a running commentary as each piece went. *"Remember the way the slots on the headboard kept popping out all the time? You always used to bitch about dusting in between them... Damn, Shelb, you made out...I can't believe Marie talked Dell into paying that much for the kitchen table...It's not even real wood..."*

She'd heeded the voice when she had decided what would stay and what would go. It had told her clearly what to do with his favorite recliner. It was not to be sold, stuffed in her mother's house or put in storage. And it didn't belong in Atlanta.

She scanned the crowd for Trish and Adam and didn't spot Trish's fire-engine hair or Adam towering above most of the men in the crowd. She might have ventured over to them and offered it if they had come. Had the last scene at their house kept them away, or were they put off at the idea of her tearing down the household she and Joe had built?

The recliner would have to stay in the basement. She just couldn't put one foot in front of the other to walk up their newly-tidy porch steps and use the recliner as a peace offering. *Sorry, Joe. Maybe someday but right now I'd be stretching my limits on that one,* she thought grimly.

Elise came over and put her arm around Shelby's shoulder. "You're making out. Can't believe Marie and Dell dropped that much for the set."

"Making out," Shelby murmured, as she watched the couple load the kitchen table and chairs into the back of a pickup. Marie and Dell had played about a million hands of Texas Hold 'Em on it at Joe's card parties. Once they'd all had to haul Joe off of the table after he'd climbed up on top of it and passed out after a gin-soaked round of Texas Hold 'Em.

Suddenly this scene was stretching her limits too and she retreated inside. The rest of the auction would go just fine without her watching it. She could still hear Dee Pinkert's incessant whine, the prices for her and Joe's things going ever higher, as she shut the screen door behind her.

CHAPTER TWELVE

Moving, Shelby decided, was definitely something to be done only if you were in the witness protection program.

And she hadn't even done any of the heavy lifting. That was up to the two sweaty men heaving a recliner up the stairs to her new apartment. One didn't look any stronger than she was. He was a ferrety-looking guy named Gil, the furniture store's manager who had sold her the furniture on clearance. The other mover was oversized, and the effect of the unbalanced recliner, Gil's side listing considerably lower, was that of a heavy and a small child on opposite sides of a teeter-totter.

She had decided if she was going to do Atlanta she was going to do Atlanta. Peachtree Street was the obvious choice. Out of 71 streets in Atlanta with a variant of Peachtree in their name, there was no mistaking the original. Shelby found herself warming to the *But wait*…quality that was Peachtree. Sigh…here's a CVS and a Starbuck's, just like in every other city in America. *But wait*, not so fast…Here's the Fox Theater, on the same street, still standing! All but left for dead, to be replaced by a big, bad skyscraper, headquarters for Southern Bell, but hell no! How many other theaters in America had been intended to be a temple? The rich, Gothic architecture made its originally intended use easy to imagine. Too much history at stake, so thousands of Atlantans had raised the money and saved it so new memories could be made. Who could forget the 1990 "Starlight Express" performance and the infamous fog machine breakdown? Skaters had hit the resulting oil slick and went down like dominoes. These were moments patrons would never forget and would never have experienced had it not been for that stubborn Southern fund-raising. Maybe she could live here. Maybe she *was* Atlanta...

Gil muttered a string of curse words as he and his overdeveloped employee tilted the recliner to fit through the apartment door. They were no doubt directed at the mover who had called out sick. Or maybe he was cursing her for choosing an apartment three flights up.

She could imagine Gil's absent employee looking at the address the day before, seeing it was a high-rise and deciding, *No way.*

Gil needed to hire some more movers, she decided as he swore again. The freight elevator wasn't working. Gil and helper's bad luck. Should she offer some encouragement or tell him apologetically that she would have waited another day for the delivery? Probably not. She wondered about tipping for moving services.

"Son of a--" Gil began a few minutes later when they set the kitchen table down on the tile of the small kitchen area. It was a far cry from the jovial "call-me-Gil" persona he'd presented a few days earlier. He pulled out an old-fashioned handkerchief and angrily dabbed at his brow with it, then quickly arranged the chairs around the table. After a few more seconds of panting he tried to be a professional again.

"Well, Ms. Norris, there's your furniture, right on time. Think of us if you need any more." His beady eyes grazed the small apartment, which was mostly empty except for a few boxes. Ever the studious bargain hunter, Shelby had ordered a living room and bedroom set from another company, but she wasn't about to tell Gil that.

"Thanks, Gil. I appreciate it." She slipped him an extra forty and thought regretfully that it wouldn't help him much with the back surgery he'd need later.

After Gil and his company of one left she surveyed her new kingdom, which wasn't much yet. The other furniture would be here tomorrow so it looked like sheets and a pillow on the floor for tonight. She made a mental note to check the status of the freight elevator before the delivery tomorrow. Those movers would take it worse than Gil if they showed up with an entire bedroom and living room set with no way to get it up to her apartment.

Now she thought about the estate sale, her own one-woman blowout extravaganza. *Everything must go.* Almost everything. Her prized 100-year-old Deacon's bench with the wondrous curvy design etched into its wood was now sitting in her mother's basement, along with Joe's recliner.

Why hadn't she stopped by Adam and Trish's to tell them goodbye, give them the chair? Maybe it was best. She didn't know if she'd ever be ready to forgive Adam the sin of deeming Joe's life unsalvageable. The final trip south without a word to them, the boxes stuffed in her car, free of most of the physical trappings that had made up her home before. *Everything must go.*

She sat down in the cream-colored recliner. Nice and neutral, more streamlined for an apartment. It was hard to picture herself in it every night, reading a novel with the city lights winking at her through the window, but maybe in time. She was about ready to flip up the footrest when her phone rang.

"Shelby, great news!" the realtor exclaimed without preamble. "I took this young couple through the house a few hours ago. They're in love with it, and I think they're going to put in an offer! How's that for record time? And in this economy. Lucky you!"

"Lucky me," Shelby murmured. "That's great, Bill. You're the best."

When they clicked off she imagined Bill walking the nameless, faceless couple through the house, highlighting the craftsmanship, the crown molding Joe had put up. On the first day of owning the house they'd made an impromptu trip to Lowe's for a deep purple color to paint the walls. Passionate plum. Later on she'd yelped and laughed when he ran his thick fingers through her hair and caught them on clumps of dried paint. Joe had helped her color her world. Now she was surrounded by four white walls.

Suddenly claustrophobia kicked in. Time for a walk. When she stepped out of her apartment, the familiar aroma that drifted out of the apartment directly across from hers made Shelby stop in her tracks. Chicken mingled with the sharp tang of vinegar. Her stomach rumbled. Now the meatball and mozzarella Hot Pockets in her otherwise empty freezer didn't seem so inviting. She jumped, startled, when the voice came through the slightly open apartment door.

"*Pa-amoy-amoy ka pang pagkain, hindi ka na lang pumasok?*" When Shelby stood rooted to the spot, the same voice let out a cackle. "I tell you that I see you out there sniffing at my food, so why not just come on in?"

She pushed the door open the rest of the way, revealing a short, plump woman on the other side who Shelby guessed was of Asian descent. She was at her kitchen stove forking some rice into her mouth and impatiently motioned Shelby the rest of the way in. The rice was still letting off a small cloud of steam but it didn't deter the little woman as she continued her enthusiastic sampling. The sheer roundness of the face added to its friendliness factor.

"You should really be careful about leaving your door open," she told the woman. "It might not be a tiny, harmless person like me the next time."

"I got mace," the woman assured her. Her accent made it seem as if someone was tugging on the words that were trying to escape out of her mouth, but an undertow kept pulling them back. She seemed frustrated and impatient to get them out. "Besides, I like seeing what's going on outside my door. I can tell right away who's coming or going. Safer, don't you think?"

"Mmm, I'm not so sure about that. I'm Shelby Norris, your new neighbor. Sorry I was hovering. Your chicken adobo smells good."

"I'm Mona Abeya. You know adobo?" the woman asked curiously.

Shelby shrugged. "Fan of the food network. I used to try all of the different recipes out on my husband, poor guy. I cooked the one for adobo enough to get pretty good at it." Shelby caught the words after she said them and was grateful the little woman didn't ask any questions about the absence of said husband.

"Pretty good at it, eh? Well I think I do better than pretty good. Wanna try some?"

"Mona, I will never turn down good adobo." She stepped into the apartment, feeling instantly at home. The small space was crammed with furniture and woven baskets. Colorful paintings and ornate crosses hung on the wall. A lamp that hung in the corner of the living room was made of delicate white shells. Beside it was a picture of a young man with a perfect white smile and flawless skin like Mona's.

"That's gorgeous," she commented, pointing at the lamp. "I've been feeling sorry for myself, wondering how I was going to make my little white box next door home. Now I'm starting to see the possibilities. Young man in the picture's gorgeous too."

"It's a Capiz lamp and that's my grandson, David," Mona answered as she ladled some rice into a bowl and placed the chicken on top. She happily pounced on the opportunity to talk about him. "Picture next to it is my daughter Sue, his mama. He lives out in LA, wants to be an actor. Been in some movies as an extra. Done a few walk-ons on some TV sitcoms and dramas, too. Bet you've even seen him. You watch ER? He was a patient on a gurney. He's smart, got a real job too."

"Let me know what he's in and I'll rent it. You'll just have to tell me where to look in the movie."

"I make you a list. He been in a lot. So you're ha⸺ just because you're tiny, eh? I got a scar on my ɦ suggest that kind of thinking is faulty."

"How's that?" Shelby asked, interε took the hand the older woman thrust toward ⸺ the pale white line that slashed across its little ɪ.

"When I was about ten years old got bit by a dog. Took a pretty good chunk out of my hand, and the dog wasn't a big, scary looking thing either. Little bitty cute-looking one. That's why I thought I could pet it in the first place. I bet you get people that way too. You look cute like a Chihuahua but maybe you like a German Shepherd inside. I know that expression, 'it's not the size of the dog' and all that." Mona cackled again.

"I *wish* I was a Shepherd in Chihuahua's clothing, Mona." Shelby forked the rice and chicken into her mouth, groaning with satisfaction. "Now *this* is adobo."

"No matter what our size, we all got teeth. Well, hopefully I do for a little bit longer, anyway." Mona clicked her own perfect rows of white together to punctuate her point, then chortled. "Just have to know how to use 'em. You remember that, Shelby Norris."

CHAPTER THIRTEEN

Shelby pulled up to the cluster of buildings without a real plan. She had pitched the story idea to Maura, insisting she could do better than just a three-sentence quote from someone who lived in the projects. Her speech had been passionate and long, painting a sad picture of a family fearing they would have no place to go, distrusting politicians' promises of vouchers for alternate housing when their home was torn down. It had done the trick and Maura had finally told her to get the hell out of the office with an annoyed, dismissive wave. Maybe they'd use the story as a sidebar.

Bankhead was scheduled for gentrification, which was politicians' fancy way of saying they were going into an urban area to improve it or start from scratch. Some of Atlanta's housing projects, which had dated back to the thirties, had been the very first built in the country. They had started as a solution for the working poor and were now ground zero in the fight to rid Atlanta's Bankhead area of large housing projects. Doing so was also supposed to help stamp out gang and drug-related violence there.

The last of the projects would be history around 2010 if everything went according to plan, and would be replaced by smaller neighborhoods. Spreading the poverty out instead of having it condensed into one area was the name of the game. If the poverty wasn't all in one place, officials reasoned, neither would the crime be. It was meant to have the added bonus of a better life and more opportunity for those who remained in the area. Atlanta was at the top of the list for a teardown of its urban projects since the number of its residents living in publicly funded housing was the highest in the country.

Talk to people, that was rule one Leo had taught Shelby when she'd gone to work for *The Layton News* as a junior in high school. Talk to people. She scanned the parking lot and watched a little girl twirling around in circles with her arms outstretched, all lovely, almond-shaped eyes, braids, and coltish legs. A little boy on a rusted tricycle pedaled furiously in a dizzying circle around the girl, as if he was trying to corral her or surround her with some kind of protective force field. He was shirtless and sweat dripped down his tiny, wiry brown arms, caught by the faded blue sweatbands he wore on each wrist. Base thumped from a car in the distance, mingled with music drifting out of someone's open window. Sounds of upbeat hip-hop music clashing with the low, repetitive beat of a rap song seemed muffled by the thick, humid air. Tempting dinnertime smells also floating out of the open windows mixed with the sour decay of the dumpster near where the kids were playing. The light tan brick buildings looked mostly tired and worn-out, not ominous or home to the drug violence that was regularly reported on here.

Excuse me, gorgeous, Shelby thought ruefully. *I just want to talk to you and your little brother for a second. I'm doing a story. Do you think it's possible to decentralize poverty?*

She walked toward the children and waved. The girl waved back and continued the fun of making her world spin. The little boy took a break from his pedaling to give her a manly little salute.

Well, she certainly couldn't go knocking on doors. Shelby circled around the first building slowly, marveling at the sheer stupidity of the situation she'd created.

"Well you don't look like somebody out trolling for little kids," the male voice stated. It was deep and rusted-over, like the engine of an old car getting started.

Shelby turned around to face a man who was in a flannel shirt despite the heat. His shirt sleeves were rolled up, revealing muscular forearms. He wore a white tank top underneath and had a doo rag stretched over his head. Tiny black freckles

dotted the type of ageless face that made it impossible to guess
how old he was. He seemed to have appeared out of nowhere
and sucked casually on a cigarette while he waited for her to
respond.

"Are they yours?" Shelby asked. "They're beautiful."

"They everybody's kids, we all look after them," he told
her with an odd sort of pride in his voice. "That's Terrence and
Bethie." Posing the obvious question, he asked, "What you doing
here, lady? I think you took a wrong turn at Albuquerque."

"Would you believe I actually started out in Indiana?"
she asked dryly. This little venture had not been wise. "I'm
Shelby."

"Ernie Thompson. So why you here?" he repeated.

"I've come to see for myself what scares the hell out of
people who make decisions about housing," she responded
in what she hoped passed for an official, commanding tone.
"What do you think about the plans to tear down the projects?"

"Why you care?"

"I'm a reporter, actually, and I'm doing a story."

"Oh, a *re-por-ter*." He broke the word down into syllables,
trying for her inflection.

"That's right, a *re-por-ter*," Shelby told him with a half-
smile. "I'm sure you know there's been lots written about it,
and some papers have even talked to people who live here.
But mostly the stories have lots of crime statistics and facts and
figures. Just a quote or two from the people who are going to be
the most affected by it."

"So you think our lives are going to change when these
buildings are torn down, Miss Re-por-ter?" he asked, almost
amused.

"I don't know, are they?" Shelby knew what his answer
to the question would be but wanted to draw it out of him,
prolong the conversation.

"What you think, lady?" Ernie feigned exaggerated
patience, as if preparing to explain a simple truth to a child.
"Me, I've lived around here all my life. Looked just like little

Terrence over there when I was six. Even had a little bike too. And so it goes."

"So you're saying little Terrence's kids will be riding their bikes around a dumpster, and so on and so forth?"

"Well it ain't gonna be this dumpster, obviously. Does Terrence look unhappy to you? Does Bethie?" Ernie asked impatiently. "How you know everybody around here is so miserable?"

"I don't," Shelby told him evenly. "That's why I'm talking to you. To find out."

"Well, everybody's got their problems, don't they?" Those kids live right next door to a nasty drug dealer. Mean dude, beats his girlfriend up and pimps her out. You lucky you didn't pick him out for an interview. Yeah, we've got our problems here. They worse than yours? Maybe yes, maybe no. Don't know you. Probably mostly just different. Thought about moving before."

"You must want a different life if you've thought about leaving," Shelby pointed out.

Ernie took a long drag while he considered this. "Might've tried. But a different location, different building's pointless. Wherever you go, there you are. You think this plan they've got going to change a damn thing about how I live? I don't know how to do anything else, be anything else, or live anywhere else. Might want to, but..." His words trailed off and he looked over at the children again for a long time.

"How do you live, Ernie? What do you do with your time?" She couldn't help but take the risk and ask the pointed question.

"Yeah, you in the right profession lady. Full of questions. I'm a professor at Georgia Tech. Teach English, okay?" he said derisively.

"So what do you think I'm going to do? Grab you, wrestle you to the ground and make a citizens' arrest if you tell me the truth?"

"I sell drugs, okay. Try to do better things with the

money than the scum next door to those kids. Give some to
their ma, make sure they live right and don't end up doing the
same thing. Do something wrong for the greater good, guess
that makes me a Robin in the Hood. Get it? Robin who lives in
the Hood?"

He threw back his head and chuckled. Shelby couldn't
resist a little smile. They stood there for a while in silence and
watched the daylight fade.

Ernie stubbed out his cigarette and declared, "It's going
to be different for everybody. You'd have to interview the whole
damn building. Got enough paper in your little notebook for
that? The ones who know how to look at it will see this as an
opportunity. Of course I want to see those kids get out of here,
whether I think they okay for the moment or not. They still got
a chance. Their ma's still got a chance." She thought she saw a
touch of longing flicker in Ernie's eyes when he said this. "No
chance for the scum next door to them. Don't care about him."

"Maybe you shouldn't write yourself off along with
him, Ernie."

He smiled now. "Right, 'cause I'm a *good* drug dealer.
You know Bankhead's not all bad. We got us come culture here.
Even had a movie filmed here in the old school building over
by English Avenue. Ever seen *One Missed Call?* Japanese horror
film. Old Ernie will never look at that building the same way
again. Also got some rappers from here but you probably don't
know 'em. Shawty Lo, Dem Franchise Boyz, and D4L. They
all from Bankhead. We even got our own dance. Call it the
Bankhead Bounce. Wanna learn?"

"Why not? I got up today and said to myself, I think
I'll go learn a hip hop dance. By the way, I'm a very big fan of
Shawty Lo. Love him more than life itself."

"Yeah, I bet you do, re-por-ter. Don't hate. Just trying
to teach you some culture. Here's what you do. Move your
shoulders up and down and bend your arms toward your
chest." When he demonstrated, the effect was something like
jumping on a pogo stick, but going about it in a very cool,

subdued way.

"Okay." She dutifully hopped up and down, which sent the kids into fits of giggles.

"Now rock your upper body back and forth," Ernie instructed.

"I can't believe what I'll do for a story," Shelby complained as she started to rock.

"There you go. You can do a coupla variations. You can go fishin'--just act like you castin' a line."

"Well that I can handle." She threw out her arm and cast an imaginary line.

"Or do a touchdown. Throw down your imaginary football for a touchdown and do your own victory dance."

"I am not doing that," Shelby told him firmly. But she bounced an invisible football off of the pavement and did a half-strut.

"Last but not least, the running man. Move your arms like you running but in slow motion."

"Technically, that would be the walking man," Shelby corrected.

"You was one of those kids always interrupting the teacher in class, weren't you?"

"Could be," Shelby told him, trying for a convincing running man.

The kids continued to giggle as they watched. Terrence cast his own invisible fishing line, and Bethie skillfully demonstrated a "running-girl."

After this Ernie took a few minutes to scan his small kingdom with a watchful eye. "Terrence, Bethie!" he finally barked authoritatively. "Get your behinds inside, your momma's probably got dinner ready. Go on. And Terrence don't be leavin' that bike outside. Get even more rusted up or disappear and then what'll you do?"

The children reluctantly retreated from their spot near the dumpster. Terrence drug his bike up to the second floor of the building and a young woman appeared at the door, waved to Ernie, and regarded Shelby with curiosity. She had glossy black hair that was smoothed into submission and the same lean, stretched out look her daughter already had. Shelby thought she caught a longing look pass across Ernie's face again. They watched the family, along with the blue tricycle, disappear into apartment 242.

"I've got to go, Ernie, but I want to come back. I'm sort of curious about what you decide to do after they're done taking down the buildings. I'd like to know where those kids end up too."

He looked amused again, as if she had much to learn, then laughed and shook his head. "You're going to do a follow-up story on us, re-por-ter?"

"That's right, a follow-up," Shelby agreed. "I'll be back. Be good, Robin in the Hood."

He chuckled, made his way up the steps, and disappeared inside of his own apartment on the other side of where the children lived.

Shelby tried to quiet her thoughts as she drove home. Something in the way Ernie Thompson had talked, the way he saw more of the same in his future, disturbed her. When she finally stepped inside the tiny apartment, Shelby paced around with Toonces not far behind. There couldn't be anything sadder or more frustrating than a person trapped in a way of life they were so used to they couldn't see their way out. She understood.

A different location and a different building's pointless, he had told her. *Wherever I go, that's where I be.* Still the same Ernie. *Not going to change a damn thing about how I live. I don't know how to do anything else, be anything else, or live anywhere else.*

Didn't she tell herself that same thing every time she wanted to call Leo up and beg him to let her type out the rest of her days in the dusty little *Layton News* office? Hard to judge Ernie when she was having trouble with that all-important step away from the known herself. She paced some more as the hours ticked by, tried to eat but ended throwing half of her frozen dinner in the trash.

She thought about knocking on Mona's door for some conversation and leftovers, but it was late. Instead she wandered over to the window and looked down on the street at a couple arguing, in the throes of an intense conversation right in the middle of Peachtree. The girl had a mop of curls that were flying every which way. There was another girl trying to pull her away, sandwich herself in between the couple. The man was tall and even from here she could see the intensity when he gestured. Maybe she had danced with someone else, paid another man a little too much attention and the evening had soured. Or maybe he'd eyed another girl.

A few groups of people passed the trio, ignoring the heated exchange. Now Mr. Intensity pulled his girlfriend in and kissed her, ignoring the friend. Girlfriend slapped him in response and whirled away from him. The fifth group of people to walk by deftly sidestepped the scene. Mr. Intensity rubbed his cheek and hurried after her, but she shook him off. The women disappeared up the street at an angry, purposeful pace with the man still tailing them.

Shelby moved away from the window, remembering she had never taken her injection at dinner. After pulling the insulin out of the refrigerator she pressed the cold glass vial against her cheek, considering. What Ernie had said was true. *Wherever I go...*

"To hell with it," she muttered, and tossed the vial in the trash. As she watched the glass container lay there on top of the middle of discarded coffee grounds and food, the fake newspaper article she'd been given at her party caught her eye. In the picture above it she and Joe were laughing at something, freshly married.

After a long look at it Shelby gingerly pulled the vials off of the pile, laid them on the tile of the kitchen, and brought her shoe down on them decisively, like a newlywed breaking glass at a Jewish wedding. She heard the squelching sound as the glass mingled with the liquid inside. *Good.* It was only a matter of time now before her body would start to break down.

She thought about Joe giving up, Ernie too, and just couldn't make herself care.

Miranda flew up Peachtree Street with Clint not far behind. He had caught her at 404 again like he had some kind of damned radar or GPS on her. Lately his intensity was a rabid thing and she couldn't go anywhere without him knowing about it. When she had pulled into the parking lot at the bar his jeep had already been there. He'd been waiting at the door like a Doberman snapping from the end of a leash, denying her entrance. He had the bouncers pulling for him, and they'd done nothing when he had moved her towards the parking lot. They liked Clint and had pretended to busy themselves with checking the IDs of other customers while she'd screeched in protest and tried to drag her feet into the pavement. When she'd wrenched free she and Cora had headed for her favorite all-night diner. Of course Clint knew most of her little escapes and had had no trouble tailing them

"I don't even understand how you do it," she tossed over her shoulder, moving up the street at a quick clip. "You've got two jobs. Make that three. Being my keeper doesn't pay very well."

"Stay away from 404 and Jon," he old her shortly, and grabbed her wrist. "Stay away from the whole damn scene, it isn't you. Besides the obvious fact that this shit is going to kill you, you'll get yourself into more trouble than you know. Just stay away. How could you do this? I thought the baby was enough. Obviously not."

"Hey Clint, I think it's clear she wants to be left alone," Cora hissed.

"I'm this baby's father. Stay out if it. You're part of her problem. You're a real good influence right now with your drugs. Why don't you let us finish this conversation and clack off down the sidewalk in your 'hello boys, come-screw-me' boots?"

"Hello, am I here? Mind if I join the conversation about myself?" Miranda interjected acidly. "You don't trust me," she told Clint. "I was going into 404 to find Cora. I'm moving out of her place. I can't stay in a dorm room with a baby growing inside of me. We talked about this, you knew I was going to do it soon. Either your place or back to my parents'. Why can't you believe me?"

Clint sighed. "I do believe you."

"Then why are you so relentless? I know it didn't look good, me heading out to the bar. But I can't live like this. You have to back off."

"I can't. You'll get yourself into more trouble than you know. It's important that you stay away from there."

"I'm not going to use. You think so little of me that you honestly believe I'd hurt this baby?" Miranda demanded hotly.

"I've been there, remember? I'm still there some days. You're sick and I know you're going through hell. You need help. Let's get some for you. Stop being so proud," Clint pleaded.

Miranda studied his face and momentarily wondered at the cryptic variation on the message he'd delivered so many times before. *You'll get yourself into more trouble than you know. It's important you stay away from there.* Then she sank against his chest, suddenly tired from sprinting away from him. He pulled her up and branded her with another kiss.

CHAPTER FOURTEEN

"Shelby, open up." Maura rapped sharply on the door, every bit as authoritative in personal situations as she was at work.

Shelby nearly cracked her head on the porcelain as she scrambled to pull herself upright from crouching over the toilet. No way was she letting her boss see her while she reeked of vomit in her Elvis nightshirt, her hair standing out in strange, oily clumps away from her head. She tried to pat in down and subdue it. No hope. It was the worst case of fish-hair to date.

It hadn't been as hard as she'd thought it would be, at least not at first. Extra trips to the restroom at work, slipping away from her desk more often during the day. An extra six-pack of Diet Coke brought in a cooler and poured over extra ice. A little less energy and a little more time to get her thoughts fashioned into articles on the computer screen. All very matter-of-fact, this business of letting nature take over. Then her body had moved into the more serious stage of protest and she spent most of her time bent over the toilet. Work was out.

Maura rapped harder. "Like they say, I can do this all day," she called through the door.

"Just a minute." The attempt at a bright voice jammed in her throat and came out as a croak. Who was she kidding? This was Maura, she wasn't going to go away. Shelby hobbled to the door and yanked it open.

"If you paid me better I could move into a nicer place. A really ritzy complex with more security where you have to be buzzed in. Might help out in case any unwanted visitors come around. So who, exactly, is 'they' anyway?" she demanded.

"*Who says?* Now get inside, would you? You're embarrassing me."

"Nice hair. So you're into appearances? Since when?" Maura made a show of looking around and surveying the empty hallway. "I certainly wouldn't want to humiliate you in front of all of your neighbors," she said, her voice laced with sarcasm. "You're lucky you're sick, or I'd fire you for talking to me that way," she told Shelby casually. "You look like dogshit, you're coming with me."

"Well that was...graphic. Thanks. With all due respect, boss, I think I'll stay here. I'm not going anywhere like this, including any kind of doctor's office, so don't even think about it. What I need is time to rest...stress free time," she told Maura pointedly. "Without interruption."

"Get dressed and for God's sake gargle with something," Maura ordered. "Bring your ID and insurance card. Some clothes too, since they'll probably want to admit you. I'll be in the car. If you're not down there in five minutes you are fired. I don't think they're hiring over at the *Journal-Constitution* right now, either. Besides, you'd need a good reference from me. I have more pull than all of you snot-nosed reporters think."

"Maura, believe me, none of us underestimate you," Shelby half-snarled as she resentfully drug a comb through her hair. Just the simple act of combing her hair drained her energy, and she could feel the nausea building again. "Go ahead, I'll be down in a minute. But only because I'm not so certain you wouldn't ax me."

Gee, maybe I haven't thought this through, she thought derisively. *I've been hiding in my apartment, getting sicker and waiting to die, and now I'm packing my things because I'm worried about keeping my job.*

"Great. I'll be waiting," Maura told her, leaving Shelby to gather her clothes as instructed. When she painfully shuffled down the hall she saw Mona's door softly close, as if the little woman had seen what she was waiting for. So Mona had told on her, called the *Atlanta Minute* office for reinforcements. She inched down the stairs, every body part screaming in protest as she moved. Maura could have hauled her to the car, she outweighed her by about sixty pounds. But Shelby sensed Maura had left her to come down by herself to spare her any further embarrassment. She was disheveled. She smelled bad. She was weak and couldn't even stand up straight. Had she really intended for no one to ever see her like this, to just waste away in her apartment alone?

She settled into Maura's serviceable Ford and they drove a few seconds in silence before Shelby asked, "Can you at least tell me exactly where we're on our way to? I'm assuming you're dragging me to Atlanta Mercy against my will."

"Oh good, so Atlanta Mercy would be your first choice then?" Maura asked brightly.

"So what makes you think I'd need a reference letter from you anyway? I've built up a pretty good book of clips."

"Shelby, let's just stop for a minute and be serious. We're all worried about you. You're sick and you don't seem interested in helping yourself. It seems like you've given up. You lost your husband but you don't talk about it. You uprooted your life to come out here but you don't talk about that either."

"I thought it was pretty obvious. I was trying to start over," Shelby hedged.

"And do you feel like you've been able to do that?" Maura's tone was heavy, meaningful.

"Well, it's like Ernie Thompson said. Wherever I go, there I am," Shelby told her with a sigh.

*   *   *

The heart monitor blipped rhythmically, its clipped cadence almost putting her to sleep. Shelby already had a hospital gown on, which looked on her diminished frame like she was wearing a paisley tent. Maybe they figured the bright pattern would cheer patients up. Not so far, she noted.

She had uncomfortably submitted to a thorough

examination, which netted raised eyebrows when the admitting doctor came to the large purple butterfly on her lower back. So much for the strategically chosen, private location.

Shelby could vividly recall the skeptical look on the heavily pierced and decorated tattoo artist's face when she'd strolled into his shop that day. The sensation of the buzzing needle touched to her back had not been painful but an odd vibration that traveled all the way down to her leg. It was maddening and worse than a sharp, expected burst of pain; it had taken all of her resolve to lay still. But she'd been determined to be a story for any burly man who might come into the shop and howl and whine as the needle dug through his skin. She could be tougher than that.

The doctor who had introduced himself as Cole Michaels thought it would be humorous to matter-of-factly keep a running commentary on the tattoo while he assessed her. "Large, purple discoloration on the lower back, left side, that appears to have a black outline. Approximately four inches tall by four inches wide." He grinned then, with a smile that didn't so much appear on his face as spread across it slowly, like melted butter oozing across a plate.

Shelby responded to that with a croaked out, "It was college, and as the dumb-kid phrase goes, it seemed like a good idea at that time. My one act of rebellion." *I'll strangle you with your stethoscope,* she thought sourly.

Now the nurse handling the patient intake questions asked, "Are you able to get around by yourself at home and manage basic activities of daily living?"

"That's a loaded question," Shelby said, and quickly grabbed the sick pan she'd used twice already. When she was done she reached for the towel the nurse silently handed her. Then, catching the nurse's look, she added with a sigh, "Reasonably well, I guess."

"Has anyone threatened, harmed, or abused you recently? Do you feel safe in your home? That's a pretty nasty bruise on your leg."

"Ma'am, absolutely no one harmed me, until I got here." Shelby could only keep the sarcasm in check for so long when she'd been poked and prodded within an inch of her life and numerous vials of blood had been taken from her. "I only live," she continued tiredly, "with my cat, who I guess you could say indirectly harmed me. I tripped over him on my way to the bathroom. If you want I can file charges against him." Even to her, the truth sounded like a lie.

There it was again, the arch of the nurse's brow. She shifted her clipboard and continued to scribble, probably something about a potentially uncooperative patient in the intensive care unit. Maybe even a recommendation for a psych consult. Shelby tried in vain to read the notations, vaguely resenting that the nurse seemed so secretive.

"Ms. Norris, do you think domestic violence is funny?" the nurse asked archly. "I'm just trying to do my job."

Shelby winced, immediately contrite. "I'm sorry," she mumbled. "No, I don't think it's funny. I really don't think anything's funny right now."

The same thirtyish doctor with thin wire-rimmed glasses swept back into the room. He had wavy hair. Freckles dusted his face as if someone had tossed sand at him and it had landed in random spots across his nose and cheeks. She thought it odd that he had spent ten minutes with her and already knew one of her little secrets, the tattoo, something some of her friends didn't know about. Nothing like a full-body exam to get you acquainted.

"Ms. Norris, as I said before, I'm Dr. Michaels. Have you noticed a funny smell to your breath? I'm sure you've been noticing symptoms like increased urination and hunger for some time now."

"Diabetic Ketoacidosis," Shelby supplied tonelessly.

"And you've been diabetic for about eleven years now."

"Eleven," Shelby murmured in agreement.

"Well, we'll continue to pump fluids in you since you're pretty severely dehydrated. I'm also not comfortable in sending you home until we see some stable blood sugars, so I'm afraid you'll have to be admitted."

Now it was Shelby's turn to raise her eyebrows. No accusations, no recriminations, just brisk and matter-of-fact. "No lecture?" she asked curiously.

The doctor leaned forward and stared hard at her. "Would it help, Ms. Norris? If you'll be receptive I'll be glad to give you one. Otherwise I'll skip it. You seem intelligent enough to know the consequences of not managing your disease."

"Wow. I'm pretty sure that's not in the physician's handbook for addressing noncompliant diabetics."

"No handbook for that particular subject. Tell me, are you always this glib when it comes to your illness?"

It was more of a declaration on his part than a question, and he didn't wait for an answer. He just swept out of the room, leaving Shelby staring at the back of his white coat.

*   *   *

"I can't believe some people actually check into the hospital for exhaustion," Shelby complained the next morning. A night of having blood drawn and hourly blood sugar checks had netted her a solid half-hour of sleep. "Who gets sleep here?"

Shelby had been reminded of her first hospital visit after she'd been diagnosed at twenty-one. She'd been convinced she was having a fabulous dream, semi-conscious of an intense, exotic man massaging her arm. Then she'd felt the pinch and the needle as the overeager young lab tech who hadn't mastered the art of finding a good vein finished his work.

"…And good morning to you too, Ms. Norris." True to his word, Dr. Cole Michaels had stopped by to check on her. He had an oddly familiar and cheerful way of putting her in her place that she wasn't sure if she liked or disliked. She noted he was in denim jeans, a Georgia Yellow Jackets jersey, and tennis shoes. Just Cole Michaels and not the doctor for the moment.

"Sorry," she mumbled. She studied him. "Don't you

ever get sick of dealing with people who are either in the throes of extreme pain, or devastated? You see people at their absolute worst. You don't deal with them unless they have a problem. A big problem. Your job's worse than customer service."

"Sometimes I get tired of it. But on the good days I get to make it better for people."

"Are there more good days than bad?"

"You always ask this many questions?" he mimicked her staccato, rapid-fire style of speaking to perfection and she couldn't help but smile.

"Always. I'm a journalist."

His face dawned with recognition, bloomed with satisfaction at having plucked a misplaced fact out of the air. "Shelby Norris of *Atlanta Minute*. I knew I'd seen or heard the name before."

"You read *Atlanta Minute*?" she asked incredulously. "You strike me as more of a *Journal-Constitution* kind of guy."

"I try to make time in my day for both." A smile quirked at the corners of his mouth but quickly disappeared. The doctor was back, despite the Yellow Jackets jersey and jeans. "Shelby, I hope you'll start taking better care of yourself. If I was your doctor I'd recommend you be put on an insulin pump, but I don't think you're ready for that yet. That being said, I don't think you would have reached the stage of Ketoacidosis you were in unless you had stopped taking your insulin altogether. Am I correct in assuming this?" The words hung in the air as he stood there, waited.

Shelby fidgeted, plucked at the scratchy hospital blanket, and examined the bruises on her arm from constant needle pokes. The IV was secured with tape to her wrist. It was delivering fluids her body had lost, trying to restore some kind of balance to her system. Some of the bruises already seemed to be fading, the purple and yellow mingling like a child's muddy-looking watercolor project.

She knew she should feel grateful to Maura and Mona for stepping in, but she just felt ashamed. Embarrassed. She had elicited a confession from Maura en route to the hospital that Mona had called the *Atlanta Minute* offices and asked them to "persuade" Shelby to come to the hospital. Shelby smiled at the thought of the chubby little grandmother wrestling her into a white van and speeding off with her like a kidnap victim. With the state Shelby was in, the little Filipino might have been able to manage it.

"Don't you have other patients to save?" she finally asked rudely. "You're an ER doctor so why are you here?"

"I'll leave if you want me to. Shelby, I would ask you if there's something going on in your life, but I doubt you'd tell me. You seem depressed. Depression can be a side issue with diabetics, as you probably know. I'm not trying to pry into your personal life. I'm just trying to help you gain some insight, figure out if there's another issue to deal with that might be affecting your overall health."

"Okay," he said patiently when Shelby didn't answer. "I remember you telling me you don't have a regular physician out here yet. You've recently moved? What brought you to Atlanta?"

"The internet," Shelby answered cryptically. "And the mother of all kerfuffles."

"The internet? Care to elaborate on that?"

"Nope."

"Well then," he soldiered on, his bright voice not masking his irritation, "I peeked at your chart and found out your potassium level is still very low from all of the vomiting, so they'll probably start another IV for that. Potassium given intravenously tends to make the arm cramp up. Hurts like hell, actually, from what I've told," he added cheerfully.

With a few long-limbed strides, he was out the door again, leaving Shelby glaring after him. She sighed. "Dr. Michaels!" she called. He turned around.

"My husband committed suicide. He'd been diagnosed with ALS," she said in a rush. "I hated him, I still do, for giving up. And now I'm here because I tried to kill myself, just more slowly. Pretty hypocritical, huh? I drove six hundred and twenty-two miles to move out here and take another job because I couldn't stand to live in the house he'd fixed up for us anymore. I've been trying to start over for him. For myself, I should say, because that's what he really wanted me to do. It hasn't worked. I took a quiz a long time ago on the internet. It told me the city I was best suited for was Atlanta, so here I am."

He didn't offer her any condolences or apologies. His face didn't betray any shock or telegraph any pity. "Thank you for your honesty, Shelby Norris," was all he said before she watched him disappear out of the room. She didn't have time to ponder that before he peeked around the door again.

"What's a kerfuffle?" he demanded.

"It's basically a state of confusion," she told him with a faint grin. "I spend a lot of my time confused, so it's one of my favorite words."

*   *   *

The next day, at the same time, Cole Michaels appeared again in gray sweats.

"Another unofficial visit?" she asked lightly, but suddenly felt the need to start fidgeting. She commanded herself to keep still and stop picking at the damned hospital blanket. She could pick all she wanted, but there was no getting around what she had told him yesterday. It had almost been a relief, to tell someone out loud what she'd tried to do to herself. But why him?

"Something like. Well, you're looking better. Has your temperament improved?" he asked with a cautious arch of his brow.

"Don't bet on it," she told him with a smile. Was there a special thank-you card for doctors who knew the right moment to walk away? One that read "thanks for not ordering that psych consult even though I clearly need it?" She'd been replaying his exit and simple thank-you ever since he had left. His reaction had intrigued her.

"How about doing something to pass the time," he suggested.

"I have a book."

"How about Hangman? You up for a few rounds?"

"I didn't think ER doctors ever followed up with their patients. You do it by playing Hangman?"

"Not usually," he allowed. The melted-butter-on-a-plate grin oozed across his face again.

"I suspect, Dr. Michaels, that you need a life outside of the emergency ward," she told him, grabbing a notepad Maura had brought her. She produced a couple of pens from her purse and handed him one.

"Thanks," he muttered. "You come up with a word for me to guess first."

A few minutes later, Shelby sighed, "You're hopeless. And I even stuck to medical terminology to make it easy for you." She gestured to the blanks that were still unfilled, the letters he'd incorrectly barked out in an attempt to spell out the word in her head. Each wrong letter equaled a body part in the hangman's noose, and now he had "hung" himself.

"I need to know," he told her, raising his hands in supplication. "What's the mystery word?"

She filled in the blanks for him then.

"*Ketoacidosis*," he read in wonder. "You have a twisted sense of humor, Shelby Norris."

"So I've been told, Dr. Michaels. So I've been told."

"It's my turn to come up with a word," he declared, grabbing the notepad. "I've still got a few minutes left in my shift."

CHAPTER FIFTEEN

Lindy Thomason knew there were some people who didn't approve of her job, what it represented. She thought of those who disapproved as "the self-righteous many." Others, surprisingly, were the former and current heroin addicts she was trying to help.

Lindy worked as a nurse at New Horizons methadone clinic and gave drugs to the addicted to ease their withdrawal symptoms. For the past five years she had seen people at their sickest: sweating, shaking, puking, hurting, when they were trying to quit. She didn't believe they should be physically punished for trying to do the right thing. Of course, the "self-righteous many" would argue that was the price you paid for choosing to take drugs in the first place.

It did sound strange when she boiled down her job description to its bare bones: *I give a drug to addicts so they'll stop taking drugs.* That was the problem most people had with it: substituting one drug for another. Some addicts who tried standard methadone maintenance treatment saw the $13 a day cost as money they were paying for another habit.

"Methadone is a last resort," an addict had told her once. "Once you get on it it's just something else to kick. I just don't see any future in it." Another had said, "Some say methadone saved their life, but what kind of life do you have? Constipated, sweating and sedated..."

The term "orange handcuffs," coined in the early days of methadone treatment, summed up the general thoughts of non-believers nicely. The pills taken in orange juice under the watchful eye of a nurse looked just like tiny handcuffs.

But there were others, Lindy thought. Those who would swear she had saved their life. Those who were living reasonably normal lives now.

Lindy felt being constipated and sedated beat dead of an overdose any day. Not that she agreed with the "sweating and sedated" assessment. Methadone patients were supposed to be able to feel some pain and experience normal emotional reactions, another interesting part of her job. Ease the pain but leave some. Some pain, a healthy amount that let her patients know they were alive, was good. A person on methadone to help curb their cravings could perform normal tasks of daily living and even drive a car or operate machinery. Lindy smiled at the thought of 90-pound Anita Velasquez, one of her favorite patients, happily operating a forklift thanks to her daily dose of methadone. Better yet, maybe Anita could chase her ex-boyfriend /ex-pimp around with a bulldozer and hopefully catch up to him with it at some point.

"Lindy, can you come do a new patient assessment?" the receptionist's voice called.

"Sure, baby, give me just a sec." Lindy gave her dark braids a toss and set down the charts she'd been going over. She took a deep breath as she grabbed the clipboard with the necessary forms and questions. She always wondered who she would be meeting, what their story would be. A sad one, probably.

When Lindy stepped into the reception area she noticed the young woman in a ponytail anxiously twirling the crystal cross she wore around her neck. There were dark circles etched underneath the girl's deep blue eyes. A beauty, at least for now. If she continued to use she would likely go from willowy to bony, unhealthy; the mane of hair would become dull and matted, unwashed; and the vivid almost-purple eyes would become flat, no longer taking much notice of the world around her and telegraphing the intelligent awareness Lindy noticed there.

She walked up to the girl, who looked as if she had a

severe case of the flu. Patients complained of feeling the sickest the first three days after they stopped using, and described the experience as the worst case of the flu they ever had, squared. Other symptoms such as craving and insomnia could linger up to six months. All part of the fun package.

A lanky man with a tiny cross dangling from his left ear and a slight but not unattractive overbite over full bottom lips sat beside the girl, stroking her hand, trying to comfort her. *That one, he's been there already,* she thought. Lindy had a sixth sense about these things. She could always spot the battle-scarred look of a recovering addict, someone who was jumping into the fray all over again each morning when they woke up.

"I promised you I'd be there," she heard him tell the girl. "I will, even if I have to cut out of work early and drive you here myself."

"What's your name, baby?" Lindy asked as she knelt beside the young woman, who she guessed to be about eighteen or so. The girl couldn't weigh more than a hundred and five, hundred and ten pounds.

"Miranda," the girl told her in a hoarse voice. "Miranda Linn."

"You been throwing up a lot, Miranda?"

"Not for awhile…Lindy." The girl referenced Lindy's name tag and shivered involuntarily. "Past that stage. Do I have to be throwing up to get help?"

Lindy ignored the girl's tone. "But you're still having cravings, huh?"

"That's right, Lindy." The girl teetered on the verge of further sarcasm but seemed to rethink it at the last moment. The young man who was her boyfriend, no doubt, looked ready to tell her to relax and be nice. He rested his hand on her arm, but seemed to rethink commenting. Yep, he had definitely been there.

A lot of first-timers saw her as a gatekeeper, someone who could dole out or withhold relief. She hated to see the flicker of fear in their eyes once they had said something inappropriate, maybe cursed her out. As if she would hold the medication just out of reach, use it as either reward or punishment.

"You know, you can be as big a bitch to me as you want," she told Miranda. "I'm still going to help you. If you decide on methadone treatment you'll take the pills daily. There are some rules to follow--we'll test your urine from time to time to make sure you're not still using. But I never refused to help somebody just because they were rude to me. God knows I'd have a hard time doing my job if that were my policy. So do you feel up to answering these questions and me giving you a real quick medical exam, Miranda? "

The girl actually gave her a wan smile and took the clipboard.

"Okay, sugar. After you're done filling those out and reading all of the information, you can bring it back to me. Then if you have any questions or concerns, we can talk about them."

"I can tell you right now I'll only have one concern," the girl told her, an odd combination of hope and fear in her voice. Any expectant mother would have recognized it. "My baby."

CHAPTER SIXTEEN

"Well you smell better than when I brought you in, at least," Maura declared.

"Yeah, they let me take a shower and everything. Probably charged me thirty bucks for the little bar of soap. Surprised they didn't make me insert dollar bills for the hot water," Shelby told her, stuffing some clothes into a plastic bag.

"Well, you're lucky I provide such excellent medical coverage to my employees," Maura reminded her. "And just two days in the hospital, that's not so bad."

"Yes, boss. Toss me my iPod, will you?" Shelby caught the small white machine deftly in one hand as it flew towards her and stuck it in the bag. Cole had caught her listening to it on his third unofficial visit, silently mouthing along, the hospital-issued blanket jumping up and down as her feet kept time underneath. He hadn't bothered to mask his amusement, but she hadn't been embarrassed.

It was almost like in another lifetime when Joe had caught her talking to herself at the city council meeting, but she'd squelched that thought quickly.

"So...are you ready?" Maura asked expectantly, her gaze stern.

"Are you seriously asking me if I'm ready to leave a hospital?" Shelby sniffed, sure of what Maura meant but determined to avoid the question's intended meaning.

Maura continued to stare at her. "I'm assuming you're not planning any more stays at Atlanta Mercy? I can count on you to keep yourself healthy enough to keep supplying my paper with fluff?"

"No more planned stays. I'll do my best to keep myself fit enough for the daily demands of churning out fluff," Shelby muttered softly.

Cole stepped into the room, sparing her from any further discussion about managing her general well-being but opening up the door to another uncomfortable scene.

"So, you're leaving us." He shifted from foot to foot, played with the papers in his hand.

"Well, you know, every good vacation must end," Shelby told him dryly. "I wish I could say more for the food and the accommodations. I know you tried your best in the entertainment department." She flashed him a lopsided grin.

"I'll bring the car around," Maura told her with a smirk.

When Maura sauntered out of the room, he handed her the papers.

"A schedule for classes on managing diabetes? Is this a condition for release, part of my parole?"

"Something like that. They're held right here at the hospital. You can, ah, look me up if you decide to give them a try. Fare well and don't come back, Ms. Norris. If you do make it for the classes."

"Why so stiff and formal all of a sudden? Call me Shelby. We've played Hangman. You've seen my tattoo."

The nurse who had just brought a wheelchair into the room glanced up sharply, and Shelby couldn't help snickering as she flopped herself into it. As she was wheeled by, Shelby handed him a piece of folded notebook paper.

"Oh, wow. So I've got first name privileges if we ever run across each other again," Cole said sardonically, slipping the piece of paper in his jeans pocket.

"Get yourself in the news and I'll come interview you, Dr. Cole Michaels," she promised. Then she pointed bravely ahead and declared, "Well, onward," to the nurse who was in charge of wheeling her to meet Maura outside.

Cole chuckled softly as he watched her twist around in the wheelchair, narrowing her green eyes and pursing her full lips thoughtfully before she give him a final salute.

"What's the point of this whole wheelchair protocol?" he heard her ask the nurse. "If you don't trust me to leave the hospital on my own power, I've got no business leaving, right?"

Her hair was sticking up in back; orange leopard-spotted slippers were jammed on feet that barely touched the foot rests, she was so small. What a God-awful contrast they were to the red track suit she was wearing. Now he watched her disappear, facing him again as the elevator doors closed on the strange woman/child/reporter. There was no way to tell if she was any more able to meet life or start over as her husband had wanted her to do. He was interested in the answer to that question. He pulled the paper out of his pocket and unfolded it

Dear Dr. Michaels who was really only my doctor for a few hours, thanks for caring when I really gave you no reason to care. Why you bothered with a cranky bitch like myself on your own time is beyond me, but I want you to know it made a difference. I don't know of any other ER docs who would bother to check on a patient afterwards, especially one like me. The games of Hangman helped to pass the time. I'll never forget the gesture.

Sincerely, Shelby Norris

P.S. Are you really that bad at Hangman or did you just let me win?

The last thing written on the note was six dashes, indicating blanks to another mystery word. But she had filled them in and the message read, *Thanks.*

"I'll do my best to think of something newsworthy," he muttered softly. "Please take care of yourself, Shelby Norris."

CHAPTER SEVENTEEN

Miranda gathered up her books, hoisted the backpack over her shoulder, and stepped out of New Horizons into the heat. Just three weeks, but this was part of a familiar routine now, lugging her books into the methadone center and reading while she waited to swallow the small pills that would take the edge off.

After the pills she usually lingered a few minutes to talk to Lindy or the other staff, sometimes the other patients. An unlikely second family. *We're going to try, just try,* Clint had told her. And she was. They were.

Her parents had interestingly been silent and helped her pack up her things, baby books and all, to move them over to his apartment. She had heard Clint's low promise as she finished arranging the books, his assurance to her parents that he would see to her getting regular treatment. *Almost like a parent-teacher conference,* she'd thought resentfully, but she would try with him.

The move out of Cora's had been quick and painless with only her books and a single pile of clothes to shove in a small bag. No longer interested in frequenting 404 or bonding by using recreational drugs, Miranda had shifted into the liability rather than friend column in Cora's ledger.

"*Senora, sus papeles.*" It took a minute for Miranda to realize that the voice was calling after her as she unlocked her car. She slowly returned to present time and space and to the tiny, hard-looking Latina who was holding the papers out to her.

"Thanks," she told the small woman, who looked like some sort of renegade Santa's elf with dark, wicked eyes and olive skin. She saw the potential for mischief and a fun kind of wickedness in the elf's eyes, imagined her petulantly putting dresses on macho action figures she didn't approve of making for the children on Santa's "good" list.

"No problem." She had a low, scratchy voice to match the look but her demeanor was off, shy and unsure. "You're always hauling all of those books and papers around so they must be important."

"For a class. You usually seem to be coming as I'm going."

"And you're usually behind a mountain of books. I didn't really know what your face looked like before," the Latina said with good humor. "I'm Anita Velasquez."

"I'm Miranda. Let me put down this mountain of books so I can shake your hand. I really do appreciate it. So what are you doing right now, Anita Velasquez?"

The small woman looked startled and slightly suspicious. "*Nada*. Why?"

"Would you like to go get a coffee? I'll buy."

"Oh, that's not necessary, Miss." The small woman looked even more uncomfortable now. "Just a few papers."

"Not for the papers. I've decided I'm bored with myself and walking around just thinking about my own problems."

"You want to hear my problems? As a favor to you?" Now her expression was less suspicious, slightly amused and quizzical.

"If you want to tell me what they are, sure."

"Okay, just a minute." The Latina flipped open a cell phone and Miranda noticed the two marks on the woman's arm, ones that should be completely faded considering she had seen her coming in and out of the treatment center for weeks.

So the elf was still using. She spoke rapidly in Spanish and Miranda, semi-fluent, caught the gist. She was letting boyfriend know where she was going. Said boyfriend seemed to be telling her to get home now, judging from Anita's reactions. Now she was telling boyfriend where to go. The woman ended the conversation with a few phrases that were not readily taught in Spanish class. Miranda smiled.

"Snake," Anita said dismissively. Then she said abruptly, almost defiantly, "Jimmy's my sort of boyfriend but he's really my…manager, if you know what I mean. I hope you don't have a problem with that."

"I think *you* have a problem with that," Miranda told her meaningfully. "Let's go get that coffee."

Now it was Anita's turn to be arch. "Should you be drinking coffee? What about *el niño?*"

"Actually I was going to go for a smoothie. So you noticed some of the books were maternity books, huh?"

"I did. Just noticed by chance, really. I wasn't spying."

"I hope you don't have a problem with that, me being pregnant," Miranda bantered with the embarrassed woman.

"No. Do you have a problem with you being pregnant?" Anita asked now, and the two dissolved into easy laughter.

As they ordered at the café Miranda caught Anita eyeing a gargantuan blueberry muffin displayed behind the glass case. Judging by the woman's waiflike appearance she should be hungry.

"Blueberries are my thing," Miranda announced. "I'm going for it, but I can't eat that whole blueberry mountain by myself. You'll have to help."

Anita shot her a grateful look, and when the two sat down Miranda divided the muffin. As she watched Anita fight to eat her half slowly, Miranda said, "So what's with this loser boyfriend/manager you were telling off on the phone?"

Anita's mouth tweaked up as she finished slurping the white foam at the bottom of the cup. "I'll have to remember you speak a little bit Spanish. That 'loser' I'm going to ditch. I'm serious. I'm planning on moving out of his place."

Miranda scraped her chair back when both of their halves of the muffin were reduced to crumbs. "Well, today's as good a day as any, then," she decreed.

"For what?" Anita asked, suspicious again.

"You said you were planning on moving out of his

place. So let's move you out. Have you got a lot of stuff? My car's small, but I've got four hours til class."

"I didn't exactly mean today," Anita told her uncertainly.

"If you didn't mean today then you didn't mean it," Miranda dared.

The Latina licked some of the crumbs off of her fingers and considered. "If Jimmy catches us moving me out…"

"Do you have a lot to move?" Miranda repeated.

"Well, no," Anita hedged. "But you pregnant, you don't need to involve yourself. It wouldn't be right."

"I promise not to lift any heavy boxes," Miranda told her, purposely sidestepping Anita's real meaning.

"I meant…" Anita clarified with a sigh, "that he's not a nice man."

"Which is why we should move you out as soon as possible."

"All right," Anita yielded. "If Jimmy's around we just leave. We'll do it later. And if he's not we pack up fast, and I mean we beat it."

"Agreed," Miranda conceded in a satisfied, silky tone. "Lead the way. Where are we going?"

"Bankhead," Anita told her petulantly, clearly still convinced this was a bad idea. The Latina said little on the way, just gave directions to the identical rows of apartment buildings.

The apartment, as expected, was a depressing one. The carpet was brown but still showed stains and probably needed to be flea-bombed. Miranda noted the syringe wrappers that littered the worn couch and her skin instantly came alive, shifted and crawled at the sight. *This is how I've lived,* she thought. Not so long ago her purse had been filled with syringes.

"Do you have anything to put your clothes in?" she demanded of Anita.

"Just some trash bags," Anita admitted.

Trash bags which were plentiful since they obviously hadn't been used to actually take out the trash, Miranda thought, but bit back the comment. "Well, let's start stuffing."

Miranda was interested as they shoved the clothes into the garbage bags; some were heavy, bulky sweatshirts and sweats and others were barely-there shorts and tops. It almost seemed as if Anita was trying to reconcile two lives, just like Miranda had a few short weeks ago. Covering her body up as much as she could on her off time.

Now Anita carefully placed some framed pictures in one of the bags. One was of a sober couple, their lips firmly pursed together and stern expressions on their faces like in an old Western photo. The woman wore a crucifix and a man with a moustache stood beside her, his arm firmly clamped around her shoulder. Her parents, no doubt. In the other picture Anita stood proudly beside a fresher, plumper version of herself.

"My younger sister Leticia," Anita told her. "That was her *Quinceañera*. Fifteenth birthday party."

The younger girl looked like a dark, shy Scarlett O'Hara with the dress to match, her shoulders erect. Trying to take a photo that made her look the woman she was supposed to be with this rite of passage. The parents were also in this picture, their mouths tipped downwards and their eyes slightly cast on Anita's far less conservative dress. The picture said it all, seemed to tell Anita's whole back story in one captured image.

"Leticia'd be twenty-five now," Anita murmured. "Wanted to be a lawyer last I knew so I hope she's making it."

Miranda thought of how close she had come to this, leaving herself to look at pictures of people lost to her and wonder about them. She stuffed the last pile of clothes into the bag, determined, and tied the top in a decisive knot. She scanned the apartment again; it was all Jimmy except for the clothes and a few pictures. Electronics, beat-up furniture, a Carmen Electra poster tacked to the wall. The requisite neon beer sign and some pictures of his own.

In a photo that occupied a place of honor, Jimmy was boiled down and hard with coppery skin stretched over his bones. He and some friends had their arms splayed out and their fingers twisted as if they were trying to throw tough-guy gangster signs but couldn't quite get it right.

"So," Miranda asked expectantly. "Where are we going from here?"

Anita's eyes traveled downward. "Women's shelter I went to the last time, I guess."

Miranda almost made another characteristic snap decision and offered up her old bedroom at her parents.' Her Mom would readily take in Anita. Or Miranda could even sweet-talk Clint into letting her stay on the couch at his apartment.

No, she decided. The woman wouldn't accept either invitation. She was too proud and clearly had little experience with even the simplest of kindnesses being offered up to her. Miranda imagined how her father would shake his head with a smile and joke about she and her mother picking up too many strays. She thought that she wouldn't mind catching some of the best of what she sensed in Anita Velasquez if the woman did bite.

"Hey, Anita," she said suddenly, "I think you owe Jimmy a proper goodbye before we book it out of here."

Anita looked momentarily alarmed but her mind was quick. No further clarification on Miranda's part was necessary. The two girls communicated on another level and a wicked smile suddenly appeared on Anita's face. Miranda thought she could almost hear the corners of the Latina's hard mouth creak from non-use. She hoped to help her new friend oil her smile up.

"He loves this damn ball cap. I'm surprised he left it here since it's always on his greasy head." Anita dangled the cap thoughtfully and held the brim gingerly between her fingers as if it was infected.

"Your decision. Up to you to decide where you think it belongs," Miranda told her, eyes glinting merrily as she surveyed the poster highlighting Carmen Electra's bikini-clad curves. "You take care of it and I'm going to tend to Carmen over here, just based on my own personal objections, if you don't mind."

"Please do." Anita issued the invitation in a mock-formal tone, body bent low in a bow.

Miranda fished for the black marker and orange highlighters she kept in her purse to use for class and immediately went to work on Carmen. She kept the artwork simple and blacked a few teeth out. A moustache followed and then she filled in strategic body parts she decided should be more covered. Now Carmen wore a chaste black suit instead of a skimpy one.

"Sorry, Carmen. Nothing personal," she apologized brightly.

"I think I decided where it belongs," Anita called from the restroom. Miranda joined her as Anita casually let the prized ball cap hover for a second and then drop into the commode.

"He'll have to fish it out if he loves it so much, and I don't even think he knows how to use a washing machine," Anita said mirthfully. The two dissolved into laughter for the second time and drug the garbage bags out of Jimmy's apartment. The remote to the television was shoved into one of them. The girls had decreed that Jimmy would just have to get up to change the channel from now on.

Before they continued down the stairs, Anita stopped and took a second to make a final rude gesture towards the apartment that was a nice, decisive punctuation mark on the departure.

CHAPTER EIGHTEEN

"Let's see that belly!" Lindy demanded as soon as Miranda walked into the clinic.

"Have you ever heard of boundaries, Lindy?" Miranda asked with an eye-roll, but pulled her loose cotton top up to reveal her midriff. This was part of an often-repeated request to check on her "baby bump."

"Hmmph. Looks like maybe you've done a week straight of buffets at the Golden Corral, but not much more than that. You'll probably tip the scales at all of 125 at nine months."

"Yes, Lindy, I know you want me to blow up like a Macy's Thanksgiving Day Parade balloon. I'm only three months along."

"You should be bigger. In my world everyone would be bigger, pregnant or not," Lindy declared, patting her ample behind to make her point. "What's wrong with having both..."

"Quality and quantity," Miranda supplied with a snicker, rounding out Lindy's familiar routine. "The rest of us just can't pull it off like you can, Lindy."

"Well you're right about that. Let's get you your medication. We'll do a quick assessment and have you hop on the scale, see how much weight you haven't gained. By the way, how's that boyfriend of yours treating you?"

"Pampering me to the point of annoyance. But he does buy me all of the Happy Meals I want. He won't let me drink the Coke though. He makes me get milk," Miranda complained. "And he tries to get me to substitute the fries with sliced apples. I draw the line there."

"Don't pretend you're not thankful for him, baby,"
Lindy chuckled. "Now get on the scale."

"One hundred and thirteen pounds," Lindy announced
a minute later. Miranda looked sheepish as the nurse slid the
metal square on the doctor's scale back to zero.

Miranda stuck her tongue out. "I'll be well past 125 by
nine months. You've got plenty of time to fatten me up, make
me nice and round. You know I do have a regular OB doctor.
Are you satisfied, Mama Lindy?"

"Never. Let's take your blood pressure. Speaking of
waifs who weigh next to nothing, have you seen Miss Anita?"
Lindy asked with a frown.

"Not since last week. I was going to call her, check up on
her tomorrow. She hasn't been in today?"

As Miranda posed the question she felt an uneasy,
internal radar start to hum.

"Well..." Lindy seemed to wrestle for a split second with
her medical sense of propriety. She never discussed patients or
their treatment routines with other patients.

"Oh, give it up, Lindy," the nurse muttered to herself.
"She hasn't been in for four days, and I haven't heard from her,"
Lindy finally finished grimly.

"Then it's time for me to go look for her," Miranda
answered calmly. She had a knack for that. Small things, the
trivial, often became epic problems for her. Potential real
trouble, which required too much energy to waste on hysterics,
she always met without so much as blinking. "You worry about
your other sheep, Lindy. I'll find her."

"I believe you," Lindy said. "Just find her okay. And
don't get yourself in any damn trouble going about it!" she
called sternly after Miranda, who was already halfway out of
the door.

"I'll be back with Anita," Miranda tossed back over her
shoulder.

Once she was in her car Miranda tried Anita's cell phone.
No answer, but she hadn't really expected one. She had no

trouble choosing her direction and headed west of downtown, toward Bankhead and Jimmy's apartment.

As she drove she savored the memory of gathering up Anita's meager belongings and moving them out of Jimmy's apartment, the two of them giggling like teenage girls at a slumber party. She still wished she could have witnessed the aftermath, him fishing his lucky ball cap out of the commode and hunting around his apartment for the precious remote that wasn't there. She wondered how Anita had paid for the offenses on her return to Jimmy. Why hadn't she checked on her friend before this?

She had told Anita on the day they met she needed a break from her own self-indulgence. Time for another break.

When she reached the apartment building, Miranda marched up the stairs to the second floor and threw open the door without announcement or preamble. The neighborhood was so rough, drug violence here so prevalent that once upon a time mail carriers who delivered in Bankhead had required police escorts. But the door to the apartment was unlocked.

So this was Jimmy. He had wasted no time in getting a new remote, she noted. Or a new cap. He sat in front of the TV in a sleeveless T-shirt and a crisp new Braves hat that was turned backwards on his head. His trigger finger jumped on the remote, aimlessly flipping through the channels. Carmen no longer graced the walls, but no airbrushed image had been tacked up yet to take her place. Anita was on the opposite end of the worn couch, eyes glassy, her expression bored. Dirty dishes were piled high in the sink and various fast food wrappers littered the apartment, though Anita didn't look like she'd eaten for a week or more.

"I see you got a new cap, Jimmy, but I don't know why you bothered," Miranda commented to the wiry, olive-skinned man with a sniff. "She was just trying to make sure your old favorite one smelled like the rest of you."

If Jimmy held any ill will towards her he didn't show it. He stood up from the couch and stroked his goatee, a stupid grin spreading across his face, obviously on something at the moment. "So you're M'randa! She talks about you *all the time*. 'Bout time you came to see us!"

"I'm here to see Anita," Miranda clarified. "Actually to haul her ass out of here."

"No, no, no. Stay awhile. Hang out. 'Nita doesn't want to go anywhere, do ya?"

He turned towards Anita, who said nothing. She refused to look at Miranda. That, or she didn't even know Miranda was there. They were both high. In a way it had been lucky, catching Jimmy like this. Genial, unfocused. How long that would last was anyone's guess, and she hadn't been smart to come here. Clint was working or else he would have insisted on being a solid, looming presence. She could imagine him with his arms folded while the girls calmly left the apartment. There had been no time to call him, and now that she was here she wasn't leaving without Anita.

I can handle this, she decided. But no more wisecracks. Getting herself into trouble wasn't just getting herself into trouble anymore, she thought, imagining those tissues and cells inside of her body continuing to mold themselves into a human being.

"Thanks, Jimmy. Do you mind if Anita and I go out for awhile? I want to take her window shopping. Girl stuff. We'll be back in a bit, okay?" she chirped.

"Can't be rude and just run out like that. 'Smatter with you, can't you accept an invitation?"

This wasn't good. Jimmy's bad temper was starting to seep through the drug-induced haze.

"Sure, Jimmy, I'd love to hang out. Later, after we're done." She moved over to the couch, hooked her arm underneath Anita's, and pulled the woman to her feet. Finally Anita was starting to come around.

"Miranda, what are you doing here?" she asked groggily.

Unfortunately, Jimmy was starting to come around too. "She's staying here. Got no money to shop anyway."

"Just window shopping. We'll be back, Jimmy." She pulled Anita a few steps further.

He stepped forward, a perturbed expression spreading across his face, shifting through his gears like a race car. From friendly to menacing in six seconds flat. Miranda backed towards the door, pulling a dazed Anita along with her. The tiny Latina was barely dressed, clad in a skimpy halter top, boxer shorts, and flip-flops. Hardly the right clothes to go out on a cool, misty day like this, but that was the least of Miranda's worries at the moment. She backed towards the door, facing him. It wouldn't do to have her back to him right now. He loomed over them, threatening, and shut the front door she had started to open. She could feel his breath on her shoulder and her arms and legs came alive, her skin at a full crawl.

"Well," she said with false bravado, "It's not original, but it works."

"What works?" Jimmy demanded, fury tinging his whiny, accented voice.

"This," she answered, aiming her knee at his groin. While Jimmy bent over, howling in pain, she yanked the door open and drug a stunned Anita through it. On their way down the stairs, a tall, dark man with freckles and wavy hair kept a watchful eye.

"Need any help?" he asked. "I'll do anything for anybody that gets Anita the hell out of here."

"Thanks, but I think I took care of old Jimmy for the moment," Miranda assured him. She grinned in enjoyment as she quickly replayed the scene in her mind.

"Glad to hear it. Why don't you get that girl out of here now? I'm going to hang right here and make sure old Jimmy stays where he belongs. In his nasty little apartment by his nasty little self."

After dragging Anita the rest of the way to the car, Miranda nearly threw her inside and took a second for a lecture. "If you weren't high right now, you'd be able to remember this later," she panted. "Once you get your head straightened out, it's the kind of moment you'll want to come back to."

"Trust me, I'm gonna remember this no matter what," Anita reassured her in a foggy voice.

Miranda didn't allow herself the laughter until she had peeled out of the parking lot. She was pleased when Anita joined her and chortled in a deep, guttural smoker's laugh. The voice was scratchy, too old and low for Anita's age, but Miranda was still happy to hear it.

When they were a safe distance away, she stopped at a gas station and picked up a Coke and turkey sandwich for Anita. She opened the trunk of the VW Bug and pulled out a blanket her mother had made for her. It was stitched with yellow moons and stars, along with personality characteristics of each astrological sign. She'd harangued her mother, but had been secretly pleased when she'd placed it in her trunk.

"Mom, it's Georgia. It's not cold for ninety-nine percent of the year. I'm not going to get stuck in a snowstorm. Why do you want me to keep a pretty blanket like this in the trunk of my car?"

"I put a lot of love into that blanket. I want it to go wherever you do. You never know when you might need it."

She placed the blanket over Anita's shivering form and handed her the food silently. Questions and demands swirled around in her brain, but now was not the time. She wanted to ask her friend, *What was the moment? What made you abandon all of that hard work and all of the promises you made yourself? If I could just find that out, get a better explanation than it being a simple moment of weakness or a craving, maybe I can keep it from ever happening to myself.* She craved an answer but knew there was not a generic, universal one to the question.

"I'll be damned," was all Lindy said when Miranda and Anita came through the door. Anita's hair was slightly matted; her eyes had the telltale, glazed-over look. She wore only flip-flops on her feet. But she was safe.

"Told you I'd be back with Anita," was all Miranda said.

CHAPTER NINETEEN

Clint sang off-tune in front of the skillet, the radio and his singing mingling with the sizzle of dinner as he worked on some three-cheese scrambled eggs and sausage. Miranda was a fan of breakfast for dinner, and this one was trumped only by blueberry pancakes. They had already done those this week.

Clint warbled along with an Outkast song on the radio. *Tap tap tap.* The stove doubled as a tinny drum set, the spoon in his hand keeping time.

When he felt Miranda's hand on his shoulder he turned around, smile already forming, anticipating a new, creative insult about his singing. Her expression was blank and when she spoke it was in the eerily calm voice that always sent chills through him. The more composed she was, the worse things were.

"Clint, let's go to Atlanta Mercy. Now." No hitch or waver to her voice, but her hand lingered on his shoulder as if she needed to prolong the contact before she would be able to move or speak again. As if she was trying to draw strength from him for what would come next.

He took his cue from her, did not ask why but instead said in the same even, measured tones, "Okay. Right now." He turned off the stove, the sausage still sizzling in the skillet and the eggs piled high on the platter next to it like a bright, sunny promise.

In the jeep the DJ on the radio was telling listeners, "And that was Outkast with *Hey Ya*. We'll be back after these messages for another long music sweep."

He held her hand and tried not to clutch it too tightly

or telegraph any fear. She returned the light pressure but said nothing, still stoic.

She had even thought to bring a towel to avoid staining the upholstery with the blood that was seeping through her pajama bottoms. She was still Miranda with her sassy teasing and put-downs, but she did things like that since she'd moved in with him: cleaned up after herself right away even though she was notoriously messy, as if she was a guest in his apartment. It was almost as if she felt she'd caused him enough trouble in the past months and didn't want to create any further chaos in his life. He tried not to speed or fixate on the image of the red stain on the front of the blue cotton bottoms.

                *   *   *

When Clint returned three hours later he dumped the sausage and eggs into the trash. Now his apartment smelled like old grease. He gathered Miranda's favorite blanket and a change of clothes for her, along with some shampoo and the novel she was halfway through re-reading. The doctor had said something about Miranda's electrolytes being off. She was weak from the blood loss so she was being admitted.

Just last night she had set the book down with a half-smile and proclaimed, "This heroine is unimaginably dumb."

"And why's that?" Clint had asked with a low chuckle.

"She thinks she's stupid to have remained innocent all her life. Thinks she should have mixed it up and lived more. Well, some of the stupidest things I've done have been anything but innocent," she declared. Then she had laughed wryly and situated herself in his lap. She'd shifted after awhile and fallen asleep with her legs stretched over his.

They were just kids, too young for such a comfortable, domestic scene to play out, but there it was. He'd thought then that he was watching them age years before his eyes, their wild beginnings almost impossible to reconcile with the now-nightly routine of reading and dozing on the sofa. A few short months ago she'd regularly stay up for days while she wrote papers and constantly fed her need. Now she finished up early and never made it through Conan. With each day that passed at his place they marveled that they were doing this and more so that it was working. Now they had both aged another hundred years in the space of an evening.

The bright yellow sticky note with the date of Miranda's next maternity appointment caught his eye, and he pulled it off of the refrigerator so she wouldn't see it when she came back home. *Dr. Kemple, August 13, 9:30 am. Be there, Dad!* The note warned. He would never miss one and it was part of the constant ribbing he enjoyed.

The note went into the trash and he threw the garbage into the dumpster before tossing the duffel bag he'd packed for Miranda into the jeep. He slammed his fist into the side of the driver's side door before he climbed in and drove back to the hospital.

CHAPTER TWENTY

Bethie and Terrence were right where they had been on her last visit, playing beside the dumpster. Shelby stepped out of her car, not feeling the same apprehension this time. She hadn't caught sight of Ernie just yet but she was sure he was hovering somewhere out of the line of sight, keeping a watchful eye. She walked over to the children and noted that Bethie was nearly as tall as she was.

"Hello Bethie," she said softly. "Hi Terrence." She smiled at the little boy, who was of course perched atop his blue tricycle. She imagined he saw the tricycle as a necessary comic book character accessory, like Captain America's shield or Wonder Woman's lasso of truth.

"Is this your favorite spot?" she asked them. "Last time I visited you were playing here too."

"You see, that's the ship," Terrence explained, pointing at the dumpster.

"Ohhh," Shelby nodded seriously, as if she understood perfectly. "Tell me more about the ship."

"We wait here every day," Bethie chimed in. "The ship's gonna open up one of these days and we'll be able to take a ride in it wherever we want to go. There's aliens in there." She dropped her voice to a whisper and looked around, as if there might be enemies lingering who would exploit the secret if they knew. "We have to do a special dance to get them to come out. Sometimes it takes awhile."

"I see. So that's what you were doing last time. Your special dance."

"That's right," Bethie confirmed solemnly. "They were just about ready to come out last time but you scared them away."

"I'm sorry about that," Shelby told her in an equally solemn tone. "I hope I didn't scare them away this time too."

"Nah, we hadn't even really gotten started this time," Terrence reassured her. "So why you back here?" he asked her, mimicking Ernie.

"Well, Terrence, I got very sick after I left here last time. I'm feeling much better now but I thought it might help me even more to come back and say hello, make sure you're all doing all right."

"We doing fine. So you all better now?"

"Well I'm working on it, Terrence."

That was mostly the truth. The part about coming back to say hello was wholly the truth, she thought as she considered Ernie. *Maybe he can find his way out. Maybe I can too.*

"Good," Terrence told her empathetically, in his manly little way.

"Well I didn't mean to interrupt your dance," Shelby told them. "Go ahead, by all means."

Bethie looked embarrassed, as if she had no choice but to reveal a worldly, uncomfortable truth to Shelby.

"I'm sorry miss. But you see, they won't come out when grown-ups are around. It's not that they're not friendly," she said in defense of their alien-friends. "They're just shy."

"They can't even get 'em to come out for me," the tires-over-gravel voice stated.

A smile spread across Shelby's face and she turned to face Ernie. "You've been around all this time? You seem to have perfected the art of lurking."

"Didn't actually expect you to come back here, re-por-ter. So you been sick, huh?"

"What was wrong with you?" Bethie wanted to know. "You never said." Her tone was a mixture of childish curiosity and sweet concern.

"Well, I stopped taking some medicine I need to be well." She didn't dare toss a lie in the direction of the brown eyes and braids.

Bethie knitted her eyebrows together, puzzled. "Now why would you do that?"

"Well that's a very good question. I think it's because I was also sick in here." Shelby pointed a finger at her chest and then placed it directly above her heart. "I've been very sad."

"Ohh," the little girl breathed, nodding her head. She asked no further questions and neither did her brother. Neither did Ernie, who studied her curiously.

"You want to meet our mama?" Terrence asked.

"Please," Bethie implored. "I don't think the aliens are going to come out today anyway. We'll try again tomorrow. 'Ventually they will." She seemed undeterred, up to the challenge of coaxing her otherworldly playmates out. Eventually she would get her ride to some far-off, unknown place. It would just take time.

"You can do more research, re-por-ter. Their mama Lucinda can be another interview and you can write another story, make it a series," Ernie told her in a half-serious tone.

"Well, okay. Why not?" Shelby allowed Bethie to grab her hand and drag her up the stairs while Ernie and Terrence brought up the rear. Terrence drug the tricycle carefully up, taking care not to scratch or bump it unnecessarily.

When Bethie threw open the door she announced at the top of her voice, "Ma, we have a visitor!"

The same lean, stretched-out woman who had peered curiously out of the apartment before materialized from a bedroom. Today she had a green scarf tied securely over her hair and hoops dangled attractively from her ears.

"Well," she said in slight surprise. "I thought today was the big day where I'd finally get to meet some space people so forgive me if I seem disappointed. Seen you before."

"Just a mere earthling, Lucinda. Nice to meet you."

"Ernie told me about you. How you doing an exposé on

our neighborhood."

"Not exactly," Shelby told her with a smile. The woman's grip was firm and cool when they shook hands. She didn't look any older than twenty-five, but the smooth, unlined face had the self-assured and dignified air of a woman who had been ushered quickly into maturity by unplanned circumstances.

"I think I lost my special ring!" Bethie wailed suddenly.

"Oh Lord, child." Lucinda sighed. "Have your Uncle Ernie and your brother help you look for it."

"You need to keep better track of it if it's so important. C'mon, now." Earl shooed the children out of the door again.

Shelby looked around at the afghans draped over the furniture and the plants hung in the room. Pictures of Bethie and Terrence were arranged in neat, decorative blocks on the wall. "You've created a little oasis here," she told the woman.

"I've tried hard to make it a place that would make my babies forget about what's outside the door. A place where they feel safe."

"Well you've done a wonderful job with the place and with your kids too, I think. From what I've seen they're happy kids who'll use their imaginations when they venture outside of the door."

"The aliens," Lucinda said. "I probably read too much into it, they just doing like kids do. But their favorite game is playing at trying to get a ride away from here."

"I think you're definitely reading too much into it. That's just kids being kids."

"Ernie told you about the man next door?" Lucinda asked.

"He did."

"And you know what Ernie does for his money." Lucinda stared her down now, as if daring her to judge.

"I do."

"You wrote that article for *Atlanta Minute*. You done research, you know the police out here a lot because of drugs. My babies, they want to know why the police always here.

What am I supposed to tell them?"

Lucinda opened up the window and produced a cigarette out of her pocket. "Got to hurry up with this while I got the chance," she commented, quickly lighting up. She inhaled deeply and on the exhale directed the smoke out of the window, shooing it out the way Ernie had the children a few minutes ago. "Time's not your own when you've got little ones. Don't know what I'd do if I didn't have Ernie."

"He's very...fond of you," Shelby told her in a neutral tone.

"And my kids," Lucinda added levelly. "Anything you see between him and my babies is genuine. Not just 'cause he angling for something with me."

Shelby was pleased at the woman's immediate defense of Ernie's intentions. "Yes, I believe that."

"Don't know what's going to happen if and when we all end up scattering. To my babies but mostly to him. I worry about him more. People like him got to have purpose, something that keeps 'em straight. And even then, as you can see, he goes a little crooked 'cause he just don't know how to make it otherwise. Never was taught. But he got some goodness in him and that can't be taught."

As if she possessed some internal radar, Lucinda extinguished her cigarette into a green ashtray and snapped the window shut. Thirty seconds after the snap of the window the door flew open. Bethie triumphantly produced a plastic pink ring. "We found it!"

"Can't imagine where," Lucinda said dryly. "Any chance is was laying by the dumpster?"

"If you knew that, Ma, why didn't you just tell me so I wouldn't worry?" Bethie rebuked. "You know I need it for 'munication with the aliens. If I lose it I might never see them again."

"If you want to talk to them you'll always find a way," Lucinda told her daughter, dropping a kiss on the top of Bethie's head. "It'll take more than some distance to stop you from seeing 'em." She sent Shelby a placid smile and then shifted her gaze towards Ernie. The woman seemed to have answered her own earlier question and was pleased with the response. The quiet moment in the apartment was interrupted by some sudden, high-pitched cursing. The walls were thin. An indirect introduction to the man who was surely the aforementioned neighbor from hell, Shelby thought.

"Alright, headphones on everybody. Time for some music, y'all know the drill," Lucinda ordered. Two little bodies scattered and a moment later came back with a small gray Walkman apiece. They sat on the worn couch and each placed a pair of headphones over their tiny ears in a synchronized fashion.

"Mommy makes us put these on so we won't learn any swear words," Terrence explained.

"Ernie bought 'em each a Walkman the first time we heard that nasty man go off on one of his tangents," Lucinda elaborated.

"I told Luce the kids can learn swears the old-fashioned way, in school, but they ain't going to learn 'em from that heathen next door," Ernie declared. He seemed pleased with his resourcefulness.

Shelby watched two sets of small feet bounce in time to their respective music and thought she would ask the children what they were listening to whenever the screaming fit next door subsided. She had to hand it to Ernie with his humor and $15 walkmans used as survival mechanisms.

In the apartment next door Jimmy Lamoras paced angrily, swore, and thought about the many creative ways he'd make Anita pay when she came back. She'd been gone for some time but it didn't matter how long she stayed away; an insult he never forgot. He would replay it in his mind and plan her comeuppance until she finally came crawling back. A beating wouldn't do this time. He wanted to make her hurt on the inside. And he'd fix that friend of hers, Miranda, who'd humiliated him and helped her leave both times. Anita was not the kind to walk away without help. Nobody walked away from Jimmy and nobody took cheap shots when he wasn't expecting it, either.

He still wasn't over the first insult, let alone Anita's latest departure. He reflected now on Anita's first transgression. The first thing he'd noticed when he had come back to the apartment that day was the poster. Most of Carmen Electra's body had been blacked out and there was a moustache above her teasingly parted lips. Some of her perfect teeth were blacked out. The bitch responsible had signed: *Love, Miranda.* He'd yanked the poster off of the wall in a single motion and wadded it up into a ball. He was tired of this one anyway, he reasoned. Maybe he'd tack up a centerfold for Anita when she came back. Miss September for her to look at every day.

Then he'd done a quick loop through the place. Jimmy had seen red when he stopped in the bathroom, where his cap sat in its final resting place. He'd grabbed a hanger from the closet and fished it out, letting the dripping cap drop into the grimy bathtub.

Inspection of the bedroom revealed that Anita's clothes and her few belongings were gone. Not one thing remained because he had looked hard for something of hers to tear up or throw out. When he had flopped down on the couch and went to turn on the television, he noticed his remote was gone. With a fresh string of curse words he'd put his fist through the thin wall.

He chalked up the injury as something else to blame her for when she came back. She'd buy him a new remote, a new cap, and a new poster too. But this would cost her plenty more than the price of everything she'd messed with.

Now Jimmy thought about Miranda Linn and what she had done. It sent him into another howling fit of rage. He'd wait if he had to and practice an unknown virtue to himself, patience, in order to make sure both of the bitches got what was coming to them. He'd find a way if it was the last thing he did.

CHAPTER TWENTY-ONE

Miranda had already finished signing the discharge papers and was coming out of the hospital's restroom when she heard Clint's voice at the nurse's station. Two days in the hospital was too much time to lay there and think about what had happened, and she had to get the hell out of here.

"I'm here for Miranda Linn. She's still being discharged today, right?" He had the same hyped-up, authoritative tone he always used when it came to matters of Miranda. The one he used when he thought he should step in and solve things. But she noticed the undercurrent to his voice, flat and anchored down by grief and exhaustion.

"Well, she just signed her release papers and she was waiting for a wheelchair right over there a second ago. You're the one picking her up?" the nurse queried politely.

"Yes." Clint's voice had an impatient edge now. "I sure don't see her sitting over there, do you? You didn't see where she went?"

Miranda stood with her hand on the slightly propped-open door and continued to listen as Clint spiraled up. Now he was starting to yell about the hospital ignoring patients. She wanted to push the door open, tell him to calm down, but she didn't make a move to come out. She was paralyzed and couldn't make the last few steps to leave with him.

Even as he'd held her hand the past two days had the same voice in her head nagged him too, questioning whether her carelessness had led to all of this? She didn't deserve to drift off on his shoulder as the steady vibration of his jeep coaxed her into sleep, or to be wrapped up in the stars and moons blanket on her parents' couch and drink her mother's homemade herbal tea. For now the uneasy alliance was still in effect between Clint and her parents. For the sake of Miranda. She couldn't stand the thought of them continuing to do an uneasy dance around each other. What was the point of that now?

Miranda eased back into the bathroom stall and shut the door. She closed her eyes and pulled her legs up, waiting. Sure enough, the door opened two or three minutes later and she heard the nurse's voice softly call her name. She halfway expected the door of the stall to come flying open, like when someone is hiding from the bad guys in the movies, and tried not to make a sound. But no kung-fu kick ensued to reveal her cowering there and soon the nurse's retreating footsteps echoed softly on the tile floor. The door closed.

She wondered how long it would take for Clint to give up and leave the hospital. She knew he'd pace up and down the floor, yelling demands at anyone with a uniform, and search everywhere they'd let him, relentless. Her legs were starting to cramp hitched up underneath her, but she clasped her arms around them and stayed in the same position. She couldn't believe she was being such a coward, but there was no way she could face him, tell him to go away, and make it believable.

Miranda finally let her legs drop and massaged them as the feeling returned. She wondered when feeling would return to the rest of her. She'd answered in monotone while the attending physician asked her questions. *How many weeks along? When did the cramping start?*

No one had bothered with any platitudes or reassured her that she would be able to have children in the future. She was grateful for that. Her Mom and Dad had come and stayed until she had commanded them, "Go home. Please."

She'd been filled up for awhile and now she was hollow and emptied out again. The experience had also been physically painful, which seemed fitting. It should feel as if an invisible hand was reaching inside and forcibly yanking something precious out. *Miscarriage,* she thought. *Noun. The birth or natural expelling of a fetus or baby before it has developed enough to survive.* Well, screw the dictionary. Nothing about the experience had felt natural to her.

She slipped out of the stall and kept her head down as she slunk down the hallway and out of the hospital alone. She had no other way home, had no idea where she was headed. But wherever it was she wanted to go there by herself.

She kept walking and didn't stop until the McDonald's sign beckoned her in. Oh, to taste some real, fresh grease after a couple of hospital meals that equated to nutritionally balanced TV dinners. Her breakfast, lunch and dinner had been brought cheerfully hidden underneath plastic pink covers.

A Happy Meal with Coke instead of milk this time, that was the ticket. No point in avoiding caffeine or anything else that was bad for her anymore. Clint would be frantic, this wasn't fair to him, but she pushed that thought away as she fingered the toy that came inside the cheerful box. It was a children's book about a Hispanic girl who had lost her mother. It schooled its young readers about the girl's culture and was tied with a ribbon. The book's pictures of the shy-looking girl reminded her of Anita's little sister.

Her phone vibrated. No question who that was. She let it go to voice mail, then sighed and listened to the message.

Clint's young/old voice had the expected worried edge to it. "Miranda, look. I know this is hard but I'm asking you to just lean on me. If we help each other through this maybe you'll wake up one morning and be surprised. You'll find out you actually want to wake up that day. It'll take time. We still have each other, so pass the time with me. I'm worried about you. Please call me. Don't do this. Love you."

Sheer determination. That was one of the best and worst things about him. He made it sound so easy, as if the answer to every problem in her universe was that simple: *Just take my hand.* She dialed his number.

"Let me come and get you," he said immediately, before

she even spoke. The phone had barely rung through before he'd picked up.

"Look, I love you too, but there are some things you just can't fix, including me," she told him wearily. "And don't you dare tell me you wouldn't try and put me back together. We both know that's a lie."

"Right now I'm just interested in being with you."

"I know, Clint, but I just can't right now."

"Miranda, where are you?" he pressed.

"Love you," she told him, and clicked off. She walked out of the McDonald's, ignoring the vibrating as he called again.

Now where?

Just as she walked out of the parking lot, a beat-up Mazda pulled up.

"Hey, aren't you Miranda?" the Mazda's driver called. She was a dark-haired girl Miranda recognized from 404. "Need a ride?"

"Guess so," Miranda shrugged, and climbed in.

*   *   *

Four hours later the Mazda screeched to a halt in front of the plain white brick building. Miranda was stuffed in the middle of its backseat and climbed over the lap of one of the other passengers before she jumped out of the car. She took a minute to survey the small, ugly building she had come to so many times for help. She'd made friends here with people she'd trusted. *I thought I could trust Lindy. I tried so hard to do everything the right way, and she told me everything would be all right.*

The building looked different at night, dirty and unwelcoming devoid of the faces and voices she usually associated with it. Or was she seeing it for what it really was now? She couldn't believe she'd pinned her future on a place that was nothing more than a dump. A tiny, ugly square box where she was still coming to get drugs every day. She reached into her oversized purse for the can of spray paint she'd picked up at Wal-Mart.

"Hey, Miranda, whatever this place is, it looks like it's closed. Let's go," one of the people she had been doing speedballs with for the past four hours slurred from the car. He was a real observant one. No one else in the car commented; they weren't the most inquisitive group around. They hadn't bothered to ask where they were going when Miranda had told them she wanted to make a stop that would only take a minute; they probably assumed she was going to meet someone to buy more drugs.

"Thanks for pointing that out," she told him acidly. When there was no response from the car she sighed. Being sarcastic just wasn't fun when your target didn't get it, or in this case was too high to know where he even was. She calmly walked up to the building and began spraying the blood-red paint against the white brick.

As she continued spraying, the car's driver called out in alarm, "Hey, M'randa, what the hell are you doing? Let's get out of here! You want to get busted *now?*"

"Just…one…minute…" Miranda licked her lips in concentration as she finished with a flourish. She stood back and examined her handiwork, taking in the unsettling effect it created with satisfaction. Finally she hopped into the car and it screeched away, leaving behind a stark message on the front of the New Horizons Methadone clinic.

She knew Lindy always came in early, and hoped that the message would greet her first when she opened up. She could imagine Lindy strolling tiredly up to the clinic, a cup of her precious Starbucks caramel macchiato in her hand, not comprehending the red slashes on the front of the clinic at first. Her hand would fly up to her mouth, the coffee splashing to the ground in a muddy pool as she dropped the cup in surprise…

*   *   *

Before the sun had even started to completely burn

through the atmosphere, Lindy made her way up to the clinic with her distinctive strut-shuffle. She hummed Sade's "Taboo," coffee in hand, as she mentally prepared for the day.

She froze angrily in her tracks when she noticed the graffiti on the front of the building. Damned kids, some of them actually considered their tags or obscene messages sprayed in fat block letters art.

Then she read it. The message was slashed across the building like it was trying to cut into it, and it was meant to cut her too: *Lindy Thomason sells false hope. This shit will not save you.*

The coffee fell to the ground, forgotten, and splashed on the pant leg of Lindy's purple scrubs. Her first thought was, *One of my babies is in trouble. One of my babies has relapsed.*

Anita again? Lindy ran back to her car. Marla could open up, she was always early too. The other nurse would just have to pull double duty until she got back. Then she realized she hadn't seen Miranda in a few days... *Dear God, she hadn't seen Miranda in a few days.* How had she let that go after Anita? After five years of doing this was her mind so resistant to the possibility of one of her favorites backsliding that she couldn't recognize when they were in trouble anymore?

She slammed her hands down on the steering wheel once she was inside of her car. Where to go first? Miranda could be anywhere. She dialed a familiar number on her cell phone.

"Lindy." The voice that picked up seemed tense and on edge. First thing in the morning, but the person on the other end of the call sounded wide awake. Awake enough to pounce on his phone and check to see who was calling. That wasn't a good sign. "I was getting ready to call you…"

"Clint, was Miranda was at the clinic last night? Is she in trouble? Do you know where she is?" Lindy demanded.

The sigh that followed was definitely not a good sign. It seemed to echo through the phone, telegraphing the deepest kind of fear and sadness all at once. "Lindy, Miranda lost the baby a few days ago. I don't know where she is right now or who she's with. I wanted to call but she threw a fit and wouldn't let me. After she was released from the hospital she took off. I've been looking everywhere for her. I haven't slept...I don't know what to do."

Lindy let out an involuntary half gasp, half sob. How many times had she assured Miranda that things would be okay, that she had the answers? *Methadone is completely safe for your baby, sugar. We encourage expectant moms to get on methadone so they're not tempted to use during their pregnancy. Trust me, this is the much safer route.*

And now Miranda had lost her baby. Deep down, she knew Miranda didn't hold her responsible, but the girl needed someone to lash out at. That certainly explained the chilling message.

"Lindy, you still there?" Clint's voice brought her back.

"Clint, I'm going to look for her. You don't know if she's alone or with somebody? She might've even taken off with someone from the clinic..."

"I don't know, Lindy. I'm all wrung out. I told you, I've called everyone we know, even powwowed with the freaking Linns, been everywhere. I can't think anymore."

"Then I'll do the thinking, baby. Sit tight and keep your phone on," she ordered. "I did see Miranda talking to some of my other patients from time to time, I'll start there. Maybe Anita knows. Believe me, I know where they all go."

"Thanks, Lindy," Clint told her in a hollow voice.

Once they disconnected, Lindy squealed off, spurred on by the defeated sound in Clint's voice and the message Miranda had left. *She's hurting and she's angry at me, but she wouldn't have left that message at all if she was done with everything. She wants help.* But she couldn't help but play Miranda's stark indictment over and over in her mind. *Lindy Thomason sells false hope...*

Lindy's adrenaline spiked along with the famous guitar solo when Lynyrd Skynrd's "Freebird" came on the radio. The song reminded her of Jenny, the troubled addict in the movie "Forrest Gump." Lindy had been transfixed when she'd watched the scene in the theater years ago: Jenny tottering around on the ledge outside of a hotel room in her seventies style disco heels, trying to decide what to do, with the very same song playing in the background. The audience had sighed in relief when the girl pulled herself back inside. Lindy had cheered inwardly when Jenny left the seedy room and started over. She hoped the song was a good omen, that Miranda could do the same.

As she drove she thought about Miranda helping her track down Anita not so long ago. Miranda, though younger than Anita, had wrapped a blanket around the shivering woman and told her it was going to be alright. Now she was sure Miranda would be the one who needed help. A quick and typical reversal of fortunes in the world of the addicted: the star, the poster child for staying clean, would be the one who took the tumble while it was the three-and-four time loser who finally managed to claw their way upwards and turn things around. All it took for the tumble was a bad day, a setback, a disappointment. That didn't even begin to describe what Miranda had gone through in the past few days.

Lindy drew in a steadying breath. She would start out with an obvious place. It seemed too cliché for Miranda, but she'd found a few of her other patients there when they'd relapsed.

"I'm coming for you whether or not you want me to, baby," Lindy muttered as she took a corner a little too fast. "You say you've given up on Lindy but she sure as hell won't ever give up on you. Damnit, Miranda, you better be my Jenny."

CHAPTER TWENTY-TWO

Halloran park, a Mecca for drug abusers, was deserted at the moment. It was probably on some up-and-coming politician's list for urban renewal or "gentrification," but in the meantime it was a long way from gentrified, Miranda thought.

It was a desolate place, really, but that was fine with Miranda. The grass was patchy, half dead from neglect. It was mostly brown with longer green shoots poking up in various places. The effect reminded Miranda of a man with green hair plugs. A rusted-over swing set that was cemented into the ground stood to the left of the splintery, peeling picnic bench she sat on. The grass, swing set and bench were all reminders that there had been life and activity here once. Everything seemed dead now. She imagined children shrieking and playing here before the decay. This shell of a park was like her insides, where something good and hopeful should be happening but wasn't anymore. *Oh, that's rich,* Miranda thought. *I ought to write that down.*

She pulled her journal out of her purse and started to scribble furiously. Even now it was instinct to let her frustration seep through her pen and onto paper. She had always amazed teachers with her essays in school, starting with a spelling assignment in the third grade. It had been her job to incorporate spelling words like "explore" into a paragraph about space. Her third-grade teacher, Mrs. Lemmuns, shook her head in wonder when she read eight-year-old Miranda's opener. "We have the chance to improve our own world, our own planet, but instead we explore space," it read. The short essay had continued on with a laundry list of almost everything Miranda could think of that was wrong with earth, from hungry kids to pollution. No paper about how "awesome" space travel would be for Miranda Linn. Even at eight years old, her view of the world had leaned toward the overcast, the darker. When asked to describe herself in a freshman English writing assignment years later, Miranda had proclaimed, "I'm a new England autumn and I just happen to be stuck in a hot Georgia summer." She had laughed when she wrote it--how melodramatic--but it was true.

Here she was still, at nineteen years old: in the midst of a hot, sweaty Atlanta morning, still feeling chilled inside, still feeling out of place. She even had a hoodie on despite the make-the-devil-sigh Georgia heat; she couldn't seem to get warm. She didn't have a single thing in common with the people she had just spent the past few hours with, except the fact that they all shared a drug habit.

They had left a few hours ago, and she hadn't been interested in going with them. She'd been sick of the drugs and sick of the company by the time she refused the OxyContin pills and Jack's they passed around. They hadn't protested too much when she told them to go ahead. No doubt she wasn't much fun to be around.

She wanted to be alone. She didn't feel like sharing something so personal, this humiliating need to shoot up and numb herself, with people she barely knew. It didn't matter if they did the same thing or not. None of them knew that just a few days before, a tiny life had been growing inside of her. Just a few days ago, there was no way she would have contemplated doing this.

She was tired, so tired, and she didn't want to think anymore. Not about the baby, or Clint, or her parents. The pain she had caused everyone. She could blame Lindy all she wanted, but…

She just wanted to sleep. She tried to as she laid her head down on the worn picnic bench. She felt a bone-crushing exhaustion weighing her down, but still felt ready to jump out of her skin. That's what you got for putting different types of drugs in your body that were at war to speed you up and slow you down. If she could just sleep, it would be a blessed relief from the thoughts banging around in her nineteen-year-old brain, slamming up against her forehead and making her temples throb.

Finally they quieted some and then started to still. She pulled out her cell phone and checked her messages. Everyone had called: Mom, Dad, Aunt Viv, Arli. She felt a loneliness that made her stomach ache as she listened to each voice in turn. Stupid, since she could hit "call" right now and talk to any one of them.

It was Clint's message she listened to last. *"You'll wake up one morning and be surprised to find you actually want to wake up...Don't do this..."*

She played it again as things started to fade, her mouth slackening and her eyes closing as the cocktail of drugs finally nudged her out of consciousness.

*   *   *

Lindy screeched up to the park and jumped out of the car almost before she cut the engine. At first it looked deserted and Lindy shivered. The place looked like an ominous forest out of a children's book that the little hero and heroine would unwittingly wander into. Then her eyes wandered to the picnic table and she thought someone had left a pink hoodie draped on top of it.

As she moved closer she realized that there were slim, pale fingers protruding from the sleeves of the hoodie. They were draped over a cell phone. The curls sticking out from underneath the hood and cascading onto the table were unmistakable. The tiny body lay there like a doll.

"Miranda!" she screamed, and dialed her phone frantically.

CHAPTER TWENTY-THREE

Cole was having a bad day at work. A bad day for him meant someone really *had* died. He was seven hours into his shift when he thought about the conversation with Shelby Norris. *"Don't you ever get tired of seeing people who are either in the throes of extreme pain or devastated?"* he remembered her demanding.

He'd been honest. *"Sometimes I get tired of it…"*

Today was one of those "sometimes" when he didn't feel like he was making anything better. He still couldn't believe the way he'd talked to the reporter. He had never talked to a patient like that. Something about her irritated and intrigued him at the same time. She'd been defiant, wordlessly daring him to skip the niceties and be blunt. So he had.

Then he'd been jarred away from those thoughts by a pretty young woman who was wheeled into trauma room one, unconscious, her long, dark hair cascading off of the side of the gurney. Her right arm also hung off of the side, limp. Cole had been quick to move it and place it on her chest. No matter what the situation was, he always noticed details like that.

A hysterical friend of the young woman's had fought like hell when they asked her to leave the room. The friend kept chanting, "I told her he was going to do it! I told her, and he finally did! I told her! Why wouldn't she listen…"

The girl was the victim of multiple stab wounds to the chest and abdomen by an ex-boyfriend. He had made good on his promise and ended her twenty-two years of life. During the attack he had punctured her lung and nicked an artery. She was dead of internal bleeding, and Cole had been the one to call her time of death. He also had the unpleasant task of confirming the hysterical friend's worst fears when he walked around the corner with a grim face. He watched the girl's face rearrange itself when she read his expression. He had not said a word when she dissolved into shrieks of denial, and she had beat on his chest when he steered her over to a chair and eased her into it.

It was as bad as notifying her next-of-kin would be. When Cole passed by a few minutes later he noticed she was still there, silent and weighed down. The initial burst of energy had been expended. Everything around her likely looked different than just a few minutes ago, the surroundings transformed by grief. She was in the After, her world changed.

He considered the small waiting room with semi-comfortable chairs, the tables with magazines and the vending machine that offered a choice of coffee or cocoa. What a shitty place to have a full spectrum of human emotions play out, usually in full view of strangers. He'd decided then that he needed a quick cup of coffee.

Cole didn't have time to finish the coffee or reflect any further when he was paged. *Feast or famine*, he thought as he dumped the rest into the sink and left the tiny break room. *Let's hope this one is a fixer.* He sprinted down the hall towards his next disaster, or miracle.

"What have we got?" Cole barked at a familiar EMT, who was wheeling in another unconscious young woman.

"Nineteen-year-old female, suspected overdose of heroin, unresponsive at scene. B/P ninety over fifty eight, respirations five at last check two minutes ago. Started her with point four of Narcan and gave her another two units about four minutes ago."

"Wow, okay," Cole considered. "So we might want to be prepped for a tussle if she wakes up."

Sometimes overdose patients woke up in what doctors and EMTs liked to call "OD fighting mode." One EMT who had brought Cole an overdose patient a few weeks ago had stated flatly, "You can give him more Narcan. Hopefully he wakes up on *you*." Then the EMT had pointed to his two front false teeth, slightly whiter than the rest, which had been knocked out by another patient who had come to swinging. But Cole would welcome this small, frail-looking young woman waking up, swinging and cursing some.

The ER team transferred the girl from the gurney onto a bed. "Let's get another blood pressure," Cole ordered as he held open the girl's lids and examined her pupils. "I'm just not liking her breathing," he muttered. "Hey, guys, let's…"

Cole was so focused on the OD his brain didn't even register the commotion until his sentence was cut off by a wild-eyed kid bursting into the room. A couple of front-desk nurses the kid had obviously blown past came running in after him.

"Miranda, oh Jesus, is she okay? Oh God Miranda, please be okay! I'm her boyfriend, somebody tell me what's going on…"

"Sir, you need to leave so they can focus and help her," one of the nurses who had trailed the kid told him in a steely tone. She was the resident champ at talking down distraught boyfriends/husbands/family members. Nobody did it better or softer. She'd be that person after she got the kid the hell out of there. Almost everyone in the room had seen it at least once in their career: a relative or boyfriend unglued at the sight of tubes, blood, sometimes death. If you let the situation escalate you'd need additional gurneys afterwards.

"Has she said anything? Is she breathing? Jesus, somebody tell me something! Miranda!" the kid bellowed. He tried to lunge forward to get a better look at what was going on, but the nurse grabbed his arm. He tried to shake her off but lost some of his steam.

"I'm going to call security if you don't calm down," she told him, her tone growing colder. "Go sit down in the waiting room, now. That's the best thing you can do for her."

The kid was sobbing now. "I don't want to leave her! Please!"

"You're not leaving her." The nurse kept her viselike

grip on the kid's arm, in control now. "You'll be right outside." As she pulled him away, he never reversed his direction. He walked backwards and never took his eyes off of the girl in the bed.

Cole, who had done his best to ignore the outburst and do his job, thought that the room was almost too quiet now. Eerily so. No one spoke except when necessary as they tried to stabilize the girl.

CHAPTER TWENTY-FOUR

Eileen Linn strode into the emergency department of Atlanta Mercy, her face drawn, and headed for the front desk like a homing pigeon trained firmly on her target. Her sandals made a flat slapping sound on the cold tile of the floor before she reached the nurse. She had moved so quickly that her husband was still several feet behind her. It was the second time in a week her daughter had been taken to Atlanta Mercy.

Lindy Thomason's voice, one that clearly struggled to keep its own composure in an effort not to upset her, echoed in her brain. *They've taken her to Mercy, Mrs. Linn.*

Even with the immediacy of the situation Eileen found that it nagged her as much as where and in what condition her daughter had been found: *She* should have been the one to find Miranda, *she* was her mother, *she* should have been there. But she had not felt the resentment once she clasped the smooth brown hand of the woman who hopefully *had* been in time for her daughter. Her shoulders tensed and she waited for a blow as Lindy told her the news, which was nothing yet.

"Lindy, thank you," she whispered to the woman who had become a mother number two to her daughter. Lindy Thomason understood the struggle that had been a part of Miranda's life for the past year better than she ever could. It was one that had made she and her daughter strangers for awhile but Miranda and Lindy friends. She was barely aware of promising to keep the woman posted when Lindy reluctantly left. It seemed as if Lindy had been privy to her thoughts and had decided to leave the waiting to the family.

This was a case where the equation was not equal to the

sum of its parts. Her daughter had so many people who cared for her, yet somehow she had ended up almost dead on a picnic table. One group of people plus love plus determination plus good intentions did not equal a safe Miranda. Not when the top part of the equation was divided by confusion, hurt, a personal tragedy, and a generally restless and rebellious spirit. Even with a small and vigilant army there was always a moment alone for a person in pain. Eileen didn't know what this troubling equation that included a lost grandchild equaled yet. She didn't know if she wanted the nurse behind the desk to complete it for her.

"My daughter, Miranda Linn. She was brought in about an hour ago. Can you tell me anything new about her?" Her words were clipped, tense. They sought information she might not want.

"I know the doctors have been working to stabilize her," the nurse told her in a careful tone. "But I really think you should talk to Dr. Michaels. When he's free he'll come and talk to you."

Should she feel relief or dread? There was no interpreting the nurse's careful tone and that cursed addendum at the end of the answer. She would know when the doctor was free? Free to what? Free to come and tell them he had saved their daughter or free to tell them there was nothing he could do?

At least no one had told her Miranda was gone, though Eileen sensed that even after she talked to the doctor most of her questions would remain unanswered. She felt some kind of journey beginning and sat down to wait. How to gather strength and prepare when you didn't know what for yet?

Jim joined her and she repeated what the nurse had told her in low tones. He clasped her hand and a few moments later she felt his entire being stiffen. She followed his gaze and saw the source of the tension. Mother's blinders had stopped her from noticing Clint sitting there in the corner of the waiting room, his hair disheveled, his eyes swollen.

"Oh for God's sake, Jim, let it be. He's here for her too.

Don't you think this is the time to put it aside?" she asked wearily.

A minute later Clint warily joined them. They all sat quietly and waited for news, but she noticed how he leaned unconsciously to the right and away from them. Together but separate.

A lanky doctor with freckles dusting his face appeared. "I'm Dr. Michaels," he told them, and mercifully launched in to giving them what they needed without any more preamble. "We've got Miranda more stable than she was when she was brought in. She's breathing with the help of a ventilator right now, but she isn't conscious or responsive yet. It appears that she overdose-"

"We know about all of that," Clint cut him off flatly. "Is she going to be okay?"

"It's too early too tell," he told them honestly. Eileen felt everything slow down as she heard medical TV drama phrases like "the next twenty-four to forty eight hours" reverberate off of the white walls.

Eileen asked the only important question the doctor could answer. "When can we see her?"

"Right now. Remember, she's breathing with the help of a machine and she isn't responsive yet."

"Thank you, Dr. Michaels, but I don't really think it's possible to ease into these things. My daughter. Please."

The three were led to the room in intensive care where Miranda lay with a tube in her throat. The machine on the side of the bed breathed for her as the doctor had warned. The effect was not as jarring as Eileen would have imagined. It was just baffling to see her daughter, all motion and kinetic energy, stilled.

Even when Miranda slept she was restless. Eileen's mother, when she kept Miranda for overnights, had always clucked: *How can one little girl make such a mess of a bed?* Miranda's bed always looked like she'd been fighting someone in her sleep or running from something, the covers twisted and jerked free from the careful tucks. *Not from something,* Eileen corrected herself. More likely *to* something knowing her daughter.

No one in her life seemed able to catch up with Miranda, not even the kid on the other side of the bed. She studied Clint. Not surprising to find him on the opposite side.

Eileen noticed that Jim was too jarred at the sight of their daughter to protest or stiffen as Clint bent over and kissed Miranda on the forehead. Her husband ignored him and took Miranda's hand, studying it as if the grooves and lines in its palm contained the answer to his questions. The heart monitor was the only reassuring proof of life to hold on to when they had to leave the room.

CHAPTER TWENTY-FIVE

Shelby ignored the general chaos of the *Atlanta Minute* office as she tipped back in her chair and stared at the tiny faces in the photo. One of the two little girls had barely learned how to use her voice, and now it was silenced.

Jasmine and Carrie Hoskins, two and five years old, had burned to death along with their mother, Miriam, in a house fire. Too late for Miriam and her girls by the time firefighters had arrived. It was a very suspicious tragedy. Nobody slept through burning to death, and Carl Hoskins had conveniently not been home at the time. The investigation was ongoing but there was little doubt that Carl had decided his wife and girls had become an inconvenience.

When and how had he decided that they were three someones in the way? The question was as disturbing to Shelby as the thought of Carl casually placing his dead wife's hand around a cigarette and walking out of the door, leaving her and the sleeping girls behind. A sloppy attempt to make it look like an accident hadn't fooled anyone.

Shelby put her head down on the desk. "Why did I ever want to be more like Christine Amanpour?" she muttered. It was more than just what Carl had done. It was the picture itself, the way Carl was looking with pride at his wife and girls. No hint, no clue how things would go bad later on. It was the same expression Joe wore in the wedding picture that was hung up in her apartment. All pride and reverence. No clue in that picture either about how things would go bad later on. She and Miriam had never seen it coming.

Glenda's voice jolted her out of her reverie, yanked her

away from the questions she could not answer. "You need some Starbuck's," Glenda told her as she sashayed over to Shelby and offered up a Chai Latte.

"Thanks. Got anything I can lace it with? It's been that kind of day and that kind of story. My old boss kept a bottle of single malt in his desk. Somehow I can't imagine that Maura has any booze stashed here in the office. I don't suppose you've got any handy?" she asked hopefully.

Glenda shuddered. "Sorry, I go for the frou frou umbrella drinks. I've thought about bringing a margarita machine into work."

"Normally I wouldn't turn one down, but too festive for this type of story."

"Still working on the Hoskins thing? Time to put a big 'thirty' on it and go home for the day," Glenda instructed.

"Almost done." Shelby aimlessly continued to rifle through the sea of scrawled notes on her desk.

"Carl Hoskins is going to get what he deserves. Now get the hell out of here and go get what you deserve. I know telling you to go have some fun is pointless, so at least get yourself a decent dinner and a bath."

"Not in the mood for fun right now. But I will consent to going out with you sometime. I'd love to see you margarita'd up."

"Deal. Be warned that it will involve bad Karaoke." Glenda pulled a marker off of the desk and prepared to use it as a faux microphone.

"Bring on the Glenda Adams version of 'I Will Survive.' Can't wait. And no, I doubt that you can get me liquored up enough to be an active participant."

"We'll see about that. Now get."

"I'm getting, I'm getting," Shelby whined as she shut down the computer. She took a minute to steal another look at the picture, already having memorized the slope of the girls' tiny noses and the exact shade of their hair. It fell around the girls' shoulders in a beautiful curtain of crimson that framed pale white skin. Miram had the same red hair as her daughters, but the girls had inherited Carl's dark eyes. How had he looked into those eyes like his own and done what he had done? When was the moment he had made his decision? When was the moment Joe had made his?

Shelby was in mid-gulp, halfway though her Latte, when the phone on her desk rang. "*Atlanta Minute*, Shelby Norris speaking," she intoned as she picked up the receiver.

"Have you taken any time out of your busy schedule for a diabetes education class, Miss Atlanta Minute?" the voice on the other end of the line demanded.

Shelby dropped the cup in surprise, depositing half of the Latte on her slacks. "Shit," she muttered.

"Now there's a greeting. And here I thought your disposition would improve when you were out of the hospital," Cole told her.

"So, Dr. Cole Michaels. You're awfully obsessed with my health." Shelby grabbed a paper towel and frantically dabbed at the stained mess on her pant leg.

"Just call me your friendly neighborhood doctor/ stalker."

"Well, the office's number *is* public. So, have you done anything newsworthy?"

"I did save a life today, but it's my job."

"Coming from anybody else that would sound arrogant." Shelby started to twirl a pen around on her desk while Glenda studied her from across the room.

'But not from me?" he asked hopefully.

"From you, not so much."

"I'll take that as a compliment." Cole sounded pleased.

"If you want to." She glared at Glenda, who had draped herself across Shelby's desk. *Go away*, Shelby mouthed. Glenda just shook her head, smiled widely, and rested her chin in her hands to get more comfortable.

"Do you really want me to come to a meeting that badly?" she asked Cole.

"It would be nice. So would dinner afterwards. What can I say? I like patients who talk back to me, give me a little bit of attitude."

"You gave it right back, as I recall, Dr. Michaels. But that's okay. I deserved it, and it made my stay more interesting."

"Call me Cole. I've seen the tattoo, remember?"

Shelby laughed. "Okay, *Dr. Michaels*, I'll think about it."

"I understand your situation, Shelby. I'm not trying to be inappropriate here. You can still have friends here in Atlanta, though. So which is it—you'll think about calling me Cole, or you'll think about going to dinner?"

"Both," she harangued. "But seriously, Cole, I appreciate everything you did for me. You'll never know what it meant that you didn't offer up any of the usual platitudes. I already consider you a friend," Shelby told him softly. Then she sent Glenda another poisonous look. "Speaking of friends, I've got one who's invading my personal space right now. Give me your number. Maybe I'll page you sometime, and maybe we'll go to dinner."

"Who was that?" Glenda demanded after Shelby had taken down Cole's number and clicked off. "Did you seriously just answer with a coy *'maybe'* to a doctor?"

"A good-looking doctor, too," Shelby shrugged. "The kind you'd call 'tasty.' Who says I can't reel 'em in with my ratty hair, bad breath, and bad attitude due to a medical crisis? All it takes is a trip to the emergency room. Actually I really wouldn't recommend going that route."

"And here all along I've put my faith in eHarmony," Glenda mused. "Who knew? No more online dating for me. I just have to fake some symptoms and beat it over to Atlanta Mercy. So are all of the doctors over there ones you'd want giving you a full-body exam?"

"You know, he actually did give me a full-body exam, but just for medical purposes. And I didn't really notice any of the other doctors there. If I'm ever admitted again, and sick as hell, I'll be sure to ask around. 'Yes, I know I need a transfusion, but are you single? You'd be perfect for my friend Glenda. Can I give you her number before you prep me for surgery?'"

"You *like* him!" Glenda shrieked jubilantly, her voice cutting through the buzz and hum of activity throughout the room. Another reporter popped up from behind his cubicle, studying them like an alert Meerkat on the prairie. Sensing danger in the gathering of more than one female, he slunk back down behind the cubicle to safety.

"I didn't notice anyone else because I was in pain. Dehydrated. Medical crisis, remember? Wasn't exactly focused on any testosterone in the room. I happened to be very aware of him because he had the orders for the Demerol and the IV," Shelby qualified.

"Now there's a great meet-cute story. At first I just liked him for the Demerol, but it grew into something more meaningful." Glenda sighed.

"Stop trying to cheer me up," Shelby muttered.

"Let him cheer you up. Go to dinner. I know there's no timetable on when you should be ready for this type of thing, but it can be whatever you want it to be."

"I have no earthly idea what I want it to be," Shelby hedged.

"That's why you should go to dinner. So you can figure it out. Call him back and tell him yes," Glenda instructed. "I'm going home."

"You're not racing out of here to cancel your eHarmony account and start researching life-threatening illnesses, are you?" Shelby demanded.

"One never knows. By the way, Flanagan's is a nice place for dinner. 'Night, Shelby," Glenda chirped.

Shelby considered Cole's phone call, the possibility of a date, of all things. Her life was nowhere near recognizable, she thought as she tucked the picture of the Hoskins family into her purse. She didn't have a clue when that moment had happened, either.

CHAPTER TWENTY-SIX

Day one.

Miranda focused on the clattering sound and the familiar voices. She also recognized the scent that hovered in the air. Sandalwood and roses.

She reached out for her mother but nothing happened. She couldn't open her eyes and tried to let out a startled cry but again, nothing. Something was jammed inside of her mouth and down her throat; she felt as if it was anchoring her down.

Her mind flashed to a story she had seen on the news and a term she had learned: *anesthesia awareness*. The polished newscaster had schooled 10 p.m. news viewers about the trauma a man had suffered when he'd been conscious but unable to move during surgery. This happened sometimes when patients weren't anesthetized properly. Those who experienced the phenomenon were awake but couldn't move or cry out when they felt the pain. The man had been severely traumatized by the event and now Miranda understood on some level what he must have gone through. He'd had nightmares afterwards about being buried alive. To be there, helpless, unable to communicate but aware and feeling everything, the cut of a surgeon's knife…

The thought would have made her shiver if she could have done so.

I'm obviously not having surgery. What has happened to me?

"It's day one at your new home, Miranda," she heard her mother tell her. "You're at Chapel Hill Nursing Home. You live here for the time being. I'm going to bring in some of your things when I get a chance to make it feel more like home. You are on a ventilator to help you breathe. The doctors say you've likely suffered some brain damage due to lack of oxygen. Screw them. I'm going to be with you every day until…"

Her mother's voice trailed off. She had summed up the situation with an eerie matter-of-factness. They shared that trait, understating things with a calm delivery when the situation was hopelessly bad. A mother and daughter survival mechanism.

Until what? Miranda wanted to know, but did not hear herself form the question out loud. She panicked again at the inability to speak, to see. There was no way to convey the horror she felt. She was at the bottom of a well with disembodied voices swirling around in it.

What have I done to myself? Miranda wondered. She lay there and willed some sort of memory to come until images of herself alone in the park, and then earlier ones of herself taking drugs with a group of near-strangers, returned. She remembered the baby but could not cry. And then Clint, how she had been unable to face him afterwards. The anger and then the park.

There was nothing after the park, only these disembodied voices. She wanted to grab her mother's arm and tell her not to go, even though her mother hadn't said anything about leaving. She had pushed her mother away so many times, and now that she needed her most, she was physically incapable of reaching out for her. *There's the irony that I love so much,* Miranda thought bitterly. She calmed some as she continued to listen to the same serene, even tones.

Her father was there too, and as he bent over and kissed her she smelled the Werther's candy he was always popping. She and her Dad both had a weakness for it, so much that her mother had taken to hiding it and rationed it out four pieces at a time in a tiny crystal candy jar. She was certain her mother had always known about the secret trips she and her Dad would make to the store to get more. Eileen probably knew where the hiding places for the candy were but was the kind of mother who would say nothing. She wouldn't want to interrupt a bonding ritual between father and daughter and had probably even pretended to withhold the candy to encourage the trips.

What Miranda wouldn't give for a Werther's right now, to feel it dissolve into a velvety smoothness on her tongue. That and a Happy Meal. Not with milk, either. She wanted to feel the bite of a Coke in the back of her throat.

Where was Clint? The thought of him insisting that she eat right sent another unwelcome pang of loneliness coursing through her. She cursed herself again for not grabbing on to the people she loved when she had the chance. *Now I want to and I can't.* Why wasn't he here? How long would she be like this? More questions she could not voice.

She considered that she might have the answer to one but did not see how it could be, exactly, since she was able to wonder about it. Another definition: *Coma,* she thought. *Noun. Deep unconsciousness that is the result injury or disease.*

No, that wasn't right. She decided on her own term for her state of being: *Half-life. Noun. A state of being when a person is capable of thoughts but not able to convey them, capable of loving and hurting but not able to express that either.*

Day one of my half-life, she thought as she slipped back under again.

CHAPTER TWENTY-SEVEN

Clint pulled up to Atlanta Mercy, putting the jeep in park and jerking the keys out of the ignition in an almost single, fluid motion. He hadn't seen Miranda in two days between his shifts at the Varsity and riding along with Wally on a repair job. Wally was always half-joking that you did not want to be distracted when you were working with electricity, but Clint certainly had been. How could he be anything else, with Miranda unconscious in a hospital bed?

He'd never give up on her, no matter if one of her last conscious choices had been to leave this very place without him. He thought he understood why, but still felt a searing disappointment that she had chosen not to lean on him after losing the baby.

His fingers had drummed on his phone for his entire lunch break, but he had stopped short of calling the Linns for any news. Things were a little more tense each time they all showed up to visit. They were always jockeying for position around her bed and he thought he saw Jim Linn's expression grow more sour and disapproving with each day his daughter did not improve. Eileen didn't look at him at all.

There was talk of moving Miranda to a long-term care facility. Though Clint felt a stab of dread at what that meant-- did they really expect her be like this forever?--he would visit her there every day until he was eighty. He would. And in the short term, it would be a relief not to run into Jim and Eileen at every turn. Probably visitation would be more flexible in a long-term place, he guessed. Less chance for the uncomfortable silences and the sour looks, though Eileen was just about as persistent as he was. The woman was always there talking to Miranda, combing through her hair, reading her a book. It was a strange, sick twist on the old boyfriend/girlfriend dilemma. *We just can't get a moment alone.* Alone was unfortunately the key word in the scenario, since even when they were alone he felt alone. He wanted to but couldn't feel Miranda there.

He'd started scouring books about other people whose loved ones were comatose, how they could feel their presence and knew they were in there. Well, good for them. Personally he thought that was bullshit. The girl laying there wouldn't be Miranda until she said something sassy, tossed a casual, teasing insult his way, and cursed at the doctors some. For now he was just waiting on her, like always, like even before this had happened. Always waiting.

He punched three once he was on the elevator, rode up to the third floor expectantly, and marched down the hall to room 342. He had learned to use the short ride to prepare for a few minutes of one-sided conversation.

Once he stepped inside the room he stood there frozen, felt the blood drain from his face. The bed was empty. Oh, God. Wouldn't the Linns have called him if something had happened? Did they hate him that much? Had he been walking around the past couple of days without knowing she was gone?

He backed out of the room and was out of breath by the time he made the short trip to the nurses' station. He didn't recognize this nurse, a plump woman whose mass of blond curls were almost as crazy as Miranda's.

"The patient in 342, Miranda Linn. Has she been moved? Has she…"

The way the nurse peered at him was an invisible, stilling hand on his shoulder, an almost physical command for him to calm down.

"She's been transferred to a long-term care facility," she told him evenly.

"Already? Which one?" he demanded, relief coursing through him.

So the Linns hadn't bothered to call and let him know she was being moved. Typical, but it didn't matter. His apartment was just a few miles from where they lived. He knew Eileen would have her moved close by.

The nurse sighed, a clear indication she was not looking forward to the rest of the exchange.

"I'm sorry, young man. I can't give that information out. HIPPA regulations." She really did look sorry, but that didn't make him feel any better. Then her face instantly opened up, brightened. "You're a friend of the family? Just get in contact with them."

Friend of the family? *Hardly*, Clint thought. But he told her soberly, "Oh, I'll do that. Absolutely." *Right now*.

Clint felt his resentment dial up from simmer to boiling as he pulled out of Mercy General's parking lot. This was just another way for them to send the unconscious message that he and Miranda's relationship had never been legitimate to them. Never mind he would have been the father of their grandbaby. *Doesn't matter*, he reminded himself. *I'll just make nice one more time to find out where she is and then I'll work around them. Doesn't matter. Doesn't matter…*

His mantra had stopped working by the time he pulled up to the tan Craftsman style home. He was not in the mood to make nice as he jabbed the doorbell once, then again when no one answered. Finally Eileen opened the door, her gray hair falling around her shoulders and a weary look on her face. She was wearing one of her hippie getups, a simple sheath-type thing that was probably hand- sewn from all-natural fabric or some shit.

"Oh, Clint." The words indicated a touch of surprise but she didn't look startled to see him, didn't look anything. She had a flat, vacant expression, all of her energy and feeling apparently drained by her daughter's ordeal.

"What, your third eye couldn't sense that I was coming?" he asked sarcastically. "Look, I just went to the hospital. Imagine my surprise to find Miranda's bed empty. Almost had a heart attack. Then a nice nurse informed me that I should talk to the family and find out where she's been moved to. A family you'll obviously never consider me a part of whether Miranda comes out of this or not. But that's fine," he said tightly. "Just tell me where she is, and we can work around each other. You won't have to see me."

Something closed off and shuttered up in Eileen's face then. "I am sorry we didn't call and let you know right away, Clint," she said stiffly. "We've been a little distracted with the uncertainty of whether our daughter will ever regain consciousness again. You might want to squelch that temper of yours. It's not going to help Miranda get better."

"Neither is you blaming me for everything that's happened. That's not exactly sending a lot of 'positive energy' her way, now is it?" Clint seethed. *I blame myself enough, you don't need to bother.*

"Leave," she told him shortly, and shut the door decisively in his face.

"Tell me where she is, damn you!" he screamed, and pounded on the door. He heard the lock click and continued pounding for a minute more. Then he left, cursing, figuring she would call the cops if he stayed any longer. She probably had already.

CHAPTER TWENTY-EIGHT

Eileen yanked the telephone book off of the kitchen counter. For a moment when she'd seen the kid standing on her doorstep looking hurt she had felt ashamed that they'd never thought to contact him.

It was a depressing juggling act, trying to navigate through each day of visiting Miranda while struggling to keep the shop going. It seemed wrong and inexcusable, but she had honestly forgotten. She's been ready to tell him so, felt her heart bruise slightly when he stood there and talked about realizing he would never be an accepted part of their family. Then he had made his sneering comment about sending positive energy Miranda's way and she had felt the compassion, a delicate and tenuous house of cards being built in her mind, collapse. This was, after all, the son of a bitch who had gotten her daughter addicted in the first place.

And so her fingers did the walking, settling on the first lawyer who specialized in domestic abuse cases and restraining orders. She tore the ad out of the phone book after the pounding stopped and heard Clint's jeep start and pull away. *We'll see if you ever see her again.*

*   *   *

The next morning, in the office of Graham Barrett, attorney-at-law, Eileen wiped her damp hands on her skirt and was uncharacteristically fidgety. She wasn't usually prone to the stomach-churning dread or stress headaches that come with wondering if you're doing the right thing. Eileen was a woman accustomed to being sure of herself, secure in her decisions.

She tried thumbing through an old *Home And Gardens,* then put it back down on the coffee table in the reception area. Were most of Graham Barrett's clients the *Home And Garden* type? She caught sight of a *Field and Stream* magazine. He covered all his bases, then. She shot a searching look at her husband and posed the unspoken question.

"Yes, we're doing the right thing," he said patiently, reading her. It was a skill that had been honed and sharpened over twenty-one years of marriage. The buttoned-up accountant and the hippie with a crystal shop. People always commented on the marriage with the standard, "They balance each other out."

"He's a thug, Eileen, and he doesn't need to be anywhere near our daughter. Most of the time Miranda didn't even want anything to do with him. He followed her everywhere and wouldn't leave her alone. God only knows what he did to her when they were together."

"I know he was relentless at times. But I think he was trying to protect her from herself, Jim. How many times did we try and do the same thing when she was growing up?"

Jim put his arms out. "Eileen, you're the one who suggested we go this route. I just happen to wholeheartedly agree, and I'm not about to let it go now."

"I'm just afraid that when I made the decision to try and get this order, I did it out of anger." Eileen wiped her palms again.

"Of course you did, Eileen!" Jim let out an exasperated sigh. "Because you have a right to be angry! That's almost as senseless as a woman who's been knocked around by her boyfriend fretting that she's making the wrong decision because she's pissed off about it at the moment she walks into the police station. *She should be.* We've lost our daughter and we may never get her back."

"I think about that every day, Jim," she told him tightly.

"Eileen, I'm not trying to bully you here."

At that moment the receptionist walked up to them, and Eileen didn't have a chance to answer. "Mr. and Mrs. Linn? Mr. Barrett is ready for you." She led the way into an office where a man with steel-gray hair and eyes almost the same color waited. His suit was also gray, well-cut, but somewhere in the middle when it came to expense and quality. The all-gray effect added up to a wolfish appearance. Only a maroon tie added a burst of color. He probably figured it was important not to go too cheap or too expensive when dressing, or with his office furnishings. Clients wouldn't appreciate staring at the expensive trappings their money bought him, but go too cheap and it wouldn't appear that he was successful enough. His desk wasn't Office Max, assembly required, but it wasn't solid oak, either, she noted. The result was carefully chosen Pier One chairs, lamps and other accessories placed strategically throughout his office. On sale, likely. Creams and mauves jazzed up by a vibrant plant and interesting, colorful knickknacks here and there. He had probably given his secretary a medium-sized budget and instructions to create a relaxing atmosphere. *Nice try*, Eileen thought fleetingly. She felt anything but relaxed.

"I'm Graham Barrett," he told them, and squeezed each of their hands in turn. "The circumstances of this protective order we're going to be seeking are...well, interesting."

"I want to be clear about something," Jim told the lawyer gruffly. "We don't want this situation to be used for publicity or any kind of legal showboating. We just want you to keep this kid away from our daughter."

"I understand," the lawyer said slowly. "I think we're a ways away from having to worry about any of the local papers taking an interest in this. And they're not going to hear about it from me. Here's how it works. I have to file a petition for a protective order in the office of the Clerk of Court. Once the petition is on record in that office, it's assigned to one of the Superior Court judges for consideration. If the judge grants a temporary order, a hearing is scheduled in the next thirty days. At the hearing there's a chance for a permanent order to be granted. If we want to even get to the stage where we're granted a temporary order, we're going to have to prove this young man is a threat to your daughter, or that he harassed her in the past."

He stopped to take a delicate sip of coffee, courtesy of the Bunn-O-Matic coffee maker on the table beside his desk. He offered them some but they declined.

"So I want you to tell me everything you know about your daughter's relationship with her former boyfriend. We're going to have to go the extra mile here since your daughter can't speak for herself. Did your or anyone else ever see Miranda's boyfriend harm her in any way? Was he threatening or harassing her?"

Eileen could almost hear him mentally reviewing the rest of an invisible checklist. *Did he ever prevent her from eating or sleeping or endanger her health in other ways? Did he ever hurt any pets, destroy her belongings, or cause harm or damage to anything else that was especially important to her?*

So this was a critical moment. She thought of the misguided young man who had made the mistakes her daughter had made; he had asked her daughter to follow him into oblivion. Now from what she could tell, he was trying to correct the mistakes, start a new life that included her daughter. He wanted her to follow him out. But even as relentless as he was, in spite of all of the entries in Miranda's diaries about his showing up and dragging her out of places she shouldn't have been, he couldn't save her. He'd taken her hand and they'd jumped off of the cliff and it was too late. Somehow he'd caught a rope on his way down but her daughter had gone tumbling into the abyss. He'd lost track of her when it mattered most and couldn't find her at that critical moment. So now it was too late for him. She set her jaw firmly, made the choice.

"No, Mr. Barrett, I never saw him abuse her. But I know people who can tell you that they saw him forcibly remove her from places on numerous occasions, kicking and screaming. After he'd followed her there. He was definitely harassing her. He was obsessed with her, and it wasn't healthy. I have

Miranda's cell phone here, and you won't believe it when you go through the history. He flooded her with calls at all hours of the day. He wouldn't leave her alone. I also have some journals of Miranda's that detail how he would follow her around. Like I said, he was absolutely everywhere she was. He smothered her. If you want to hear from some of the people she hung out with and get their take on the situation, I suppose I can track a few of them down."

She finally stopped, winded, as if the words spoken had cost her great effort. But she finished strong. "I want you to help me give my daughter some peace. He's caused enough damage to our family, and now I want him to leave us alone."

The lawyer's steel gray eyes pierced her own. "We'll see, Mr. and Mrs. Linn. Between the cell phone, journal and friends, we'll try to get it done."

Eileen was suddenly in a hurry to get out of the lawyer's office, away from the fake but passable plants and the mellow surroundings where relationships gone bad were defined in legal terms and handled as neatly and safely as possible. They all shook hands again. Graham Barrett, attorney-at-law promised to keep them posted on whether or not a judge felt a temporary order was necessary, and whether a hearing would be scheduled.

"I'm very proud of you," Jim whispered in her ear, taking her hand on the way to the car.

I wish I was proud of me, she thought miserably.

CHAPTER TWENTY-NINE

The snack cart clattered down the hallway past room 103 and Eileen woke with a start. Usually it was full of an assortment of crackers, sugar free cookies and fruit. Juice and water too; Chapel Hill nursing home believed in keeping its patients hydrated. They did their best, satisfied her as much as any parent with their child in here would be satisfied. Not that her daughter had ever been able to eat or drink anything off of the cart; she received everything she needed through a feeding tube and IV, but it still mattered.

Yawning and stretching, she glanced over at her daughter's still figure and listened to the beep of patient call buttons going off up and down the hall. When Miranda was six she had suffered from chronic earaches. Eileen falling asleep by her bedside had become an almost nightly occurrence. Now Miranda was grown and Eileen was keeping vigil again. These days, though, she woke to the sound of a nurse moving around and the depressing perfume of the nursing home. Bleach with not-so-subtle undertones of urine. Most of the patients except for a few younger ones here for rehabilitation had already lived a lifetime. Her daughter should have lived five more decades before ending up in this place. On the worst days she was afraid her daughter had already lived her lifetime too, crammed it all into nineteen years.

She hated feeling as if she was in the way when she visited her daughter. She was just days into this purgatory that had become her existence, watching Miranda hover between the worlds of the living and dead. But it felt like a lifetime.

Strange how she had spent much of the past two years

of her daughter's life wondering who she was with, where she spent her nights. Now she knew where her daughter was every second of the day, and it was equally sad. She glanced at the calendar on the wall and noted the dark, markered slash through each day. Tomorrow she would flip the calendar over to a new month and start slashing through those days too. She wanted Miranda to see exactly what day it was when she opened her eyes.

Depending on her mood she either saw the slashes as a triumphant marker for another day that Miranda wasn't gone, or as another frustrating reminder that she wasn't quite there. She thought about the conversation with Graham Barrett, how he'd promised the papers wouldn't hear about what had happened to their daughter from him. But they might hear about it from her.

"I'll be back, baby," she whispered to Miranda, suddenly feeling an even stronger sense of purpose.

Miranda thought about her mother's visit as she listened to the nurse's twangy lilt. She sounded like the Paula Deen type. If Miranda could eat, the woman would probably bring her some deep-fried, butter-laden or cooked-with-lard Southern goodies just like the cooking show hostess. She liked the way the nurse talked to her mother, brought her coffee. She heard her mother gratefully accept it each day on her visit. Vigil was more like it, but her mother wouldn't have skipped a day even if Miranda could have commanded her to.

She hated to think of her Mom and Dad with their lives jammed in neutral like this, but she needed the visits and the voices. They drug her back and reeled her in. She had climbed in her VW Bug and taken off in a squeal of tires on Intervention Day, but she was their captive audience now.

She felt as if she was trapped behind a thick, dark curtain. She imagined yanking it aside, but there was always another one in her way each time she pulled it back. No progress. She was back in the Haunted House at nine years old: that day Miranda had felt the ropes jump underneath her feet and snake over her shoes. Even though the room was pitch black, she'd known, of course, that they were not rats' tails like the guide was trying to tell them. After the tiny bumps had briefly risen on her arms she had not been afraid. When she had screamed as the robed, white-haired ghoul jumped out at the group with an ax, it had been all in good fun. She loved horror movies, loved the delicious thrill of danger while still knowing she was going to be okay. But when they had come to the last part of the horror house and she expected to step out of the door and giggle about how dumb it had all been, she kept wading through curtain after curtain. She'd kept her hands out expectantly, waiting for them to push on something solid, but they just kept grazing the softness of another curtain to open.

Her screams had been real then with no thrilled excitement behind them, and the guide had helped her out of the door. She'd run into her mother's arms shaking and sobbing and had never been in another Haunted House since.

The nurse came back in the room and Miranda felt the head of her bed move up slowly. Oh, terrific. Dinner time. She was being repositioned so she wouldn't choke on her "food." Not since the days of childhood and enforced veggies had she dreaded mealtime. There was no getting out of this one by hiding the unwanted portion under her napkin or feeding it to a waiting dog on the sly. She was being fed through a tube in her nose.

"Here's your chicken and biscuits, hon," the nurse said lightly as she tended to Miranda's feeding tube. Yep, definitely Paula Deen. But Miranda was pretty sure she was glad not to be able to see what was being shoved into her.

She reached deep down in an attempt to startle the nurse. She'd love to open her eyes with the tube snaking out of her nose and tell the woman with mock enthusiasm, "Yum." Or the alternate, "No matter how many times you do this, I will never be okay with it." Wouldn't that make a great story for the medical journals or a *Woman's Day* article?

After "dinner" the nurse would also rub Vaseline on Miranda's cracked lips and sponge her mouth while she hummed the same tune. She'd been listening to it for the last fifteen days minus the nurse's days off, but she still couldn't figure out what it was. Maybe it wasn't a song at all, just something in the nurse's head. How could the woman be so happy? Wasn't it depressing tending to a still body every day, someone who never reacted and couldn't show you any appreciation?

God bless the woman, Miranda thought. *I wouldn't want to spend my days cleaning me up or shoving things up my nose.* She hummed along in her head, trying to match the parts where the song was slightly off-key. For the hell that she was in, this realization of one of her biggest childhood fears, there was still something about today that felt different.

Clint sat in the parking lot of Chapel Hill with a mixture of relief and quiet pleasure coursing through him. He thought he felt it roll to the edge of his fingertips and refresh them like the tide coming in at the beach.

He lit up and scanned the outside of the place for awhile. Nice lawn, plenty of landscaping. If Miranda was able to look out of her window she'd be able to see trees and some punches of color. Of course she couldn't though. Could she? He doubted it but he'd gone for days without hearing a word about her. He hadn't returned to the Linns' before today. That would have been pointless. When he'd received the temporary restraining order it had instructed him to stay away from the Linns' home and their daughter. No mention of where their daughter was being cared for. Wasn't Eileen clever? Actually he had always thought so. But he'd never figured her for vengeful like this.

She wasn't clever enough that she'd paid attention to the rusted-over Chevy S-10 that had been parked across the street from her house and followed her all the way to Chapel Hill. He was sure she would have noticed his jeep, which she probably saw as some sort of symbol of her daughter's downfall. So he'd borrowed Wally's old beater and just like he'd hoped, Eileen's Volvo had made a short ten-minute trip to the nursing home. Miranda would always be kept close. Eileen's third eye was a little clouded these days.

Well, he couldn't go inside without all hell breaking loose. He imagined an old black and white western-style poster of himself taped up, alerting staff to be on the lookout for him. Clint Mullen, Public Enemy No. 1.

For now he would have to bide his time, but he had ways to make Miranda know that he still cared without actually going inside. He glanced at the radio sitting on the split leather interior of the passenger's side. The cassette tape was ready to play but he decided to wait just a little bit longer. He reluctantly pulled out of the parking lot to return the truck to Wally. If he didn't hurry he'd be late for work.

CHAPTER THIRTY

"Shelby, I've got something for you," Maura announced.
    Shelby pulled the small headphones out of her ears one at a time, coming out of her story and music-induced trance. She was knee deep in another city council meeting scandal. One of the council members had attempted to be a very bad boy with a pretty young thing who had unfortunately turned out to work undercover for vice.
    Ages ago, she'd playfully schemed with Joe to create scandals for city council members in Layton. Now she had the real thing. She took the piece of paper Maura handed her. It was scrawled with an unfamiliar name, Eileen Linn, along with a contact number.
    "'Okay, who's Eileen and why do I want to talk to her?"
    "You're going to do a story on her daughter Miranda, who's currently in a comatose state at Chapel Hill nursing home due to an overdose. I hate that name, Chapel Hill. The word chapel makes me think of a damn funeral, which makes it seem like they're already dead. I sure as hell wouldn't want to spend my twilight years there. Anyway, Eileen's pushing publicly for the accepted use of personal heroin overdose kits for addicts. Seems she thinks one could have saved her daughter." Maura delivered the synopsis in her usual rapid-fire, not-a-breath-wasted style.
    "A personal kit? Are you talking about addicts keeping some sort of a rescue concoction on hand just in case they overdose?"
    "Precisely. They actually distributed these kits to addicts in other major cities in the United States. No known

side effects. It's taken up the nose of all things. Single dose costs about twenty bucks. Not hard to see the appeal."

"Sounds a lot like the clean-needle programs you hear about," Shelby said skeptically. "Kind of a band-aid on the problem, isn't it? They're giving addicts clean needles to prevent the spread of AIDS, hepatitis, what have you. That's great. I'm not saying addicts deserve any of that. But here's the thing: they're still using, aren't they? They're still headed to the same place, just via a different route. And for God's sake they're giving them the tools to do it!"

Shelby warmed to the argument and began twirling her pen thoughtfully. "This sounds a lot like that. They get bailed out, they feel invincible, so they do it again. And maybe they shoot up even more next time, up the ante…"

"Whoa, there." Maura held up a hand. "You're not in the editorial department. You want to write a nice op-ed piece on it, get paid to spew your opinion, you're going to have to be here a lot longer and come after my job. Until then, let's skip the debate. Call Eileen Linn. Find somebody reasonably intelligent that has some sort of title to interview. Get conflicting viewpoints. You know what to do. Just write the damn story."

"How effective are these rescue kits? Have they actually saved lives?" Shelby pressed.

"Happy researching, dear. For you to find out," Maura told her as she breezed away.

"Since when are you an idealist?" Shelby called after her. "I can't believe you're ordering me to write an unbiased story and all."

Maura turned and sighed. "I agree with a lot of what you're saying, Shelby, but think about it from a mom or dad's point of view. A way to save your kid. Even from a pragmatic point of view you can see it as priorities and first things first. You can't rehabilitate your child if they're dead of an overdose."

Chastised, Shelby studied the name and number for a second and punched it in on the office's telephone. A mellow-sounding woman on the other end wanted to meet her--at the nursing home where Miranda Linn was being cared for, no less.

After Shelby hung up she typed in a Google search on heroin overdose kits and clicked several hits.

Shelby's cursor whizzed through explanations of Narcan kits. Apparently they were seen as a crutch for addicts by some, as a savior for addicts by others. She marveled at the idea of one addict saving another from an overdose with a trusty backup kit. It wasn't all that hard to understand a parent wanting to latch on to a $20 insurance policy for their child.

Shelby read through endless quotes of people arguing back and forth about the safety of addicts administering drugs, the fact that an easy way out left users with little motivation to change. Some parents of addicts sounded off about the kits being a good safety net until their children could be talked into going to treatment and getting a permanent solution.

Already this story didn't have the feel of the warm-and-fuzzy human interest stories Maura accused her of gravitating towards. Shelby did a quick MapQuest, sighed, grabbed her keys, and headed toward Chapel Hill.

She pulled up to Chapel Hill thirty minutes later. No chapel, Shelby noted. There *was* a hill, and lots of lush landscaping. The outside was pleasant, anyway: red brick with old-fashioned lanterns hung at the entrance. Two elderly women in wheelchairs sat outside with white afghans draped across their laps to combat any chill. Their caregivers lounged beside them in white wicker chairs, their noses buried in smutty novels. It was a peaceful scene, but not one Shelby could imagine a nineteen-year-old convalescing in.

The woman waiting for her inside had shoulder-length silver hair pulled back by barrettes on both sides. She wore a cream-colored tunic and long, flowing skirt. The neo-hippie look was accentuated by the sandals on the woman's feet and colorful bangles that adorned each wrist.

"I'm Eileen Linn," the woman finally said. "I'm starting a foundation for my daughter Miranda and trying to raise awareness about heroin overdose kits. I hope you'll help me tell her story."

Her tone was businesslike, eerily so, almost as if they should be discussing this over an overpriced Cobb salad and tea at one of the outdoor cafés in the city, or at the *Atlanta Minute* offices. Not in a nursing home at her daughter's bedside.

"Thanks for agreeing to meet so quickly," Shelby offered awkwardly. "I'm Shelby Norris." It was hard not to feel a sense of dread as they continued down the long hallway, but the room was better than expected. Eileen Linn had done her best to make the small room with gray tile floors look like home. A very new-agey home. Small pink crystals were carefully arranged on the bedside table; a Native American dream catcher hung on the wall at the head of the hospital bed. This was a family apparently open to all spiritual alternatives.

Finally Shelby's eyes settled on the still form in the bed, the delicate features in repose. "Why don't you tell me a little bit about your daughter?"

It was disconcerting to ask for information about the girl who was laying feet away from her. She tried to pay attention to Eileen but her eyes kept straying over to Miranda.

Eileen took her time. "A little about Miranda," she sighed. "My daughter is a very complicated woman, Shelby. She's two sides of a coin, the hell raiser on a Saturday night who's sitting in the pew on Sunday. Not that she's a hypocrite. I think she honestly struggles with two real sides of her personality. I just don't think I can sum her up with a neat little phrase or quote. It wouldn't seem fair, almost like…"

"Trying to sum up somebody's life in a thirteen-inch column," Shelby supplied. She noticed that Eileen had been careful to speak about her daughter in the present tense. "Sorry, I'm a journalist and that's my frame of reference for most things," she explained hastily. "I just mean I understand what you're saying."

"I think you do." Eileen quirked an eyebrow, and Shelby had the unsettling feeling it really wasn't necessary for her to explain anything to this odd woman at all.

"I'm sorry for what's happened to your daughter," Shelby began again. "My editor didn't tell me much, just a little bit about Miranda and that you're pushing for the city to implement a rescue kit program."

"You're not quite convinced it's the right thing to do, are you? I can hear the skepticism in your voice. I've certainly heard all of the counterarguments. You think it doesn't get at the root of the problem, that it keeps the whole cycle of bad behavior going…"

Shelby shifted uncomfortably. "I've got mixed feelings. But you know what? I'm not a parent. And my editor pointed out to me that even from a purely logical and unemotional point of view, there's the fact that the immediate danger needs to be addressed before a person can think about recovering."

"Yes, there is that." Eileen Linn actually looked slightly amused. "So many addicts just aren't ready for recovery, that's a sad fact. But they might be at a later date. And do they deserve to die due to a case of too little, too late?"

She paused and wandered over to the window, stared out at the perfectly manicured lawn that most of the Chapel Hill residents could not enjoy.

"My daughter, she had been doing extraordinarily well. She'd turned things around. Then she had a terrible…setback." Eileen cleared her throat and gathered herself. Finally Shelby could see the mother in Eileen clawing through the steely self-reserve. She recognized it, the fight to stay composed. She knew the alternative was a complete breakdown. She'd been that way for weeks after losing Joe.

"But I make no apologies for the fact that I'm looking at it almost purely from a parent's standpoint," Eileen continued. "Not ashamed to use cold, hard logic to as a backup to support my argument, get me where I want to go. Not everybody weighing in on the debate has had a child of theirs overdose, after all."

"True."

"Shelby, would you mind if I do an aura cleansing on

Miranda before we talk any further?" Eileen asked suddenly.

"Sure. I can come back when you're done…cleansing. I don't want interrupt."

"No, I'd like for you to stay as long as you're quiet. Miranda used to ask me to do these for her all the time."

Shelby watched, fascinated, as the woman took a small bundle of sticks that looked like incense, placed it in a ceramic bowl, and lit the tip on fire.

"It's a white sage smudge," Eileen explained. "It's very important in Native American culture. It purifies the air and disperses negativity."

She promptly blew out the burning bundle and cupped her long, graceful hands together as if she was catching water from a tap.

Shelby glanced around nervously. "Aren't you going to set off the smoke detectors?"

"Shh," Eileen told her. "I need to concentrate." She gathered the white, aromatic smoke with her hands, seemed to corral it and move it slowly down her body. After it surrounded her long skirt like a small mushroom cloud, she inhaled deeply and murmured, "Release me from any negative energy on or around me."

Then she moved to her daughter's bedside and stroked the curly hair before placing her hands above Miranda's body. She worked her way down to the small feet. When she was done she continued to stand above her daughter and motioned with her hands. It looked to Shelby like she was fluffing up an invisible head of hair.

Eileen made her way back to the foot of the bed, looking like a priestess with her hands hovering above Miranda's head, never making physical contact. After she had worked her way downwards, she shook her hands vigorously. Shelby imagined invisible drops of…something, flying off of Eileen's fingers.

"To get rid of any of her negative energy," Eileen explained. A tear rolled down her cheek.

"Is that what you're doing?" Shelby asked in awe.

"Taking on her pain?"

"Well, that's certainly not the purpose of a cleansing," Eileen said. "But I guess that's what happens when a parent does one on their child. Probably not a wise idea. I think it's a natural tendency for most parents to want to take on their child's pain, don't you?"

Shelby said nothing. A few minutes later, Eileen told her in a faraway voice, "There's a phenomena with drug addicts called place conditioning. Drug use is very ritualized, and addicts usually go to the same place to shoot up. It's almost exactly like a Pavlovian response. When they're in their usual spot, their metabolism changes and their body readies itself for the drug. It's kind of like a survival mechanism and it increases the body's tolerance to whatever they're taking. The possibility of overdose is less likely. But when they're in a strange place they're more susceptible to the toxic effects. It's more dangerous to shoot up in an unfamiliar place. It sounds crazy, I know, but that's exactly what happened to Miranda. When she overdosed she was in a strange place, all alone." Eileen's voice cracked.

Shelby felt terrible for this woman, but strangely comforted. All of these months she had been tortured with images of Joe drifting off alone. Now she felt an odd warmth knowing he had been surrounded by his own things in a house he had lovingly rebuilt. Maybe that was the reason for the peaceful smile she hadn't been able to figure out. She would never forget that expression, as if he'd gotten answers he'd been waiting for. She could almost imagine his last peaceful sigh, him whispering, *"Oh, that's it."*

She'd never know what he had taken his last look at, but the bedside table with their wedding picture on top had been repositioned so it was directly in his line of view.

"I'll help you tell your daughter's story," Shelby told the woman. "You just have to help me understand who she was, so we can tell it in a way she would have wanted."

Eileen reached for the worn maroon book on the night stand beside Miranda's bed and handed it to Shelby. "You want to get to know my daughter, here's the best way to do it. She kept a diary, took it with her everywhere. Ever since she was thirteen she'd carry a diary in her purse and take it out at random moments, whenever something occurred to her. She's filled about ten of these books so far. Here's the latest. If you finish this one and want to read the others, I've got the rest of them at home. I know you probably don't have time for all of them, but read and you'll know her almost as well as I do. She's worth getting to know."

On impulse Shelby moved over to the bed and took Miranda's cool hand. "I'd like that," she murmured. She could only guess at the chaos that had led to this stillness.

*   *   *

Hours later, stretched out in her recliner, Shelby gingerly opened the nondescript book. This was Miranda's most recent diary, but it was still worn from frequent use. It had been awhile since she'd seen life through nineteen-year-old eyes.

"Hello, Miranda Linn, nice to meet you," she breathed, as her eyes settled on the first entry.

Today I tried to go shopping for someone who doesn't exist... yet. I feel like he's still just a part of my imagination, even though I know he's growing in there. Cells are dividing and all kinds of biology is happening. I don't know how I'm sure it's a boy but I am, and I know Noah is the perfect name. Who better for me to pay homage to than one of the first guys in the world to experience what it means to start over after total, but necessary, wreckage? I wonder if all parents-to-be feel this guilt even before they have to face the tiny creature they're answering to. What will he think when he's old enough to understand that I hurt him without meaning to before he was even born?

Most pregnant women worry about taking a sip of soda or eating enough fruit. I've shared something worse than caffeine with my baby. Will he understand that sometimes even the most loving parents are weak and selfish? The childish, optimistic part of me wants to think that maybe it's better this way, to be done with the hurting and the mistakes before he's born, before he knows. But I know there will be more. That's just how love and parenting is, I suppose.

CHAPTER THIRTY-ONE

Day Fifteen.

So her mother was searching for meaning in all of this and actually meant to start a foundation in her name. Miranda had heard her mother and a reporter talking about it; she'd been surprised at the reporter's voice and the touch of her hand.

Her mother's mission was to help people decide what would bring meaning into their lives. That was why Eileen owned what Miranda called a "one stop spiritual shop" that centered around using crystals for healing. The shop also offered numerous other alternatives for the searching. Now, just fifteen days after Miranda's half-life had begun, her mother was searching and trying to make sense out of all of this, validate the experience and lessen the pain by helping others.

Start by helping those you already know, Miranda ached to tell her. She thought of Clint. The way his life centered around her had been frightening at times. He must be crazy with grief or worry, and her mother would have helped him if he were anyone else except the kid who had gotten her daughter hooked.

She waited to hear his voice but it didn't come; she waited for someone to mention him but that hadn't happened yet, either. Miranda thought of the first night her half-life had really begun. Now that she had the time she would replay every detail she could conjure, every sight, smell, and sound. She would wonder how they had all come together to equal a choice made by her that had led to this.

Miranda and Arli linked arms and walked into the party, doing their synchronized Laverne-and-Shirley walk. More than a few male heads turned to gawk at the two curly-haired blondes who were so close in resemblance.

"Are you twins?" a heavy-lidded party-goer asked.

"No, but our Moms are," Miranda answered cheerfully.

"Huh?"

"Never mind," Miranda told him, rolling her eyes and scanning the room. She walked away as he made a lame joke about them being twice the fun.

Miranda caught a glimpse of Mr. "Twice The Fun's" girlfriend as the girl came up behind him and sharply elbowed him in the side. She cast a murderous look at Miranda and Arli but then seemed to mentally shrug. She probably sensed that they didn't seem to be angling for any attention and actually spurned it, moving through the crowd as if they just didn't have the time or patience for the male appreciation. No competition there…

Miranda took a minute to ponder one of life's little mysteries: why women, who needed as much help from other women as they could get in her opinion, were so often at odds with each other in seeking out the same questionable prize.

"There he is, Arl. Come on, I want you to meet Clint." Now Miranda was interested in some male attention. Clint's intensity matched her own. He looked like a thug but he could quote Proust. Be still her nineteen-year-old heart. His brain was home to intelligent thoughts that would surprise, except no one took the time to listen to him. She would. He looked bored and distinctly out of place but smiled lazily as she introduced him to Arli. His eyes were mostly riveted on Miranda, though, as he took Arli's hand formally and shook it.

She'd been fascinated a few hours later as she watched Clint shoot the water from the syringe onto the spoon. The water seeped outward and transformed the powder into a muddy brown liquid. Miranda flinched slightly when she felt the needle enter her arm. She almost told him to stop when she saw him draw a small amount of blood into the syringe.

"That means we've got a vein," he told her. Then he pushed

the muddy brown liquid into her body a little at a time, a series of small strokes. "You get a longer rush that way," she heard him explain. She felt the world slow down and a childish sense of happiness and well-being that would never return take over. She was barely aware of him doing the same with her Pseudo-Twin.

Miranda wished she could scream as the private, depressing home movie looped endlessly in her head. She wanted to run up, shake herself, knock the spoon out of his hands, send the syringe flying, throw it in the trash, leave the party, anything. It was maddening to lay here with her mind on replay, almost worse than if she had died. She was trapped inside of herself, unable to change anything as she committed each fatal error. It was like watching a stranger as a curly-haired girl she didn't really know put up another bar to her own prison.

After replaying the memories came the most hated moments. Her mind would jump from the past to a missed future. She pictured a boy at four...six...ten. It was a unique, tailored future: Noah running around Grandma Eileen's shop, ignoring warnings to be careful. He would fidget as Grandma moved her hands just above his squirming body, on a mission to fluff his six-year-old aura. Then he would sneak out for Werther's with his Granddad and find places to stash them that she would pretend not to know about. Finally, she saw Noah wrapped in her arms on top of Stone Mountain as she pointed out the skyline of the city. It would be his first lesson on how to look at things from a distance.

They had come so close to a cease-fire between her parents and Clint, with Noah as the unwitting glue that held them all together. It was a series of should-have-beens.

Miranda was almost glad when the nurse came in to do her feeding.

CHAPTER THIRTY-TWO

Shelby studied the sign under the striped awning. Scripted in fancy gold and blue lettering, it read *Frozen Light Crystals*. Varying shapes and sizes of crystals in endless shades of pink, blue and other colors caught the light like a rainbow captured behind the window of the pink building. The window on the left side of the door, at least. That one wasn't shattered into a thousand pieces on the sidewalk. The shards of glass that littered the opposite side caught the sun and almost looked like crystals that had spilled out onto the pavement. A police cruiser was parked out front.

Eileen was outside, calmly sweeping up the glittering mess. Today a pair of light blue crystal earrings hung from her ears like tiny chandeliers. She wore the same pair of Birkenstocks on her feet she'd had on at the nursing home.

"Eileen!" Shelby called as she jumped out of her car. "What the hell *happened?*"

She had promised to stop by Eileen's shop to bring her extra copies of the issue with Miranda's story in it. Not a necessary gesture, but somehow she had felt the need to deliver it in person. She also felt a niggling curiosity at how this odd woman made her living.

"Oh, it appears someone has a strong opinion about my strong opinion regarding rescue kits," Eileen responded, looking unruffled. "If you're passionate about your side of a debate you have to expect an equal amount of intensity from the other side, I suppose. Though I don't make a habit of smashing windows in at people's place of business. They apparently just wanted to make a point because they didn't bother to take anything out of the window. I'm lucky that no one else who happened along after that helped themselves. Remarkable, really."

"You know that someone who doesn't like the idea of rescue kits did this?" Shelby asked, still baffled.

"They left a note. They were rather succinct and to the point." She held out the piece of paper for Shelby to look at.

"Be sure not to touch that," the police officer standing next to Eileen warned Shelby sternly.

Shelby turned her attention to the note Eileen held. It read, *Junkies deserve what they get. Your daughter's not entitled to a magic ticket to bail her out of her bad choices.* The perfect loop of the cursive, the tidy penmanship, was an unsettling contrast to the venomous message.

"Oh God, Eileen, that's sick. I'm sorry."

"Well, we'll see what the police come up with. They're actually going to fingerprint it, very 'CSI' stuff. *Love* that TV show," she said for the officer's benefit. "I'll turn it over to this nice young gentleman, but I don't imagine they'll be able to do a whole lot. I can't see the full resources of Atlanta's finest being devoted to finding out who smashed in my tiny little shop's storefront window." She was almost mirthful, teasing, as if she expected the curly-haired, stern-faced officer to be amused by her casual dismissal of his abilities. No trouble at all to imagine Eileen at a sixties love-in or protest, thumbing her nose at the police and resolutely making the peace sign with her fingers.

"You know, I wonder if it could have been Miranda's ex. Seems like the type of thing he would do," Eileen murmured.

"Didn't you tell me he was an addict himself? Pretty judgmental coming from someone with the same problem."

"Recovering drug addict," Eileen supplied. "Very high and mighty about it, to use Miranda's words. Very adamant about staying clean. And very angry and hurt when Miranda kept pushing him away. But who knows? I read some of the letters to the editor after the article ran. I managed to stir a lot of people up, didn't I?" The idea seemed to please Eileen.

Shelby winced as she recalled helping Maura sift through

all of the letters that had poured in: some compassionate, some eloquent, some mean-spirited, some ignorant. All written with very strong feeling.

Eileen finished sweeping. "In the meantime, that's what insurance is for. Going to have some double-paned glass put in this time. Should have done that a long time ago, anyway, with all of these crystals sitting in the window. Might be time to install some security cameras too. Sad, not exactly in keeping with the image or ideas I'm trying to promote. Help me with this tarp?"

Eileen spread the thick blue plastic sheet out and started threading pieces of thin rope through the punched holes in its edges. She stepped nimbly through the open window and thrust the end of the tarp at Shelby. "Hold this."

"I'll show you around the shop," Eileen told her when they were done.

"Incredible," Shelby said admiringly as they stepped inside. "It's like stepping inside of a jewel box."

A dizzying array of shapes and colors stretched along the shelves. Even the painted wooden floor was multicolored, the individual planks painted in alternating yellow and blue. Along the wall a bookshelf was jammed with titles like *The Crystal Cure, The Earth's Secrets To Healing And Meditation, and Listening To The Light In Crystals.* A CD of Native American chanting played in the background, the low plaintive voices keeping a steady, timeless rhythm. A sign advertising "Yoga With a Twist" classes was tacked up on a bulletin board next to the front desk. The shop boasted the same mix of spiritual alternatives Shelby had noticed in Miranda's room at the nursing home. A hand-painted sign declared, "All bases are covered here." Spiritual whimsy?

The girl who had been tending to customers while Eileen was cleaning up looked as if she could chant with the music perfectly. Her face was all beautiful lines and angles, undeniably Native American. Her thick black hair was even roped into two glossy braids, completing the look. But her ripped jeans and tank top were decidedly untraditional. A stud glinted in her straight, proud nose.

"How did you come up with the name Frozen Light?" Shelby asked, still recovering from sensory overload.

"Well, don't these crystals look like frozen light to you? The word crystal even comes from the Greek word *krystallos*, which means frozen light."

"I like that. And I like this." Shelby gently fingered a tiny teardrop shaped pendant that was tinged with pink.

"Nice choice. That's Quartz. They're the most common mineral you can find. Quartz crystals are excellent for help in meditating and spiritual healing."

"I'll take it. I could use some spiritual healing."

"Couldn't we all, sister?" a twenty-something customer sporting a ponytail, goatee and several hemp necklaces chimed in. "Couldn't we all?"

Shelby wondered whether he had taken the healing, calm-inducing potential of crystals to heart or had chemical help for his laid-back demeanor. He didn't seem to be bothered by the tarp over the gaping hole where the front window's glass had been. She paid and had Eileen clasp the necklace for her. It was worth a try.

"I started reading Miranda's journals," she told Eileen. "She seems to be a very walk-on-the-right-side-of-the-stairs kind of girl. That's cost her a lot, but I find it hard not to admire."

Eileen's left eyebrow arched curiously. "Walk on the right side of the stairs kind of girl? What does that mean, exactly?"

"I used to walk down the left side of the stairs of the house I grew up in. The right side of the stairs creaked like crazy. I always avoided the right side so I wouldn't make any noise. Miranda would definitely *not* walk on the left side of the stairs."

"No," Eileen agreed thoughtfully. "She certainly wouldn't."

CHAPTER THIRTY-THREE

Clint was pissed, and he was going to track the bitch down. He strode purposefully down Peachtree street and didn't bother to move out of the way for anyone in the throng of pedestrians. They moved out of his way, as usual. A lady walking her poodle quickly dodged him just before he walked into the office building, rode the elevator up, and marched into the *Atlanta Minute* office space. "I need to speak with Shelby Norris," he demanded through clenched teeth. "Is she in?"

A secretary with gray hair and a smooth baby face regarded him warily. "Is this about a story?"

Clint leaned in close enough to get a whiff of the receptionist's department store perfume and some fear. He was into intimidating people when necessary. "Lady, you're damn right it's about a story," he said with feeling. He could feel her recoil slightly from behind the counter, where she was probably playing solitaire on her computer or logged into her Facebook account. He'd love to see what she would type in for her "status" update for all of her friends to read online once he was finished with her: *Taking an early lunch. Just dealt with a complete whack-job at the office. Might even take the rest of the day off.*

Finally she led him down the narrow hallway through a sea of reporters scurrying around like cockroaches, and pointed out the redhead. Shelby Norris was obviously working on a story, surrounded by scrawled-on pieces of paper. She sat in an office chair, vintage-looking horn-rimmed reading glasses sliding down her nose, head bobbing in time to whatever she was listening to on a small white iPod. She twirled a pen as she studied some notes. He thought he even saw her shoulders do an ever-so-slight shimmy to the music. When he walked up to her and towered over her chair she didn't seem to be intimidated by his size, instead peered at him from behind the glasses curiously.

"Shelby Norris," she introduced herself, thrusting her hand out. "And you are..."

"Clint Mullen," he supplied shortly, momentarily unbalanced by her friendly greeting. He let a chilly silence follow for a minute and didn't take the hand she offered. "I'm sure the Linns have told you all about me, none of it good."

"Well, how can I help you, Clint?" she asked slowly.

"How can you *help* me? You can *help* me by explaining this sentimental piece of crap," he muttered as he wadded up the article about Miranda and threw it at her feet. "You wrote this article about my girlfriend, and the last thing she would want is to be used as a 'just say no' example. 'The Linns hold a picture of their daughter, Miranda,'" he intoned in a high, mocking voice. "She's a very proud person and she values her privacy. I'm surprised you didn't go in there and take a picture of her laying there, hooked up to all those tubes and machines. 'Here's what can happen to you, boys and girls. Don't be the next statistic like her.'"

"I don't think the Linns are necessarily trying to use her an example, Clint," she told him carefully. "I think they're just trying to make something good come of all of this. It's the best way they know to get through it. Clint, I really wanted to talk to you when I was writing this. I wanted my readers to understand who she was. I left messages, but you obviously didn't want to talk to me. I know she's important to you and I wanted to hear what you had to say."

"Why, so you could get a nice quote from the grieving boyfriend? Would that have made the story better? This isn't supposed to be about me or the Linns or anybody else, now is it? It's about Miranda. They're even bigger fools than I thought, lady, and so are you, if you think there's any good to be had in this at all." The words came out in a low, enraged hiss.

On his way out Clint marched back through the activity and headed for the front desk again. He couldn't resist sneering at the receptionist. She seemed like the motherly, protective type and had a hand lightly placed on the phone as if she were ready to call 911.

"Be sure to ask for Jack Dumfries if you're calling the PD," he told her. "That's spelled D-u-m-f-r-i-e-s. He's picked me up a few times for possession. We're almost like friends."

There it was again, Shelby thought, that careful respect shown by using Miranda's name in the present tense. Eileen followed the same rule. It was a habit shared by two people who obviously hated each other but loved Miranda.

As she watched Clint Mullen retreat, the anger emanating off of him in waves and settling firmly in her general vicinity, she thought about Eileen's casual accusation of Clint. The kid could definitely reach a rage state and smash in the window of someone he hated. That, and more. But there was no way he had done that to the front of Eileen's shop. This was someone who would have done anything, used anything he could to prevent what had happened to Miranda. He would have been all for a rescue kit if it would have saved her life. She'd heard the intensity in his voice, recognized it and had felt it every time she searched for a new test trial or experimental drug for Joe. She would have done anything, used anything to keep him alive. Clint Mullen was the same.

Maybe he could have scrawled a note in an attempt to look like an *Atlanta Minute* reader who had taken their convictions too far, but she couldn't see it. He was obviously up-front about letting a person know when he wasn't happy with them. She had certainly just seen that. If he was going to smash in your window he'd probably do so right in front of you with a nasty smile on his face so you could be damn sure about who was responsible and why. He'd smile even wider as the cops led him away and assure you in a lazy tone that a little jail time was worth it for the pleasure of being able to send his message.

Now that she thought about it, she hadn't sensed any real conviction in Eileen's voice. The accusation had bubbled up like a programmed, automatic response to any trouble in Eileen's life for the past year, especially her daughter's downward slide. Easy to blame the kid, he'd gotten her daughter hooked in the first place.

The distrustful parent-boyfriend relationship was not unique but magnified by the feeling of helplessness as Miranda remained out of reach of all of them. Shelby shook her head at the thought of Clint marching around, furious that Miranda's privacy was being violated. She had to admire him a little. A lot of people his age and a lot of people in general might give up on the girl who had, so she had been told, repeatedly pushed him away. They'd go out and live their twenty-year-old lives and never look back. But not this kid. Whatever his past, he was also a victim in this whole mess.

How long would he walk around like this, all indignation and restless, raw energy on Miranda's behalf? So far his anger simmered beneath the surface, kept from reaching a boil by his apparent sense of purpose. Shelby wondered vaguely how long it would stay that way.

CHAPTER THIRTY-FOUR

Eileen glanced surreptitiously over at Clint in the nearly empty courtroom. He was almost unrecognizable in the tie and maroon button-down shirt he wore. The shirt was long-sleeved and concealed his tattoos; it contrasted nicely with the khaki pants he wore. He was even wearing loafers, for God's sake. His cheeks were uncharacteristically smooth and pink, the color rosy from a thorough shaving and nerves. He had obviously read the dress code in the same "Courtroom Do's and Don'ts" pamphlet she had received a week ago in the mail. *Do dress as you would for an important event…Don't wear T-shirts with messages…Don't dress down to gain sympathy…*

Even the small cross that usually dangled from his left ear was gone. Nothing about jewelry, but he hadn't taken any chances. He looked like one of those nervous, innocent kids who knocks on your door and wants you to buy magazines for a fund-raiser.

It was the courtroom behavior Clint would have problems with. *Do exercise self-control…Don't negatively react to the answers of witnesses to the questions from the opposing attorney…Don't argue with the other party's attorney…*

Graham Barrett sat beside them, looking more wolfish than ever in a gray suit. He had chosen electric blue for his punch of color this time.

Cora, one of Miranda's friends, also sat ready to tell a judge how they had seen Clint bodily remove Miranda from various places on various occasions, against her will. She had mixed feelings about the girl giving a statement. If Cora had been there with Miranda, in places she shouldn't have been, she hadn't been much more help than Clint had. He had at least realized his errors, though too late. Wasn't he the only one of the two who had really tried to do what was best for Miranda in the end? *But too late*, she reminded herself. *She wouldn't have needed rescuing if...*

There was no one with Clint. She forced her eyes straight ahead and felt Jim squeeze her hand. *Repeat after me*, Jim had coached her in the car just before coming in. *He destroyed our daughter, he doesn't need to see her...He destroyed our daughter, he doesn't need to see her...*

It had always been like this with Clint. Separate sides. This just made it official.

The hearing began with less pomp and circumstance than Eileen had imagined. Judge Myrna A. Harold was a fortyish woman with sleek black hair that was threaded with gray and swept completely over one eye. Eileen had done some homework and was hopeful. Judge Harold was not a woman accustomed to thinking in in-betweens or ruling with much thought given to outside circumstances. Stalking would be stalking. Unwanted attention would be unwanted attention. Harassment would be harassment, not to be confused with anything else or deemed acceptable because of "good intentions" on the stalker's part. Legal definitions would not be changed or twisted in Myrna Harold's courtroom out of sympathy. *Would they?*

"Okay," judge Harold said. "We're here today to rule on a final protective order, filed on behalf of Miranda Linn by her parents, Jim and Eileen Linn. The temporary order has been issued against Clint Mullen, and today I'm going to hear statements so I can make a decision on the final order. Does either party want to give me an opening statement?"

Clint cleared his throat. "Yes, I do."

"Alright, then. Go ahead."

"I'd just like you, and the Linns, to know that I was only trying to protect Miranda. I love her and I felt responsible for her behavior. I was trying to keep her out of trouble, get her away from places and situations where she was going to abuse drugs. It's true I followed her around, but it was never to threaten her or harass her. I was trying to keep her alive. I'm not sorry I did it. I only wish it would have helped."

So much for him having issues with courtroom behavior, Eileen thought. Where had this Clint come from? She'd expected the sneering, sarcastic, every parent's nightmare her daughter had introduced her to a lifetime ago. He was so…*composed.*

"Thank you, Mr. Mullen. Mr. and Mrs. Linn?" the judge asked expectantly.

The Wolf stood up. "Your honor, I'm Graham Barrett, and I'm representing the Linns in this matter. While they understand Mr. Mullen's intentions may have been good, the fact remains that the attention he paid their daughter was unwanted. She clearly viewed it as harassment, which she shared with several of her friends on numerous occasions. We have one of them here today to tell you just that. He repeatedly ignored Miranda's requests to leave her alone and stop following her and contacting her."

Eileen thought she saw Clint flinch at this declaration. *She wanted nothing further to do with Mr. Mullen...*She was ashamed that Graham Barrett was speaking for them, but she didn't have the resolve to talk about the hell that had been her life for the past few months.

Clint sat in silence the next few minutes while he listened to Cora tell the judge how Miranda had complained about him, what a nuisance he was, how he wouldn't leave her alone.

"So you saw Clint Mullen physically remove Miranda from different places?" Barrett asked Cora now.

"Yeah," she said, imperiously flipping her hair. "Lots of times."

Bitch, Clint seethed, watching the face that was freshly scrubbed, the outfit that was uncharacteristic of her. A sham, just like his. Beige flats on her feet? *Really?*

No doubt the change of wardrobe had been on Barrett's

advice. Clint wanted to ask Cora where the thigh-high, "Hello boys, come screw me" boots were. *If you were a real friend to her you'd have done the same thing, drug her ass out of there. But you placated her instead of trying to do what was best for her. Too wrapped up in the same habits to really care.*

And then Cora sent the real zinger flying past his head. "She was afraid of him," she stated, her eyes boring into Clint's. "She was afraid of what he might end up doing."

When it was Clint's turn again, he stood up. "Your honor, I would just like to point out again that the places I followed her to, more often than not, were places Miranda went to buy drugs. I love her and she loves me. She was just angry at me because I was getting in the way of a very powerful addiction. I understand how blind a person's need to satisfy that craving can make them to everyone else and everything else in life. You give up relationships, you give up everything, for it. You don't care about anything else anymore. But she did care. She actually did realize what she had given up for a time. When Miranda was clean we resumed the relationship and stayed together. Even her friends can tell you that much. I also need to point out that Miranda was *living* with me just before her relapse. We were going to have a baby. She obviously wasn't too afraid of me."

He tried not to let any more venom seep through, stare daggers at Cora. He couldn't screw this up. He also tried not to fidget while the Linns' lawyer stood up again to make his final statement. What, they couldn't even speak for themselves? It was so damn important for them to shut him out of their daughter's life, but they had to have somebody else do it for them?

"Whether or not Mr. Mullen feels he was acting in Ms. Linn's best interest, he wasn't respecting her wishes," Barrett stated. "Whatever his reasons, he was stalking her, and that's against the law. It's true that she did live with him for a time, but many women who are battered physically or emotionally return to people they shouldn't be with. That's a sad fact. I respectfully request that you grant a final protective order today."

I respectfully request that you kiss my ass. You've got no right to talk about what she wanted, Clint thought bitterly. Then he felt the sudden stab of fear that comes with the likely realization of unwanted possibilities.

He had been foolish to come here alone today. As if some nicer clothes and a few carefully thought out statements could change anyone's perception about who he was, what had happened. Why hadn't he thought to find someone who really understood his situation, what he was trying to do? Lindy Thomason, maybe? Would she have stood up for him, told Myrna Harold how he had held Miranda's hand in the methadone clinic? He hadn't even thought to ask for Lindy's help. She at least understood he had offered Miranda a hand, led her out of the maze he had pulled her into, didn't she?

Not quite, his inner voice taunted. *You came close, but no cigar. Miranda didn't exactly make it out.* He was barely aware of judge Harold announcing a half-hour break. She would have a decision when they got back.

In the bathroom, Clint splashed some water on his face. In situations like this, not so long ago, he might have taken the opportunity to slip into a stall and shoot up to chase the stress away. He was tempted now. God, he missed Miranda with her deadpan sense of humor and over-the-top, melodramatic ways. She was the only one he would really trust to help him out in a jam like this, and she was the one he might be losing. The one they said had never wanted him around.

Clint's stomach churned when he made his way back into the courtroom and sat down. His left leg seemed to have a mind of its own and wouldn't stop vibrating. He put a hand on his knee to still it. Eileen and Jim looked just as anxious as he felt. Why the hell did *they* look so nervous? They knew damn well he would never hurt their daughter, they were just worried they might lose the opportunity to be spiteful.

"Okay," Myrna Harold said without preamble. "After reviewing the documents that were submitted and hearing statements from both parties, I'm going to rule in favor of a final protective order, which will be good for one year. In these circumstances, that means no entering the facility where Miranda Linn is receiving care, or any written or telephone contact to her at that facility. I do commend you for trying to help Ms. Linn, young man. Unfortunately we can't force help on those who we think should seek it. It does appear that the help, and the attention, was unwanted, at least for the majority of the relationship. So that's my ruling today."

A scrape of the chairs as everyone stood up to leave, and that was that. When Clint looked at the Linns on the way out there was pure hatred in his eyes. "You know I'd never hurt her," he told them tightly as he walked past. "But I know you hate me so I guess I'm not surprised that you'd let that fucking suit talk about me like I'm some kind of *abuser*."

Jim and Eileen didn't acknowledge his fury, just turned and left without a word.

CHAPTER THIRTY-FIVE

Still leaving newspaper offices at obscene hours, Shelby noted as she punched the down button on the elevator. Same. Only the assignments were different. Carl Hoskins was being arraigned, and she was depressed again at the thought of him casually walking out and leaving his family to die.

She needed a very good book or a very bad Women's Channel movie. She'd signed off of her computer at 11:58 p.m. and pored over the notes about the Hoskins family until two. Now it was quarter after two and there was no telling what kind of shape her apartment would be in. Toonces had probably redecorated it by now. She wondered if "Call me Gil" had any really outlandish lamps for sale because hers were probably laying in tiny cream-colored shards on the carpet. One indignant swat by her monster-sized cat would be all it took.

Well, so much the better if that was the case, she thought idly. She'd gone too bland in an attempt to be stylish and make the apartment seem streamlined and modern. Time to color her world again. She would have to do it on her own this time.

She cursed herself for the lapse in judgment when she heard the footsteps behind her and quickened her own stride down the street. She had visions of returning to Mercy General's ER beaten, mugged or worse. Cole would frown at her injuries and chastise, "You were only supposed to come back for a class."

She was still dodging Cole, but now was hardly the time to ponder that. She tried to shift her eyes slightly to get a better look at whoever was behind her. Reaching into her purse for her phone, she prepared to let forth the most ear-piercing scream she could manage. Didn't all of the women's defense literature say that you were supposed to look at any potential attacker and acknowledge them? If they thought you got a good look at them they might be deterred, right? Should she turn around, smile brightly, and make some innocuous comment like "Nice night"?

"I'm not going to hurt you." The voice was deep but it sounded young for some reason.

She spun around at the sound of the voice. "I might hurt you," she told the stranger. The man smiled now, since he outweighed her by a hundred pounds at a minimum. His teeth were like white Chiclets perfectly arranged in his mouth. Nice orthodontia for a potential mugger/killer. His hair was wavy and black and he wore wire-rimmed glasses. She couldn't tell what color his eyes were but they studied her intensely and seemed intelligent.

"You don't know what I have in my purse. Back off, okay?" she warned with all of the bravado she could manage. She was definitely the Chihuahua trying to bark like a Shepherd. Shelby thought of Mona and almost laughed.

"I don't want to hurt you," he repeated. "You're Shelby Norris, right?"

She didn't know whether or not to answer him. What was this? Did she have groupies now, some sort of weird following of people who worshipped her writing? She should be so lucky.

"I sent a letter to the editor about one of your articles," he told her casually while he pulled a pack of cigarettes out of his jacket pocket, tapped one out, and lit up. "It wasn't published." A few people straggled by now and she guessed he wasn't going to assault her in plain view of potential witnesses.

"Let me guess," she told him. "The Miranda Linn story."

"How did you know that?" He didn't seem surprised but patient, expectant. His body was still as if he were an animal waiting, poised, completely centered around what she would say or do next.

"We got a lot of mail about that one. It inspired people to write in. Something like that people usually feel strongly about, one way or another."

He reached into his pocket, and Shelby considered that she must be six kinds of crazy not to run from him at this point. He handed her an envelope.

"Well I do feel strongly about it," he told her. "That's the letter. I'm Shane McCurty."

"Well, Shane, you scared the hell out of me. This is not the best way to go about it, tailing me at two in the morning."

"I was going to leave it in the drop box outside, and there you were. It's a very important and personal issue to me. Do you always work this late? You looked upset, like something was bothering you. I was having a hard time deciding whether or not to disturb you."

"I'm bothered and disturbed that you're following me," she clarified. "I'll read your letter. I used to write letters to the editor from the time I was thirteen, ache to have my feelings acknowledged in print when a story struck a chord with me."

"You're awfully patronizing for a new reporter," he told her, and actually laughed. "You haven't worked there very long, have you? I've only seen your byline for a few months. I told you, it's a very personal issue to me. I don't care about seeing my name in *Atlanta Minute*. I mostly read the *Journal* but they're not the ones who did a story on it."

"Well, ouch," Shelby said with humor. "So you mostly read the *Journal*? I've heard *that* one more times than I'd care to admit."

"Would you like to have a coffee with me so we can discuss the letter?"

Now he wanted to go get a coffee? Who was more nuts in this scenario, he for suggesting it or she for considering it?

"Noni's? Want to meet there?" he persisted.

Was he giving her a chance to bug out if she felt too uncomfortable? A predator with good manners, or did he want to make it sporting?

"Noni's. Half an hour," she decreed.

He disappeared down the street and Shelby hurried up to her apartment, found her lamps still intact, and grabbed her car keys. She was certainly going to drive there. Toonces hissed indignantly when she sailed past him. "If I'm not back in an hour or so--" she began.

Noni's was a little all-night café frequented by just about everyone, from college students to club goers to grandparents. Perfect for tête-à-têtes with strange men who had largely unknown purposes. She spotted him as soon as she stepped inside and he motioned her into one of the green booths.

He revealed his perfect teeth again. "Wasn't sure you'd show up."

"So you really were giving me a chance to bow out."

"Sorry for the way I approached you," he apologized. It was impossible for her to tell if he meant it.

"You must feel very strongly about the story if you were out at two in the morning dropping off your letter for a second time," she ventured cautiously.

"I do. Have you read it yet?"

"No, I hurried over here against my better judgment." She pulled the envelope out of her purse and studied the meticulous, perfect curve of the handwritten address on the front. Before she could read it they were interrupted by a tired waitress who took his order for a ham and cheese omelet and hash browns. Shelby stuck to coffee.

"Keeping to coffee in case you have to make a speedy departure, huh?" he noted.

"Oh, I think I've written off the potential for any grave danger, but I'm still sizing you up," she told him. "You mind?" she asked, gesturing toward the unopened envelope.

"Go ahead with the letter and with sizing me up," he encouraged. Shelby lifted a corner of her mouth in response and tore into the letter. She read it silently.

I felt compelled to write in about the issue of Narcan kits since

I lived with a heroin addict for years. I lost my brother, Jake, to heroin addiction eight months ago. Someone like me should be in favor of a kit like this. I might, after all, still have my brother had one been available to him. At least that's the argument from the people trying to push these kits and make them more accessible. But Jake had been in and out of treatment several times and had many setbacks. Believe me, a ticket out of trouble that night wouldn't have changed the outcome for my brother. I would prefer that other users understand there are consequences to their actions. A way out, a free pass, is an excuse for them to keep hurting themselves and their families as well. I wish things would have turned out differently for my brother but I know they wouldn't have no matter how many times he might have been "rescued." In fact, a "magic kit" would have kept him from getting any real help.

Shane McCurty

"I'm surprised Maura didn't print it," Shelby said uneasily. Her feelings on the issue had subtly shifted and clouded over after seeing the face of a girl who might be lost for good. She'd watched Eileen perform a heartbreaking and personal ritual as much for herself as for her daughter. The letter chilled her but there was something more to that than his matter-of-fact attitude about consequences. The anger towards his brother was a cold, steely thing but it was also the use of the word *ticket* to describe the kits, the perfect loop of his penmanship. She had seen it before. She stood up and felt her stomach turn over.

"I don't know how I can prove it, but you smashed in the window at Frozen Light Crystals, didn't you, you bastard?" Shelby asked in a low, furious whisper that twisted and caught in her throat. "I'm telling Eileen Linn to go to the police."

He sighed. "That's not necessary." His expression was resigned, not alarmed, as if he'd wanted her to know.

"Now there's a surprising statement coming from the vandal."

"It won't be necessary because I told her," he clarified.

"You *told* her?" she demanded incredulously.

"This afternoon. I told her what I'd done and we talked about her daughter and my brother. Would you believe the woman told me to pay her for the tarp she had to buy and then actually made me some damned herbal tea?"

"Yes," Shelby said weakly, "I would." It wasn't a stretch to conjure up Eileen's face, first uncomprehending and then a touch angry. The look would fade as she and Shane compared stories and the brows that had been knitted together in a hard, even line would start to separate and soften. She'd probably even warned him to let the tea cool before he took a sip. Had she tried to fix him up with her pretty Native American cashier?

She slid back down into the booth and rubbed her temples. "How could you write that, considering the fact you've been through something similar? Ever hear of empathy? It wouldn't have been a big stretch for you in this case. Jesus, what's wrong with you?"

"Hurt," he told her. "Don't you know hurting can make people dangerous?"

She thought of Clint now. "Yes, it can."

"So what would you have done if I'd walked into your shop and told you I was responsible?"

"I don't know what I'd do now. I know what I did a few months ago, when I found out someone had betrayed me in what I felt was a pretty monumental way. I found out about it in the worst possible way, on accident. Different than these circumstances but I was shocked, probably the way Eileen was when you walked into her store and 'fessed up."

"What did you do?" he asked, leaning forward in that still, animal way of his.

"Well, I slapped him as hard as I could manage and ran out of his house."

Shane sat there, his mouth twitching. "Is this something I should laugh at? Somehow I don't think it seemed very funny at the time."

"Well, it wasn't. But with all things, time," Shelby managed. "I haven't seen him since. It's had a lot of time to marinate. I must have a little Eileen in me because I mostly just miss him and his wife."

Shane lifted his brow then, but Shelby cut him off. "Not even close to one of those cheater-done-me-wrong or weird love triangle situations, trust me." The waitress reappeared and topped off her cup. She added two creams and two Sweet and Lows.

"Well it's marinated so that's good. Means it might be possible to salvage things. I think you wouldn't change slapping him then, though," he decided after pulling in a long look at her.

"Probably not. So, it seems as if eight months hasn't been nearly long enough for your loss to marinate."

"No."

"You hadn't really given up on your brother so that's where the venom came from. You were disappointed and pissed."

"Are you going to tell me now that I don't want to see other families sold false hope? That's why I'm against the kits? This is becoming a very enjoyable therapy session. I'm going to fire my shrink." He cut up the last of his omelet and she noticed he had a slow and deliberate way of eating. The way he moved and talked, everything, was calculated and choreographed. Had he considered just how to arc whatever he had sent smashing into Eileen's window, positioned the note just so after the job was done?

"Don't just yet," Shelby told him lightly. "No offense. Anybody should need help for losing their brother. And trust me, if you knew some of the things I've done in the past few months you'd forgo any of my advice or supposed insight."

"Why would I do that? Empathy, right?" he reminded her. "Like knows like?"

"Maybe so," Shelby allowed. She finished up her coffee and nixed a third cup when the waitress reappeared. When she put the ticket on the table Shane picked it up.

"Let me pay." He considered the bill. "Cheap session.

Can I walk you to your car, Shelby Norris?"

"Please do," she told him as he dropped some bills on the table. "You never know who's out there in the early morning darkness waiting to sneak up behind you."

Shelby mentally shook her head in wonder as he formally extended his elbow for her to link her arm through. Was she really receiving a gentlemanly escort to her car by the man who had sent Eileen's glass flying?

CHAPTER THIRTY-SIX

Shelby stood on the stepstool and squinted through the peephole, nervous now. The white stool had been one of her first purchases for the apartment, as crucial as any of the other setting-up-shop incidentals. Toilet tissue; cleaning supplies; butter and oil; and a stepstool for all of the out-of-reach places for her in the apartment, which were a lot.

Well, she had asked him to come over and she couldn't just leave him standing out there.

"Nice place," Cole told her when he stepped inside. "It's all a little too…tasteful for you, though."

"Oh, thanks. The master of the backhanded compliment."

"What I mean is, I expected lots of bright colors. You're not a toned down and tan kind of person. It's all very neutral." He glanced at the hangings on the wall. "Nice picture of you and the cat. These seem more your style." He paused at the article about her finding a handyman and again at the candid of she and Joe sitting at a decorated table in their tux and gown.

She was uncomfortable as he studied the hopeful expectation on her face, and Joe's, in the picture. You didn't have these kind of pictures snapped thinking they would become some sort of unhealthy shrine to the past. "I'm thinking about some different furniture. You figured out my taste from just a couple of days in the hospital?"

He snorted. "This was not a difficult thing, Shelby. It didn't take a lot of deep insight on my part to figure out. You wore leopard print slippers at the hospital."

"You noticed the slippers I was wearing?"

He colored now. "So I brought some books I accumulated during my residency. *Caring For The Comatose Patient* is pretty good. What's this about? You were very mysterious on the phone."

"A story I did recently. I just wanted to understand what this family's going through. They started a foundation for their daughter who overdosed on heroin. She hasn't regained consciousness yet. Who knows, I might do a follow-up. I thought you could offer me some insight, tell me what you know about the awake state of the brain and all of that."

"Wow, whatever you make they don't pay you enough. Seeking out consultants to better understand a story, I'm impressed. I'm hardly an expert. I should put you in touch with some of the neurologists at Mercy."

"That would be great. In the meantime you'll do," Shelby fumbled.

"Well thank you very much. Can I have a seat on your nice beige couch?"

"Sorry," Shelby muttered. "Manners. I suppose I should offer you something to eat. There's Hot Pockets and Hot Pockets. Just one variety. Diet Coke, Sam Adams, cheap wine or water to drink."

"Glad to see you're paying attention to your diet and all," he told her meaningfully.

"You're forgetting that you're not my physician anymore."

"Pity I only had that *pleasure* for a few short hours. I'll take one of those Hot Pockets," he decided.

"That's more like it. I'm going grocery shopping tomorrow," she told him defensively, moving to the freezer.

"Mmm hmm."

"I promise to buy lots of fruits and veggies."

"I'll take a Diet Coke too."

"That's right, Cole. Be nice and neutral, like the couch you just insulted." She poured him a Diet Coke and a Sam Adams over ice for herself.

He laughed and opted to sit Indian-style on the floor. She joined him after the microwave dinged and they ate while she fingered one of the textbooks.

"Neurology was one of my favorite rotations as a med student," he told her. "Like the book says, you can replace pretty much any organ except the brain. There's so much we don't understand about it, let alone what's going on in there when a person can't communicate."

"So why didn't you choose neurology?" she wanted to know.

"Can't do the long-term thing. I could never watch a patient die slowly or deal with a chronic illness. In emergency I either fix them and send them on their way or I fail and cope because I took my one shot and did my best for a person I didn't know."

"I find that hard to believe. You sought me out in your jeans the next day to see how I was doing. You let me humiliate you at Hangman."

He colored again. "Well, ah, that's my point. Imagine how I'd be with long-term patients. I'd follow them home and check their refrigerators to see how they were eating." He finished the last of his Hot Pocket.

"And tell them to drink more water and less cheap wine and Diet Coke?"

He smiled. "I was invited here."

"Yes, you were. I'm enjoying the company. Just me and Toonces most the time."

"That is one ugly cat." Toonces had meandered into the room and sniffed the air. Now he sidled up, hoping for a handout.

"I wish I could say he resents that but he's truly not smart enough." Shelby absentmindedly stuck her hand out and Toonces licked the remnants of the meatballs and mozzarella Hot Pocket off of her fingers.

"That's disgusting," Cole groaned, but stuck his hand out too. The cat obligingly licked Cole's hand when he was done with Shelby's.

"What if she was in there?" Shelby asked suddenly. "What if she could hear and feel but just couldn't communicate? Lots of people believe that about comatose patients. I can't think of anything that would be worse for a person."

"That's an awful thought to entertain," Cole allowed.

"It's not something I can ask her mother about but I've wondered a lot. Does she think her daughter's trapped in there or is she already privately mourning the loss of her child?"

"Doesn't seem like a mother would be able to survive either of those possibilities, does it?"

"Well I'm really just getting to know the family, but she's got this incredible strength. I don't think I could make it through that."

"You've made it through an awful lot yourself, Shelby," he noted. She thought she saw his eyes stray to the picture of her and Joe again.

"I suppose I was also in a damned if you do or damned if you don't situation. Maybe that's why it gets to me. Neither possibility was good. I was either going to watch Joe get sick and waste away or lose him instantly. The end result was going to be the same. Quick or slow in my case. He made it quick."

Cole looked as if he didn't know what to say so wisely said nothing.

"The worst part," Shelby admitted with a catch in her voice, "was that I know he did it in a way to spare me. I know that's a big part of why killed himself and I wonder, if he had felt I was stronger, would he have hung on longer and tried to deal with it?"

"You've been wondering that ever since your husband died?" Cole asked in wonder. "It's not surprising you ended up as sick as you were."

"Just so you know, this apartment is a no-pity zone," she told him, dragging her arm across her eyes to wipe away the moisture. "Violate the rule like I just did and I'll have to throw you out."

"No pity, Shelby Norris," Cole decreed.

"Good. Doctors are supposed to be cold and unfeeling anyway."

"I try."

"You fail." She sent him a lopsided grin. "Want another Coke?"

"I'm fine, Shelby. And you will be too."

"How do you know that?" Shelby asked softly.

"Don't think I kid myself that it's all about me when a patient comes through the door. It's mostly up to them, their constitution and will to pull through. You were in bad shape but no way had you completely given up. You came to the hospital and you'd have eventually pushed a needle in to save yourself if you hadn't," he decided.

"I'm still embarrassed. It seems like such a childish, desperate thing to do when I look back on it. Can't imagine what you must have thought of me."

"I thought you needed help, like most people who come into the ER. You think a lot of yourself, don't you? I've seen a lot more childish and a lot more desperate than you come through the door."

"So you either fix them and send them on their way or cope because you gave it your best shot. Is it really that easy? How do you tell the families? I couldn't do it," Shelby told him, admiration in her voice.

"I do the only thing I can, just try and think about how I would want someone to handle it if I was in their situation. I remember that it's a terrible moment they're going to remember for the rest of their lives. I give it the respect it deserves. By the time I have to talk to the families I figure I can take a minute to focus on them and remember the moment too since they always will."

"That makes you quite something else, Cole Michaels," Shelby declared as she walked him to the door. She noted Mona's always propped-open door and decided she might as well give the little woman some entertainment. She stood on tiptoe to peck Cole on the cheek and couldn't help but feel satisfaction as she watched his face heat up again.

"This girl's name," Cole asked to divert attention away from his embarrassment. "What is it, by the way?"

"You told me you read *Atlanta Minute*, but you missed the story?" Shelby asked, pretending offense. "It's Miranda," she told him. "Miranda Linn."

Cole looked like he had been hit by a freight train.

CHAPTER THIRTY-SEVEN

Clint was waiting there when Shelby stepped out of Chapel Hill and into the heat. Today she'd felt drawn to the nursing home to talk to Miranda like a friend and had left the room feeling lighter. Until now. She sighed, unsurprised he was here.

"Clint, you shouldn't be here. Right or wrong, fair or not, you're violating the order. You'd better get out of here before somebody who works here and cares about it recognizes you. The Linns could be here for all you know. It's almost like you want to be thrown in jail. You willing to let that happen just so you can thumb your nose at them?"

The words sounded hollow and meaningless even to her own ears. She brazenly took his left arm and studied the full sleeve of tattoos he sported. His right arm was also completely covered. Shelby noticed Miranda's name inked in fancy blue script halfway down Clint's arm. "So how many hours do you think you have invested in all of these, anyway?"

"I figure I've sat for about ninety or so, all told," he said thoughtfully, blowing a stream of smoke into the air. He made no attempt to jerk his arm away and continued to let her examine. "That's about four days of my life devoted to somebody dragging a needle through my skin because I thought it was a good idea. So why would I stay away from Miranda just because I'm told I should?"

"Pretty impressive person doing the telling," she reminded him. "A judge. Look, Clint, I don't think you're a bad guy at all. I understand what it's like to love someone you can't have a future with."

"Do you really? I wonder if you know just how many

times I forcibly put her in my jeep and drove her to meetings. I tried to check her in to rehab but they wouldn't let me since she had to consent. It was all me pushing her along before she found out she was pregnant. It was a fight almost every single day up until then. Got her started at the methadone clinic. Doesn't seem to matter how much good I tried to do. Maybe you're like the Linns and all you see is a druggie. You know these tattoos? They're just old scars, that's all they are. And those old scars are covering up the fact that there isn't a single track mark on my arm. They're all people see. Not easy to tell my arm's clean underneath all of this old ink. You get me?"

"I get you, Clint. Like I said, I don't think you're a bad guy."

"Thanks," he said sarcastically. "That means a lot. By the way, you're halfway missing the point about loving someone without a future. Aside from the fact that I'm not in such a damned hurry to give up on Miranda, she and I have a past. That counts for something too." He turned his back on her and strode away, his second angry departure in the short time she had known him.

"Clint," she called after him. "What's the significance of the dates?"

She had noticed three dates underneath Miranda's name in the same fancy blue script: *8/13/08. 10/24/08. 8/30/09.* The coloring on the last date was darker, the detail sharper. That tattoo was recent.

"The day I met her, the first time I convinced her to shoot up, and the day she overdosed," he answered shortly. "Kind of a timeline of our relationship, not one of that I'm proud of, but that's how it happened." With that, he turned and stalked away from her. Again.

Shelby shook her head in wonder as Clint's green jeep peeled away. She thought about him waking up each morning, yawning, stretching. One of the first things he would see was the sad chronology of their relationship, in blue. She wondered if Clint's tattoo artist was the chatty type who'd asked for the story behind the tattoo. Or had the artist mistaken the pain in Clint's face that day for physical discomfort?

If only the Linns knew what kind of penance he's been doing all this time, she thought. *He's even wearing his guilt on his arm.*

*   *   *

Patsy Cline crooned on the radio as Shelby carried Toonces around the apartment, stroking underneath his chin. She was walking after midnight with Patsy. Miles and miles from the kitchen to the living area and back to the kitchen again.

She thought of the sad road map of Clint and Miranda's relationship etched into his skin. No weeping willows here, she noted as she listened to the teardrops in Patsy's voice. Shelby was feeling caged in again, but she wasn't going to go walking up and down the city streets at one in the morning. These months in Atlanta had flown by in a blur of research, interviews, writing, and good-natured bickering with Maura. But the nights…

If she didn't do something soon there would be a repeat of last week. On Tuesday, at around four in the morning, she'd turned to infomercial therapy. After she'd been offered late night T.V. help for a bad body, bad psyche, and bad cookware, she'd opted for the psyche and cookware solutions. The cookware people had come up with a solution for a problem she didn't even know she had. For that alone she figured they deserved her money. She didn't have a clue how disastrous it could be to drain a pot of pasta until the commercial for a drainable lid told her so. She had to admit the cloud of steam rising up from the pot and the way its entire contents of pasta and water went sliding into the sink, with the potential for burning its cook/victim, looked pretty ominous.

So she had called about the ingenious attachable lid, and a program on curbing depression and anxiety (both rush orders). The attachable lid turned out to be useful. She had even tried it out by boiling some bow-tie pasta. Voila, no fuss, no mess, flip the pot and the excess water drained in the sink where it belonged, the pasta stayed in the pot where it belonged. Handy. The program for depression and anxiety, not so much. She'd returned that one. Her exchange with the poor customer service operator had probably gone straight into the woman's crazy customer stories file.

"No, Sheila, the materials are just fine. It's just that spending that much money, well, it added to my stress and depression instead of taking it away. Sent me into a panic, actually," Shelby told the woman cheerfully.

"We do have the option to pay in installments," Sheila answered carefully, ever the professional. "We could cancel out the order. After five to seven days your card will be credited, and then we can bill you in smaller payments if you like. What we like about our program is that it's a lot cheaper than traditional therapy." *And boy, do you need it, lady,* Sheila was probably thinking.

"That's okay, Sheila, but thanks. Since this call's recorded I want whoever your supervisor is to know you've earned every penny tonight. But I don't think there's any helping people like me."

Shelby was snapped out of her reverie and yanked away from Patsy's final, plaintive notes when she heard the soft tapping on the door. At the sound Toonces twisted in her arms and squirmed to freedom, streaking away towards a hiding place.

"Thanks for the backup, Toonces," she muttered. She drug the stepladder to the door (*survive and adapt,* she thought ruefully), climbed on it, and peered through the peephole.

"*Hindi ka makatulog?* Can't sleep? Neither can I," Mona announced, stepping into the apartment without invitation when Shelby opened the door. Mona sported a faded floral nightgown and her feet were adorned with fuzzy blue slippers.

"Oh God, Mona, sorry. I woke you up. I thought I had the music low enough."

"Wake me up?" Mona answered with her trademark,

birdlike laugh. "When you're old you don't get much sleep. Body's getting ready to sleep for good, how much does it need?"

"Mona...what *is* all of that?" Shelby took the huge grocery sack out of the old woman's hands.

"Little beef tripe, some oxtail, peanut butter, and *bagoong alamang*. That's shrimp paste to you. You want me to go through the whole list here? You and me, we going to cook. I'm gonna teach you how to make *Kare Kare*. Filipino dish for family dinners and special occasions."

"*Kare Kare*? Right now? What's the special occasion?"

"*Kare Kare*. Right now. You're up. I'm up. Special occasion is we alive. You doing anything else?" Mona challenged with good humor.

"You really have oxtail in there?" Shelby asked skeptically.

"Beef tripe too, like I said. You gonna love it. You wolf down everything else I make. Might as well learn how to cook some of it."

"Point taken. But maybe I'm better off not knowing what's in it. Easier to eat it than cook it. That's my whole gig. I actually asked for the apartment next to yours. Checked you out before I moved in, found out you could feed me."

"Sure you did." Mona busied herself laying out the ingredients on the kitchen counter. "Get out a pot," she ordered. "Got a really big stock pot? We gonna boil the tripe and oxtail first. Take about an hour so we gotta get it started."

"I have one with a drainable lid," Shelby told her helpfully. She eyed the rest of the groceries on the counter, her stomach turning over. The oxtail was cut up into small sections and the meat looked like a tiny heart with a bone in it. "Peanut butter and shrimp paste, all in this same dish?"

"Like I say...you never complain while you're eating my cooking," Mona chided.

"Okay, okay."

"We need a cutting board. We gotta slice up some vegetables. Here's some eggplant, string beans and onions."

Shelby sliced as directed and listened to the *click-click-click, whoosh* as Mona started a burner on the gas stove. "I hardly ever entertain, and now I'm getting personal cooking lessons in my own home."

"You alone too much, that's a problem," Mona answered, and moved on to putting the beef and oxtail in the pot. "But hardly ever entertain? Not even that tall good-looking man, glasses, ringing your bell a few days ago? Pity."

"That's why you keep your door open," Shelby muttered accusingly. "It has nothing to do with some misguided idea of keeping yourself safe. You really just want to see what's going on with everybody in the building. "

"That too," Mona responded without hesitation. "But to keep safe, I have to know what everybody else is doing, don't I? All serves the same purpose."

"He was sort of helping me with a story. He's a doctor and he very kindly consented to drop off some research material for me. Let's just call him a source of information."

"A source?" Mona snorted. "Come off it. Looked nervous to me. Kept running his hand through his hair, like he was really caring about how he looked. Kept fidgeting and took forever to ring the doorbell..."

"Okay, so what am I supposed to do with this garlic?" Shelby asked in a higher-than-normal voice. "Just peel it, or chop it up, or what?"

"He coming back for any more stories?" Mona asked, undeterred, enjoying herself.

"He was the doctor who saw me during my short vacation at Atlanta Mercy Medical Center," Shelby muttered.

"He's not gonna still be your doctor, is he? He just works at the hospital, right?"

Shelby smiled in spite of herself. "It's some kind of coincidence that he actually treated the girl I wrote about when she was brought into the emergency room. You know, you're making quite a leap there, you nosy little Filipino."

"Just saying...awfully nice of him to help you out with

your story. Give you his professional opinion and all. The girl, that's sad. A waste. You can learn something from her, right?"

Shelby blinked in surprise. "I think I have. You know, Mona, I don't think I've ever really thanked you."

"For what?"

"For being the kind of person that'll show up at my door at one in the morning with oxtail. For making this place seem more like home. For calling Maura when you knew I was sick and wasn't helping myself."

"You're welcome," Mona told her softly, then shooed the thanks away. "Next time we do *lumpia*. Sort of like little egg rolls. You can make hundreds if you want, freeze 'em up for later." They were silent for awhile, the only sounds in the room the soft music on the radio, the crunch of more vegetables being chopped, and the water rolling to a boil.

When the *Kare Kare* was finished Shelby and Mona made up plates and moved over to Mona's apartment. As they flopped down on the brown wicker chairs in the jammed living room, Shelby dubiously watched the *Kare Kare* steam for a minute. Then she and Mona dug in at the same time.

"Genius, Mona," she declared. "Peanut butter and oxtail, who'd have thunk it?" The peanut butter had dissolved into a silky peanut sauce that coated the dish.

"I told you to trust old Mona."

Shelby laughed. Then a picture on the wall, one she had meant to ask about before, caught her eye: Mona forty years ago, in a tight red dress with her hair gathered up into a smooth black knot. A vibrant red flower was tucked into the knot and Mona flirted with the camera, her shoulders thrust backwards and her chin tilted up. Her skin was perfect, like unstirred cream. She stood in front of the Fox Theater with her husband Adan, who looked at her with solemn, admiring eyes.

"Mona, you were gorgeous. A total biscuit. So you had yourself a night out at the Fox, huh? Bet the shows back then were really something."

"So you think I just had myself a fun night out, huh?

Old Mona was performing that night, Shelby Norris," the little woman informed her proudly.

"No you weren't. You're kidding me."

"Do you know what they called me? The Filipino Fantasy."

"You're making that up." Shelby licked her fingers and stared, willing the image of a younger Mona on stage to come.

"Cross my heart. I sang. I was pretty good too. Opened for Bob Hope. Got more pictures, you wanna see?" Mona asked eagerly.

"Do I want to see?" Shelby demanded. "All this time I've been living next to a celebrity and didn't know it."

"Where do you think David gets his showbiz tendencies? I quit to have my baby, went back to Antipolo to raise my family. But I always wanted to come back and be close to the Fox. So I did after Adan died and I'm happy. Passed my love of entertaining on to my next generation."

"I can't believe you have this whole former life, Mona. It's incredible."

"All the same life. Just lived in different stages," Mona clarified. "Maybe you need to start thinking same life, but different stages, Shelby Norris."

Shelby considered that as she forked the last of the *Kare Kare* into her mouth.

"Since you don't believe me," Mona told her indignantly, "I'll have to prove it." She stood up, threw her shoulders back exactly like the young woman in the picture, and began to warble the words to "Moon River" in a voice as clear and delicate as glass.

Mona swayed to the music as she sang, and kept her hands cupped around an invisible microphone. As she watched the little woman, Shelby thought she couldn't imagine Cole Michaels and Joe as two stages of the same life.

CHAPTER THIRTY-EIGHT

The knock on the door alerted Shelby to her rumbling stomach, and she hoped that Mona was there for another impromptu cooking lesson. She flipped the footrest of her recliner down and deposited *Caring For The Comatose Patient* on the floor. "What's for dinner?" she called through the door. "I'm hungry, so let's get to it. Please tell me it won't involve anything with anchovies…"

"Well," Cole said when she threw open the door, "that's vaguely scary. You read my mind. I'm hungry too. Let's go grab a bite. No anchovies where we're going as far as I know." He leaned up against the wall in the hallway, relaxed, his arms folded casually.

"Oh, wow!" she told him, flustered. "I thought you were somebody else." When she caught his questioning look, she added, "A seventy-year-old Filipino woman, if you really want to know." *The same one who was probably watching you through her propped-open door just a minute ago.* She wondered what Mona might tell her later about the moments before the knock on the door. Had he nervously run his fingers through his hair and rolled up the sleeves of his shirt to look more casual?

"So where are we going?" she finally asked, conjuring up a final image of Cole Michaels using one hand to spritz with breath freshener while the other one rapped on her door. She ushered him the rest of the way in, choking back her nervous laughter.

"To enjoy one of Atlanta's finest dining experiences. So what's funny? Were you watching a sitcom? Is my hair sticking straight up and I don't know about it?" He unconsciously ran his fingers through the brown waves, completing the vivid picture Mona had painted for her at their cooking lesson.

"I promise it has everything to do with you. Not in a bad way. Are we walking or driving?" she babbled.

"Is that a journalist's trait, speaking in code, or just a Shelby Norris thing?" he asked. He didn't wait for an answer. "We're walking. Isn't that why you chose to rent in this prime location? Everything at your fingertips?"

"So you wrote that slick advertisement for my apartment building," Shelby goaded as they stepped out onto Peachtree. "It was very persuasive. My work and any kind of food, just outside my door. Kind of keeps my life in a neat little box. I can map out my day and accomplish everything I need to by walking in a perfect little square, almost."

"You make your world sound very small."

"Maybe it is. I came here from a town with eleven hundred people in it. On the surface Atlanta's a big change. But in a small town you don't have to go very far or expend very much effort to reach out and grab the necessities either. I could do a perfect square from the little newspaper office to the coffee shop to the grocery store there, too. I made a big move but maybe it hasn't changed my life much at all," she admitted.

"The view outside of your window's different," Cole observed.

"The view is different," Shelby agreed.

They walked in silence the rest of the way, until Cole put his arm lightly on her shoulder and stopped her. Shelby smiled at the familiar red and silver sign that stood out on North Avenue. "Sometimes I still feel like a tourist," she told him. "I haven't even been inside the Varsity yet."

"Do not ever, ever admit that again," Cole admonished. "Besides, a tourist would already have hit the Varsity up. How long have you been here, anyway? It's about time you became a real Atlantan. Too bad we couldn't have visited in the days of old Flossie Mae and listened to him sing the menu. That would have been something, to have been here when all of this wasn't just for show."

They entered the world of red and silver and listened as the expectant, pushy cries of "What'll ya have, what'll ya have?" filled the air. It was almost like stepping inside of a slick classic car. A very large, slick classic car. Lots of chrome-looking things and stripes. She could almost see the famous carhop's smiling brown face and gleaming white teeth as he made hot dogs and burgers musical. The Varsity's setup was a gimmick now and didn't quite recreate a time that was lost. But at least they knew its worth. At least they were trying.

"You'd better know what you want," Cole told her, the corners of his mouth quirking up as the line of customers inched forward. "They tend to get cranky if you waste their time and hold up the line. In the old days they used to send people to the back of the line if they didn't know what they wanted. Humiliating, I bet. I wouldn't want to find out."

"I'm enjoying the décor. I haven't even looked at the menu," Shelby told him as someone bumped her from behind. "This place is a zoo, but I kind of like it."

"A zoo? You ought to see it after a Yellow Jackets game. I'd be deciding on your order, by the way," Cole warned.

"What'll ya have!" an attractive, mocha-skinned cashier in the requisite paper hat bellowed at them when they approached the slick, silver countertop.

"I have decision making problems," Shelby sputtered anxiously. "My husband and I used to get hungry and testy when we'd try and go out to eat because we couldn't even decide on where to go."

"What'll ya HAVE?" the cashier insisted. If it was possible to glare in a good-natured way, she did.

"A naked dog and strings! A Diet Coke to drink!" Shelby blurted desperately, after a split-second glance at the menu. The simple black-on-lighted-white style of the menu reminded her of the Diner's back in Layton, and she felt a pang. The menu board hanging up at the Diner wasn't there for effect or to intentionally create an atmosphere; Trish had picked it up at a flea market because she liked it. No gimmicks and no intended atmosphere. It was what it was without trying. If Trish had managed to get pregnant she might be showing by now. She could imagine her behind the grill, her hair escaping its knot or ponytail, standing farther away to fry the burgers as time passed and her belly grew.

"And I'll take a chili dog and a bag of rags," Cole told the cashier smoothly.

"This had better be good," Shelby told him when they approached the red and silver chairs. They looked like jazzed-up versions of the ones she remembered from back in school. "I have never taken so little time to order a meal in my life. I'm about calculated decisions. I don't do impulse."

"The fact that you moved out here on your own, well, that would seem to suggest otherwise," he reminded her.

"That would be the exception. A lot about my life since I've moved out here would seem to suggest otherwise. Though it was mostly my husband. He told my brother-in-law to send my clippings out to papers and apply for jobs for me. It isn't anything that ever would have occurred to me on my own."

"People can only do so much for you or to you, but ultimately it's up to you to decide. You went to the interview on your own, right?"

"Not entirely on my own. My cat went along for the ride. Well, most of it anyway. He joined me somewhere in Kentucky."

Cole wiped the yellow and red mixture of chili and mustard from the side of his mouth. "You picked that cat up on your way out here to interview at *Atlanta Minute?*"

"Had to leave him yowling in the car while I went in to the interview, too. I didn't have a choice. Part of the time I was interviewing I was worried about the damn cat, if he was okay in there. My car suffered way more than he did. Know how much having your car detailed bumper to bumper costs? I'm surprised he hasn't completely ruined my apartment. Turns out that for a battle-toughened warrior who had been on his own, he doesn't do very well by himself."

Cole grinned. "You never can tell. Don't be fooled by appearances and all that."

"You sound like my little Filipino neighbor. 'Maybe you a German Shepherd, even though you look like a Chihuahua, Shelby.'" She did her best to imitate Mona's accent.

"She might be right about that," Cole allowed.

"Make no mistake, I love the woman. Get this, she sang at the Fox. Opened for Bob Hope one night. Her grandson was an extra in the movie Sahara. He actually played gin rummy with Matthew McConaughey while they were waiting around to do a scene…"

"Wow, so only a few degrees of separation between you and Matthew McConaughey," Cole said. Shelby wadded up a napkin and tossed it at him.

Cole tore off a piece of his chili dog and handed it to her, a familiar gesture that was disconcerting but not unwelcome. "What's up with the plain dog? Are you against condiments? You have got to taste this. Basic ingredients, but mustard and chili together is just plain genius."

"We'll see." Shelby popped the bite in her mouth and considered. "Maybe next time," she conceded.

Cole seemed immensely pleased. He leaned back in the small jazzy school chair, slid down a few inches, and splayed his long legs out. "Maybe next time."

Suddenly this felt like a date, one that she wanted to be on, and the thought made her want to run out of the place. She almost did when the deadpan voice, familiar, seemed to rise above the others. "What'll ya have?" it shouted mechanically, without feeling.

She could imagine its owner being approached by his supervisor numerous times with a request to be more animated, more in character. He might have been subjected to a short lecture about the importance of helping to create an atmosphere. Probably he had been threatened with termination, flippantly dared his boss to do so, along with a few unsavory and graphic suggestions of what his higher-up could do with his threats.

Clint. She hadn't had a chance to entertain the possibility of running into him, but of course. He and Miranda had met while working as cashiers here. She caught his attention and sent him a half-salute. He nodded curtly in response and continued taking the customer's order.

"So what was that about?" Cole asked curiously. Then his face changed, rearranged itself into a look of shocked recognition. "Hey, I know that kid! He came to the hospital the night that Miranda Linn was brought in. I could never forget his face. My God, I've never seen anyone so torn up, and that's something coming from an ER doctor. I thought we were going to have to sedate him..."

"Then I don't have to tell you that he's pretty much destroyed," Shelby murmured. "I don't know if he'll ever recover."

"I had no idea you knew him too, Shelby. Just how involved are you with these people? Seems like this is way past just a story for you."

"Yes." Her tone was clipped and did not invite further comment or questions. "Seems I've had challenges dealing with stories that are any messier than new park benches for a nowhere town. I didn't know I wasn't a real journalist until I came to Atlanta."

"So you were faking it before?"

"Sort of," she told him, a faraway, thoughtful look on her face. "I just never had any difficult stories to write about, I guess. Now I do."

"Doesn't sound like you spend your days still walking around in a neat little box, at all," Cole said, watching Clint take orders and toss food on trays.

CHAPTER THIRTY-NINE

"You know," Shelby said conversationally as she sat by Miranda's bed, "all this time I've felt that both you and Joe were cheated. Neither of you even had half a lifetime. And I hated you both for doing it to yourselves."

She watched the girl's peaceful, impassive face carefully and listened to the low, steady hiss of the respirator. The blue dream catcher fluttered softly on the wall, buffeted by the ceiling fan. Miranda was covered, as usual, by her blanket of stars and moons. The pink quartz on the bedside table caught flashes of light from the afternoon sun filtering in, and it relaxed Shelby. The room was becoming familiar.

"I couldn't believe Joe would do it to me and I couldn't believe you would do it to your family," she told Miranda now. "Joe died purposefully and you're where you are through bad choices. I thought you both gave up. But then I got out here and struggled to live without Joe. I found out what hopelessness feels like. Maybe Joe had it figured out and he wasn't giving up at all. Maybe he was just trying to leave while his body still belonged to him. And you…"

At that moment, the notes of a familiar song wafted in through the open window. Shelby peered out and there was Clint, resolutely holding up a portable radio while the Peter Gabriel ballad blared from the nursing home's manicured lawn.

Shelby heard a nurse come into the room. "What the hell is he doing?" she asked the woman in wonder.

"He's recreating a scene from Miranda's favorite movie. Ever seen *Say Anything?* This kid stands outside of the window of the girl he loves and lets the music do the talking for him, pretty much just like what you're seeing now. Boy doesn't do anything halfway, that's for sure. Wearing a long coat, just like in the movie, even though it's about a thousand degrees out."

Clint was dripping with sweat. Even from where she stood Shelby could see that it ran down his forehead and plastered his damp black hair to his skin. He glowed from the heat and something else, lit from within by resolve and emotion. Shelby gave him a little salute and he nodded almost imperceptibly, acknowledging her. He continued to hoist the radio high above his head and resolutely held his position.

Shelby stood at the window for awhile, watching. "You know he's been here before," the nurse finally said. "I don't have the heart to tell him to leave or let the Linns know about it. They'd be furious if they knew, and that boy would be in some trouble, though half the time I think Eileen regrets what they've done. He never stays long or comes inside, or else he'd be locked up already, I suppose. It's almost like he wants to be caught some days. But he won't be stopped where that girl is concerned. Doesn't it make the hairs on your arm stand up? That's what love looks like."

Shelby just nodded in awe.

Miranda felt herself being pulled back up by something. She seemed to lose time a lot lately and it was taking longer for her to make sense of what had happened to her each time she surfaced again. The voices were fuzzier, more far away, and always the unwelcome jolt when she realized again that she couldn't make herself move.

It had taken awhile for her to decide that it was the reporter and her nurse talking. About what, she didn't know. It felt like she was doing laps in a swimming pool and hearing the noise around her, but the water kept her from making sense of what it was. She thought she had heard something musical and familiar before the voices but she couldn't be sure, only knew that it had left her with an incredible feeling of sadness and longing. Had someone been playing a song?

It had definitely been a song, she decided. One that had reached a hand straight into her chest and yanked her upwards towards precious air at the surface.

CHAPTER FORTY

Day Twenty.

Miranda decided the first thing she'd do if she could ever move again was to shut off that damned machine. The ventilator was with her day and night, the first and last thing she was aware of when she drifted in and out.

It was barely perceptible, but the steady hiss of white noise was somehow worse. It was hard to concentrate on the voices, make out words. Her ears were always straining for Clint. When he came she didn't want that steady, low hiss in her head. She wanted to be able to focus.

She thought about the song again and didn't know if it had been real or not, but it made her think of Clint. She had nothing else to do.

Now she took care of the next item on her list. It was the only other thing in her daily schedule besides listening and thinking and being fed: to try and make her arms and legs follow her brain's commands.

Her brain was still working, wasn't it? She was in here, so why wouldn't her body listen? What would it be like if she could open her eyes? Would she be able to make sense of what she was seeing or would her world be a series of distorted, fuzzy shapes painfully and sharply backlit by the sun or harsh overhead lights? Would her legs work, or were they so weak and wasted she wouldn't be able to stand on them?

She had been adrift for twenty days. Each morning her mother marked them for her in even tones. Surely her body would not be lost to her in less than a month, but she knew well how fast the body could deteriorate. She'd understood that every time a needle found her vein and chased a high that would never come again. She had understood it too when she felt sick as hell after she tried to stop chasing the high.

But, today had been a good visiting day. Her mother had brought Arli and Miranda had enjoyed the feel of Arli's wild curls, much like her own, brushing against her when her cousin bent down to kiss her cheek.

"See you later, Pseudo-Twin," Arli had whispered.

Miranda savored these moments of contact and would replay them during the lonely hours. Viv had not come this time. Miranda suspected that her Aunt was choosing to hold on to the picture of her at eight, attached to a Golden Retriever. Viv didn't want to see her like this.

Now she heard another voice, one that was becoming familiar. "Does it bother you?" the reporter asked softly. "Having something in your throat, needing something to breathe? Sometimes it's hard to think about needing to do something more than other people have to do to live. For me it's the injections. But I can't imagine what this must feel like, something attached to you day and night."

It's a constant reminder and distraction. You have no idea what it does to me, Miranda wished she could tell her.

It sent little sparks through Miranda, these flashes of understanding. It was a shock and a comfort when she would hear the reporter say something insightful, as if she was able to interpret the vibrations Miranda was sending out and understand what she wanted her to know.

"Clint was here yesterday," she heard the reporter say. "He played you a song from your favorite movie."

All of Miranda's being centered around the thirteen-word sentence. It was hard to believe that she couldn't move with all of the feeling coursing through her. The song! She *hadn't* dreamt that...

Then some of the excitement faded and disappointment edged in, backing the joy into a corner. If he'd been here why didn't she remember him talking to her? She craved little else, she wouldn't forget hearing his voice. Why would she remember the song but not his voice? Had she faded out at just the wrong moment? She willed herself to demand an answer, but if she were whole and able to form the words to that question, she wouldn't need to ask it.

Just another day in the half-life of Miranda Linn, she thought. Wondering and waiting for someone to understand what she needed to know and tell her. The reporter seemed to get it so she waited for her to say something else that would make her understand about Clint. No explanation came.

"You know you're having a birthday," the reporter told her. Miranda did know. Her mother had started a countdown to her birthday: *Ten days til your birthday, Miranda...Nine days...*

This morning the count stood at one. Tomorrow she would be twenty.

She thought about past birthdays spent on top of Stone Mountain and being woken at midnight and then again at dawn each year by her mother. At midnight to let her know the minute it was her birthday, again at dawn to get an early start on the day.

"It's your birthday and you need to savor every second, let's get up and start celebrating!" her mom would chirp as she eagerly pulled the covers off of her daughter's sleeping form. Miranda would pretend to be annoyed and pull the covers back over her head, but usually never wasted much time in hopping out of bed to stuff herself with wild blueberry pancakes. Each year a new tiara fashioned with crystals from her mother's shop would rest in the middle of an elaborately decorated breakfast plate. Miranda would be queen for the day and spend it as she chose. Nineteen tiaras and nineteen plates, a ritual started before Miranda could even understand it. Even as she became too old for it, the tradition continued.

She wondered how this birthday would be spent. Would her mother fashion a tiara and plate she would not be able to look at, cook pancakes she could not eat and make a pilgrimage out to Stone Mountain that she could not be a part of? How to celebrate the half-life of someone who was not really there but not really gone?

A few days ago she had heard her mother invite the reporter to Miranda's birthday party. It would be odd coming from anyone else, to ask a near stranger to a party the guest of honor couldn't even celebrate. Her Mom had even suggested the woman bring a guest. The reporter hadn't sounded shocked or uncomfortable at the suggestion. Apparently the woman got her mom, too.

"I'm thinking of asking someone to your party." The reporter's tone was conversational, and Miranda tried to enjoy it and tamp down on her disappointment at hearing nothing else about Clint.

It was an odd setting for the reporter's light tone with a slightly excited undercurrent, like she was seventeen and confessing a crush to Miranda. "His name's Cole. Do you know he's the doctor who worked on you the first night you were brought to the hospital? It's strange, Miranda. He's so…not Joe. Where Joe was all fun and bluster, Cole's a little quieter. A different kind of fun and more understated, I guess. God, I talk about him like I'm describing a blazer I saw on sale or something. Joe's a leather coat and Cole's a blazer? Now there's a metaphor," Shelby snorted. "And I write for a living."

Miranda laughed and then frowned inwardly, the only way she could do either nowadays. She wanted to lecture the reporter like a girlfriend. *You described him by comparing him to your husband. Not fair. You will never really get to know him by thinking about what he's not. And you think I need to wake up. Funny how it seems like I'm the one in this duo who's asleep. Not so, reporter. Not so.*

"I've spent most of the time I've known him showing my worst side," the reporter confessed. "He saw that my body was breaking down the first second he met me, and he knew it was mostly of my own doing. He saw a tattoo I don't tell most people about because embarrasses the hell out of me."

Ha, tell me about it! I did nothing but push Clint away. My body is completely broken down and it was all of my own doing! If you and I could have an actual conversation, reporter, it would be really interesting. So you've got a tattoo? I'd love to know where it is, what it is. I'd just love to see what you look like, period. Your voice has made the time go faster and the waiting easier.

"Plus I've got the baggage of a husband who's gone and who knows when I'll be able to carry on a relationship with just two people in it, if you know what I mean."

Never room for three. Not much room for your husband in any of your future relationships and there wasn't room for the drugs when it came to Clint and me.

"I know I have to find a way to be fair to Cole, whether it's attempting a strictly two-person relationship with him or telling him pursue someone else. Miranda, I have to thank you. Strange, I feel like you really are listening to me."

You're welcome, reporter. Sometimes I feel like you're really listening to me, too. Miranda felt the reporter take her hand.

"Miranda, things are a mess," the reporter whispered helplessly. "Your parents and Clint, I don't know how they're going to survive this. Or me. I've found an alter ego in you. You've taught me a few things about how I should be. I wouldn't repeat a lot of your mistakes but there was so much right about how you lived. And you could learn from me too, to slow down a little. Isn't that great? We're two halves. Maybe between us we'd make a complete person. Tell me what to do. Just tell me what to do."

Miranda sighed inwardly and thought she could feel the sadness ripple out in waves throughout her entire being. *Take the best of what you've learned from me, but you're going to have to leave a lot of it, reporter. Now call your doctor and invite him to my party.*

Once Shelby was outside of the nursing home, she flipped open her cell phone and stared at the telephone number in her contacts list. It was one she'd used only a handful of times but she had already memorized it, had spent countless times with her phone flipped open, considering but never dialing. She quickly hit the call button.

When Cole answered she asked softly, "Would you like to go to a really strange birthday party? You actually know the birthday girl. Sort of."

After she clicked off with Cole, she decided she might issue another invitation to the party. She didn't have permission from Eileen for this one, but it was what Miranda would want. And it was Miranda's party, after all.

CHAPTER FORTY-ONE

Sixteen miles east of downtown Atlanta on US Highway 78 lies a treasure that has been carved out by nature and man. It resembles a large rock that looks like it was dropped by a tired giant in the middle of nowhere.

Atlanta's Stone Mountain is the result of 300 million years of natural construction by weather and time. Man took fifty years to finish the job with a 90-foot-high by 190-foot wide sculpture after many creative differences and technical difficulties. Lofty visions of a neverending line of Southern soldiers wrapping all the way around the mountain were abandoned along the way. Now admirers looking up at the sculpture on the north face of the mountain are treated to a sort of permanent, frozen-in-time movie screen of Confederate icons Robert E. Lee, Jefferson Davis and Stonewall Jackson on their horses.

The top of the mountain is an otherworldly landscape of bare rock and small pools etched out over centuries, home to unusual clam and fairy shrimp. In a quintessential circle of life scenario, the shrimp only survive during the rainy season. They perish as soon as the pools dry up, leaving behind eggs to hatch during the next rain. On a clear day, those who venture up to the summit might be treated to awe-inspiring sneak-peeks of the Appalachians. Or they might find nothing but fog instead of a view of Atlanta's skyline.

The rock is a wonder of nature, Shelby thought as she gazed up at the mountain. Now it would be part two of one of the strangest, saddest birthday parties she had ever witnessed.

Part one had consisted of she, the Linns and a few of

the girl's other family members standing around Miranda's bed and singing "Happy Birthday." A plate and a tiara had been placed on the night stand next to the bed. It was just she, Cole and the Linns for part two; she suspected the party had been too sad for everyone else to continue. Cole had met her at Stone Mountain with an uncertain, quizzical smile.

"Gorgeous!" Shelby declared as she and Cole stepped on to the cheerful-looking red Swiss cable car and prepared to ride to the top. "When we get to the summit we'll be able to see Kennesaw Mountain to the west, the Olympic Velodrome to the south."

"Beautiful," Cole muttered. Beads of sweat had formed on his forehead and were starting to snake their way lazily down his temples. "Be even more beautiful if we didn't have to ride eight hundred and twenty five feet up to get there."

"Somebody's afraid of heights."

"Somebody is not afraid. Somebody's terrified," he corrected as the cable car jerked into motion.

"Relax. We're visiting a unique landmark. It might seem like a strange site for a birthday party, but it's perfectly fitting, trust me. Jim and Eileen said they would meet us at the top. We'll all watch the laser show together later," she told him. He looked slightly green and clutched at a metal handle inside of the cable car to keep himself steady. She saw his eyes widen as they reached the top. The car hovered, then promptly hit the side of the lift's metal railing as it stopped.

"Perfectly normal," the lift's operator assured everyone cheerfully.

"Guess you could say your job has its ups and downs," a man in a Stone Mountain visor cracked to the operator. Cole shot the operator and tourist murderous glances as everyone stepped outside.

"Fear of heights has to be the number one phobia among humans," Shelby noted with a quick chortle. "If not, it's way up there, so to speak. No shame in that."

"I need," Cole mumbled weakly, "to use the restroom."

Shelby plopped herself down on a rock as she watched him disappear inside the Visitors' Center. Five minutes later he was back, cautiously navigating over the peaks and valleys. Cole had some color back but stepped gingerly, as if his vision was off and he couldn't trust what he was seeing.

"Isn't it amazing how there's so much life on what is essentially a big rock? I mean, there are trees growing out of this thing. And the shrimp, in those tiny puddles!" Shelby exclaimed.

"It is," he agreed with a shaky smile.

"I'm sorry," Shelby began awkwardly. "I know I'm too much sometimes. But I wasn't laughing because I thought it was funny earlier. I was actually happy because I think it's good for you to be human. I happen to be a huge fan of imperfection, quirks and phobias. It's something to like about you."

"And I happen to like that you're so thrilled that trees and shrimp can live on this rock and that you're curious about everything. It's something to like about you." He moved closer and took her hand. Shelby could feel his breath ruffling the top of her hair.

She gently pulled her hand away and stepped back. *I just can't. Not yet.* "You know, I bet Miranda stood right over here," she said softly. She pointed to the slightly fuzzy outline of skyscrapers. "You can see the skyline, but it's so quiet up here. She loved it because this was the perfect spot to step back and look at her day-to-day life from a distance."

They stood there for awhile, saying nothing, just gazing at the hazy outline of Atlanta in the distance. Cole's expression read disappointed but not deterred.

They didn't move from the spot until Shelby felt a hand on her shoulder. She turned to find Eileen standing there, a peaceful smile on her face. Jim clasped Eileen's other hand.

"I know this place was an escape for her," Eileen acknowledged. "Funny thing is, she couldn't resist pointing out the darker side of things even when it came to her perfect place. This mountain supposedly has the Klan in its past. Supposedly the first sculptor had ties to the Klan. Some members even considered this hallowed ground. Miranda was horrified when she read the plaque in the museum about it. And yet, she latched on to that fact and never forgot about it. Very Miranda to remember that even the most beautiful things have an ugly side. But today, we're going to try and think about the good things…"

Eileen pulled two balloons out of her purse and blew them up. When she was done she kept the tips pinched between her fingers while Jim reached into his jeans and produced a pocket knife. He took a roll of thin red ribbon out of his other pocket and cut some off. Then he ran the knife along the ribbon slowly so it curled, creating the effect people go for at birthday parties or weddings. After the balloons were tied off, one purple and one yellow, each parent took one and let it go. Balloons were not out of place at a birthday party, but this gesture was more like saying goodbye than celebrating another year of a person's life.

Shelby didn't want to, but pitied them.

The balloons were making a fast ascent above the mountain and into the sky when Clint emerged from the Visitors' Center and stepped onto the flat, gray planet. *Here goes,* Shelby thought.

Eileen turned around and her normally serene face clouded with anger. "What is he doing here?" she demanded in a low, cold voice. It was a strange sound coming from the woman who usually spoke in low, soothing tones, like an earth-shaking Lion's roar coming from a kitten. It just didn't fit.

Shelby stepped in without hesitation. "I told him to come, Eileen. He didn't know that you'd be here too. This is a celebration of Miranda's life, and like it or not, he was part of it." She pushed past the look of shocked betrayal on both Eileen's and Clint's faces. "This is not about opposing sides here. You all have Miranda in common. You all feel the same way about her. Why can't you start from there?"

"You had no right to blind-side us like this," Eileen

whispered accusingly. "I thought you understood."

"For once, Eileen and I agree," Clint said, with the same accusing stare.

"You know what our wishes are, what Miranda's are," Jim chimed in. "You didn't respect them when you did this, Shelby."

"You know that's not really true, Jim. They were together when Miranda was clean. Clint went about things the wrong way, but you know he was just trying to protect her. You *know* it." Shelby's words sounded strangled as she nearly choked on her own frustration.

"Save your breath, Shelby. They'll never understand. Daughter's laying in a hospital bed and still they can't get past their own petty crap, take into account what she really wants," Clint tossed off over his shoulder as he started to leave.

"Hey, you son of a bitch, she's there because of you!" Jim shouted at Clint's retreating figure.

Clint turned around, his expression hurt and menacing at the same time. "You think I don't think about that every day? Blame myself? By the way, you sound awfully damn self-righteous, Jim. I know way more about your daughter's life in the past year than you do. When I was running myself ragged trying to keep her out of trouble, where were you? You tried to step in one day out of three hundred and sixty-five. *One*. And on that one day I was there too. Think about that."

Other tourists turned around to look at the source of the raised voices as Jim lunged at Clint. The older man threw himself into the punch, and Clint never backed away. He raised his hands slowly to his nose after Jim's fist landed and touched it gingerly. He considered the blood on his finger and stared Jim down. Neither man spoke.

Cole stepped in and inserted himself between the two men. "Okay, that's enough. I think we can all agree that this was not a good idea and that it's time to go home."

"Gladly," Clint hissed. Cole clamped a hand on Jim's shoulder while they all watched Clint leave.

Clint chose to walk the rocky path down the mountain, eschewing the easy cable car ride to the bottom. Shelby could imagine him winded and breathless when he finally reached the bottom, regretting his stubborn decision to do things the hard way. She had a feeling he'd been doing that his whole life.

Shelby turned to the Eileen and Jim, her face heating with shame. "I'm sorry," she whispered. "I was only trying…"

"I know," Eileen told her vacantly. "It's fine, Shelby." The woman stared up into the sun, as if she could still see the balloon she'd sent up on her daughter's behalf.

When they walked through the park ten minutes later, Shelby put a silencing hand up and told Cole, "Don't bother. I know it was stupid. I just couldn't help it. I'd rather overestimate people and hope they'll surprise me. I had to try. I thought they were capable of bridging that gap for Miranda's sake. I thought they just needed a little push."

"I admire you for that," Cole said with a sigh. "But honestly, this could have turned out really badly. That was interesting, playing impromptu referee."

"Thanks for that," Shelby told him sheepishly. She stopped for a minute and stared back at the mountain, the stone faces of the southern heroes on their horses. "I'm sorry for getting you involved. In my perfect world it wouldn't have been necessary for you to sandwich yourself between those two to prevent a fist fight in the middle of a public park. In my world…" Shelby shook her head. "I'm an idiot. Those were some nice reflexes, by the way. You move pretty quick."

Cole's lazy smile oozed across his face. "Nothing wrong with being an optimist. Although I have to say that was *really* optimistic. Besides, I've had considerable practice with this sort of thing. Oldest of five brothers. Unlike some of those situations, nobody beat the hell out of each other and nobody got thrown out of the place, so no harm, no foul."

"Really? There are five of you? I can see you keeping younger brothers in line. I cannot, however, picture you getting thrown out of anywhere, or engaging in public brawls. I'm going to have fun trying for that image though. I want to hear those stories about you and your brothers. Are you all tall? Do they have freckles like you?"

"Not today. Can't tell you everything. Maybe next time, or the next after that," Cole said as he opened her car door for her.

"No need to bait me. I'll come willingly with or without the promise of a sordid tell-all about your family life. I really am sorry about today."

"Quit apologizing, Shelby Norris, self-appointed mender of epic rifts between parents and boyfriends," he told her. "The fact that you did this, well, it's just another thing to like about you."

"I wish I got points for trying," she said with a sigh. "Their relationship certainly hasn't gotten any better, and neither has Miranda."

CHAPTER FORTY-TWO

Miranda heard the voice commanding her to open her eyes in measured tones, like it had done before.

"Open your eyes, Miranda. Can you open your eyes and blink at me?" The neurologist commanded. Now his tone was slightly louder, more insistent. "Can you open your eyes, Miranda?"

If I could I would have a long time before this...

Finally she felt him open one of her eyelids and shine a pen light into her eye. Now he was moving his finger up and down in her line of vision.

Miranda tried to make herself blink and follow his finger. *I know what you're doing…*

He let his finger drop from her lid and her world went dark again. She knew what was coming next, the part she'd bitch-slap him for if she ever came out of this. He pinched her. Hard.

Ow, damn it! That hurts. You're in a shitload of trouble if I'm ever able to move my arm again.

"Okay, grade EO for Eye Response. Eyelids remained closed with pain." Miranda could say the words along with him by now, he'd done this test on her many times before and called it a Four Score test. Apparently they were actually trying to judge how awake and alive she was.

"Miranda, can you make a fist with your hand? Can you give me a thumbs up or make a peace sign?"

I wish to hell I could. She willed her arms to move. They wouldn't.

"Okay, she is not flexing her upper limbs. No response

to pain when I press down on her suborbital nerve. Grade MO for motor response."

Now the eye drops. Miranda felt the liquid fall into her eye.

"Grade BO. No reflex of the pupil or cornea. Pupil shape is not regular."

Nothing about this is regular, she wanted to tell him.

"Now the breathing," the neurologist muttered. There was only a moment's hesitation before he declared, "Miranda cannot breathe without the help of a ventilator."

No shit…

She heard him sigh, then heard other voices in the room. What the hell were they saying?

Finally she heard the one who'd pinched her say, "I'm going to order a CT angiogram right away. If those results confirm, I'll talk to her parents."

Miranda felt the panic rise in her chest. She'd failed. Like the past times she hadn't been able to break through to him. She wanted to make her body follow the doctor's commands but couldn't. She wanted to reach up and twist the skin on his arm as hard as she could, pinch him right back. He had always treated her with careful respect when he did the tests, but this time he had spoken in flat tones. *If those results confirm I'll talk to her parents.* The room had been silent after that and that said it all. It was the sound of them giving up on her.

She didn't know why she was still here but not here. It was as if she had been cracked in two and her essence was somehow apart from her body, a separate thing but not entirely separate. She couldn't begin to understand how to put the two back together and thought she was not meant to know. She only knew what kept the last tenuous thread between body and soul from unraveling completely. She'd been trapped so long that she just wanted to let go, but she would not let herself unravel into nothing. She would hold on as long as she could, as stubborn as she had always been, and wait. She just didn't know how much longer she had.

*   *   *

The familiar cries of "What'll ya have, what'll ya have?" swirled around Shelby as she spotted Clint's lanky form. She caught his eye and ordered a Diet Coke. The Varsity wasn't exactly a typical site for delivering this kind of news.

What choice did she have? She couldn't believe she was in the middle of a hotdog Drive-In, waiting to tell someone their loved one was going to die soon. She thought about Cole, his summary of what is was like do this kind of thing on a regular basis. She would tell him the next time she saw him that it wasn't the skills he used for saving lives that she admired most. It was the courage it took to tell the families and friends when he couldn't.

She knew it was almost time for Clint to get off. He read her face and approached her chair a few minutes later with a wary look, guarded but with fear seeping through. He sat down next to her and said nothing, just waited. He looked vulnerable when he removed his paper hat. She felt sick, realized how young he looked, how young he *was* when he didn't have an angry look stamped on his face. They both ignored the chaos and general shouting around them. She sipped at her drink, trying to muster up her courage. Clint didn't push; she knew he could tell he wouldn't like what she had to say.

"Let's get out of here," she finally yelled over the din. "Let's talk in my car." Shelby could almost feel his dread growing as he followed her outside.

"Is it okay if I smoke?" he asked, once they were inside her car. "If I roll the window down?"

"I'll even light it for you if you want," she told him wearily.

"So?" He lit up and exhaled a stream expectantly, and even the smoke seemed laced with fear.

"The Linns talked to the doctors at the nursing home today, Clint. Miranda's whole team. The neurologists, everybody. They seem to be in consensus that it'd be the best thing to let Miranda go, and that's what they've decided to do."

The words came out in a rush. Straight to the point and no more delaying. He deserved that.

He jumped out of the car, as expected, and she found herself almost sprinting to keep up with him. Each long stride of his was equal to three or four of her own.

Why had she decided to tell him? *Damn this twisted sense of responsibility I feel. How did I let myself get involved in this whole mess? This should have stopped with a simple story about the Miranda Linn Foundation.*

Clint probably would have found out the news from one of the nurses at Chapel Hill he had endeared himself to, but Shelby had needed to be the one to tell him.

"I'll find a way to stop them from doing it. I won't let them kill her. I'll go through everything she ever wrote to me and find something that proves how much she wanted to live, that proves this would be against her wishes," he told her wildly, never breaking his stride as he continued up the street.

"Clint, they don't want to kill her, and you know that. They just want her at peace." She hesitated a moment, unsure of how to phrase her next words. "You know Eileen gave me Miranda's diaries. Well, what I've read...she did want to live, Clint. But not like this. One of the first things you said to me was that she's a very proud person. I don't think she'd want to just exist. Deep down you understand that."

"I never dreamed, never dreamed, they'd want to let her die," he muttered through clenched teeth, not hearing her. "God knows the Linns and I have precious little in common, but I thought we all at least had some hope she might come out of this one day. Now they're giving up on her...they've decided to put an expiration date on their daughter. And you agree with them. Big surprise. All you've done since I've known you is follow me around, telling me what great people they are and how I need to understand where they're coming from."

"Clint, stop it! It's not like that," Shelby protested, panting with the effort of keeping up with him. They had made a full circle around the Varsity and now they were headed down North Avenue at a sprinter's pace. "You do need to understand. They're with her every day, getting more and more pressure from the doctors, listening to them say that the best thing to do is let her go. The doctors are planning to do a final test on her brain that will probably take the decision out of anybody's hands. They're in an awful limbo that isn't doing anybody any good. They know it isn't fair to Miranda anymore. They're doing it for her, not themselves..." Shelby stopped, suddenly horrified at what she'd told him and how blunt she had been.

He skidded to a halt. "Hey! Aren't you sick of chasing us all around, playing go-between when it comes to me and the Linns? Trying to explain each other's side and motivations? Didn't you learn anything from the fiasco at Stone Mountain? At least the Linns have each other to hold on to. Who do I have to carry me though this? Who's on my side? The one person I used to count on I can't even talk to anymore!"

"Damnit, I am on your side!" Shelby declared hotly. "I feel terrible for everyone in this whole miserable mess, but I am absolutely sick of it! It's the same scene time after time, rinse, lather, repeat. You, Jim and Eileen are too stupid to see the fact that you all love her as a common bond. Instead of grieving together you've all tried to hurt each other. For you to be so at odds with each other is senseless. I want to help you, Clint. I'm always running after you, trying to reason with you while you storm off yet again."

"Then don't do it anymore," he advised acidly. "Maybe the Linns invited you into their lives but I never did. I thought I made that pretty clear the first time we ever met. I'm telling you to get one of your own, and you can quote me on that."

"I told you this so you'd have a chance to say goodbye. Clint, you've got to let her go."

"Not if I can help it, I'm not," he answered grimly, still clutching the paper hat in his hand. His tone never failed to convince but his shoulders slumped and he made slow progress as he turned around.

Shelby let him head back towards the Varsity by himself. Some things even his determination and devotion couldn't change. She was afraid of what would happen now that he was starting to realize this.

CHAPTER FORTY-THREE

Day forty. Her mother had made the day count on this morning's visit in even more strained, sad tones than usual. Miranda knew why.

"I've missed you, Miranda-girl…"

Now she focused on the declaration, the voice. Could it be? The statement followed a whispered, tense conversation.

"You know you can't be in here long," the voice chastised. She had come to know it well. The nurse who sounded like Paula Deen.

"Understand…need to see her one last time…"

So many familiar voices since she had been pulled into this world of never-ending curtains, and some unfamiliar ones she had come to recognize over time. There was no mistaking this one, the one that had been missing. It was him.

"So sorry…leave you alone now…Know you need to say goodbye..." The gentle caregiver's voice again, one that had understood her family's anguish, but had also somehow understood what Miranda really wanted. Wasn't that why he was here? Miranda wished she could thank her.

Finally! She had been waiting a lifetime to hear him again…She hated that she couldn't understand every word, but the feeling behind them was always clear.

The voice seemed to reach out from across an ocean to her. Its owner had somehow kept her tethered to her body and yet made her feel it was necessary to escape it altogether. As long as she was trapped, he would be too. She wanted to move, to speak, reach out and touch. She couldn't. Still.

Was the voice real or part of an imagined escape from

the prison of her body? It *had* to be real. The presence hovered above her, strong, a palpable thing. The voice continued to talk, whisper in her ear. What it was saying didn't matter, only that its owner had finally come to complete the final, missing piece of her puzzle. She savored it, trying to ignore the rising fear that it would leave and never return. Fear of what she had to do.

Clint, she wanted to say. She willed the single word, his name, to come. It wouldn't. Still.

It felt like being buried alive, suffocating, this wanting to reach out so badly. She was sick of that feeling every time she heard her parents' voices. With Clint it was unbearable.

I'm here! It was a terrible, sickening frustration to feel like they were all just beyond her reach. The other possibility was worse: that they knew she was in here, but could do nothing to help her.

Sandpaper against her cheek. She had felt it countless times before, the roughness of his unshaven face against her smooth one. How many times had she playfully batted him away when he'd purposely rubbed his several days' growth against her face? She would do anything to prolong the contact now. She'd pushed him away so many times, in jest and then, later on, because she'd been confused. Lost. But she'd always meant to hold him close.

"I know you still loved me, even with everything that happened. I know you didn't mean to push me away."

She understood his words perfectly now. They echoed her intended message so closely that Miranda felt maybe she had spoken. Now she felt a gentle pressure on her chest, the moisture seeping through her mother's blanket. He was crying. She wished she could comfort him, put her hand on his head. She felt regret that she would never be able to again. Now she felt a light pressure on her cheek, a kiss she could not return. More murmuring.

And then, just as strongly as she had felt his presence in the room, she felt it leave. The loss was the worst thing yet, the hardest moment. How long he had stayed, she couldn't know;

it should have been longer. But he knew. That was what she had wanted, what she had been waiting for each time she tried to find a way to reconnect to her body and couldn't make it work. She wanted nothing more than to be able to open her eyes and look at him. Such a simple thing, but she couldn't do it. So many things she couldn't do. But there was one thing she could…

Knowing he understood sent an indescribable rush flooding through Miranda. She only wished she could give him, her parents, everyone else she cared about and even everyone she didn't this feeling. Bottle it up and share it with them. She knew a terrible choice was about to be made, not really a choice, but her parents would still feel responsible. She didn't want them left with that burden.

She had heard the matter-of-fact statements from the doctors and the anguished whispers of her parents. Assurances their daughter was already essentially gone would do little for them. She could help them now, save them from this after all she had put them through. All she had to do was let go of the fear.

Miranda felt the maddening weight that had been pressing down on her release, the best feeling yet. She ignored the presence of the ventilator that had been her companion since she had come to this place. She had hated it, always there. She could leave it behind forever, will it to go away, along with the pain of Clint's leaving, the fear and sadness she heard in her mother's voice every day.

She could do anything she wanted to now, and so she did. She felt that boundary and a million others crumble in an instant. An invisible, looming wall in her way toppled, seemingly with a simple nudge of her foot. *Just let go…*

Day forty…

She was free.

She was forever twenty.

She was gone.

CHAPTER FORTY-FOUR

Shelby stared down onto Peachtree, errant tears falling for the girl she had never even had a two-sided conversation with, but one who had become a friend in the truest sense of the word: a secret-keeper and a sharer of wisdom.

Death was never the end of the story. The real one would be the after, about those Miranda had left behind. Her parents, Clint. Shelby could imagine herself having finally made CNN reporter, commenting on the fate of battle-worn hurricane survivors standing on top of the rubble a monster storm has left in their wake. *What's the damage? How long will it take for life to return to normal?* Sifting through the wreckage and starting the cleanup. She didn't envy the Linns and Clint that task, knew how long it could take to make sense of the rubble. Months after Joe had died she was still sifting.

Both Eileen and Clint had called separately to tell her Miranda had died during the night, effectively making her own decisions for a final time. One day before the doctors were scheduled to remove her "supportive care."

Cole's *Guide To Caring For The Comatose Patient* had taught her that most patients like Miranda, even those kept alive with ventilators and all that modern medicine could do for them, died within six months. The cause was usually infection, or multiple organ failure. Death could be sudden and of an unknown cause.

To Shelby this felt different. Was it a final act of rebellion or something less selfish? Would the Linns have had the strength to see their decision through? Could they have stayed and held their daughter's hand as she died?

Now they would never have to answer the question that should never have been asked of them, if life was fair. She wondered if the girl had died as purposefully as Joe had.

She needed to share her grief and dialed the first two people who came to mind, her mother and Cole. After that was done, Shelby yanked on some sweats and slid a pair of Crocs on her feet.

Outside traffic was light, the street calm. She'd been in a hurry to leave her apartment but felt no less suffocated out here. She hurried up the street for a Starbuck's Doubleshot Espresso and sat among the other plugged-in customers who were working on their laptops and reading. After skimming the latest issue of *Atlanta Minute* she downed the coffee and waited for the jolt of artificial adrenaline to kick in. She wouldn't have been able to sleep tonight anyway.

When Shelby was finished she circled back towards the *Atlanta Minute* offices and keyed herself in. The lights flickered for a minute in protest when she flipped them on, then reluctantly decided to do their job and lit up the place. She shuffled over to a computer, fired it up, and began to type in earnest.

Miranda Linn, 20, an Atlanta native, died Tuesday, September 24, 2009. She is survived by her parents, Jim and Eileen Linn; a special friend, Clint Mullen; and aunts, uncles and cousins. She is preceded in death by her grandparents and a son, Noah.

Linn was at the center of a controversy involving the use of Narcan rescue kits for drug addicts. The issue sparked heated debate among Atlantans. Some see the kits, which can be used to prevent complications or death from an overdose, as a way to keep drug abusers safe until they're ready to seek help for their addiction. Others view them as something to further fuel a drug habit.

All have an opinion on what the girl deserved or didn't deserve, but few really knew Miranda Linn. She became a symbol but was, first and foremost, a girl who was

deeply loved. She was a daughter, friend, and even savior to some who knew her. A grateful young woman named Anita Velasquez is alive today and making another attempt to start over because of the chance Miranda Linn took one afternoon in marching in and dragging her out of a bad situation. Despite her flaws, Miranda Linn was already a far better human being than those who saw fit to judge her.

She thought of that particular journal entry of Miranda's and stopped to imagine Miranda Linn tossing her hair and insults around in Jimmy's apartment. At nineteen she'd still been young enough to feel invincible but was also anticipating being a mother: beginning to understand the consequences of her actions and what it would be like to live for someone else. The girl had been so brave and so foolish.

Shelby stuffed her fist in her mouth and tasted the salt from the tears on her hand. With the other she tapped the backspace button on her computer, watching the words disappear from the screen, the whole nightmare undone line… by line…by line…

She didn't hear Maura enter the office or come up behind her. "Can you believe I forgot my notes for the damn Juarez editorial?" Maura asked in her usual way, as if they were already in mid-conversation. "I wanted to get a jump on it at home. What are you doing here so late?"

Maura caught a look at Shelby's bloodshot eyes, and an internal debate about whether or not to comment was apparent on the editor's face. "Are you okay?" she asked slowly.

"Couldn't sleep so I decided to finish up a story, Miss boss," Shelby answered in a hollow voice, watching the cursor blink on the otherwise blank computer screen.

Maura didn't question her any further. "Go home, Shelby," Maura commanded softly as the lights began to flicker again. "It's late. Go home."

"I will. Soon," Shelby agreed, her thoughts suddenly centered on the home she had left long before tonight. The home that meant a diner owned by former in-laws. Coworkers who toasted you with paper Dixie cups and held your send-off party in the middle of a dusty newspaper office. A mother who posted up signs in your old room that made you feel like a guest in the home you'd grown up in, but who also knew the exact moment to distract you when you shouldn't be alone with your thoughts. "Soon."

CHAPTER FORTY-FIVE

The clock read 1:58 a.m. when Eileen sat up in bed. She hadn't slept well for months, in the past twenty-four hours especially. She wondered if sleep would ever return. Now that Miranda was at peace, maybe she could be too. No more worrying about her baby girl's safety, no more agonizing about who she was with or what she was doing. She had the sad suspicion it would never work that way for a mother.

She looked over at her husband's unmoving form. Too tired to even snore. She knew Jim had also fought sleep since Miranda had died. Now it looked as if he had succumbed to the exhaustion, the knowing that the worst had already happened and there was nothing more he could do.

So many things they should have done where Miranda was concerned. Eileen was famous for her instincts, and still she hadn't been able to step in and save her daughter in time. She crept into the living room and regarded the vintage cuckoo clock on the wall. Even after the wooden bird popped out of the clock and whistled twice, loudly, Jim still did not wake.

Eileen studied the pictures on the wall and smiled as her eyes rested on one of Miranda at ten years old. She was dressed in a bright yellow chicken costume for Halloween. The outfit was rounded out by an ostrich egg in a baby carriage. She proudly sported a wide, gapped-tooth smile and her curls peeked out from underneath the chicken's head. Orange feet tied over her sneakers completed the look.

If she'd been embarrassed by that one Miranda had never let on; she had even cried, heartbroken when the ostrich's egg had slipped out of her hands and the empty, carefully drilled-out shell had cracked on the ground. Eileen had never been satisfied with store-bought costumes. A Geisha. Orphan Annie...

All of the costumes throughout the years had been homemade, the Geisha's kimono and Annie's signature red dress stitched by Eileen in the weeks before Halloween. Miranda had been proud, even at ten appreciating the fact she had a mother who would take the time. Her wild blond hair once again revealed itself in the Orphan Annie costume, peeking out from underneath the wig's artificial orange curls as if her true essence couldn't be denied. The little red dress was short enough to reveal Miranda's skinned knees, a contrast to the shiny black shoes and lacy socks she wore. The same had been true of the Geisha. Her daughter sported an eerily painted white face with blood-red lips, draped in a kimono made of silky green and white fabric. Her hands were placed together in an attempted signature Geisha pose. Trying to be someone else, a character from another time. But those blond curls escaping again. There would be no pictures past nineteen, no photographs where an attempt was made to coax the curls into submission underneath a wedding veil or a college graduation cap.

Eileen grabbed a pair of sweats out of the dresser and quietly pulled them on. She gently kissed her sleeping husband's forehead and grabbed her house keys and cell phone. She needed a walk. She needed some fresh air. She needed peace.

Her cell phone vibrated. "Shelby," she said in mild surprise, after she answered.

"Eileen, you've got to come and meet me. Now," the reporter commanded.

CHAPTER FORTY-SIX

Clint sat in his jeep and watched people stream out of the bar. Last call. He hadn't even kept track of the time. Waiting hadn't been a problem, he had all the time in the world. He was ready to light up a cigarette and get comfortable when he saw Jon amble out and playfully flip a couple of his buddies the bird. He listened to the crunch of gravel and drunken laughter as people left.

This was going to be easier than he thought. No shaking hands, no shallow breath, no sweat sliding down his forehead or making his shirt stick to his back. He felt anticipation but not the kind that makes a person fidgety with impatience, like a basketball player seconds before tip-off. Just a sense of looking forward to what was going to happen and knowing it would in due time.

He felt great about what he was about ready to do. Fan-freaking-tastic, actually, he thought, as he fingered the Glock 20 pistol. It was capable of firing ten rounds but he wouldn't need that many. He saw one of two people still alive that were responsible for Miranda's death lumbering out of the bar. The other one he had to face in the mirror every day. Both would get what they deserved tonight. He jumped out of the jeep and fell into stride beside Jon, slinging a companionable arm around his shoulder.

"Hey, can you hook me up?" he asked, his voice a cross between casual and needy. "I really need something. Bad."

"Since when?" Jon asked suspiciously. "Thought you were mister twelve-step these days, too good for the likes of me."

"What can I say?" Clint shrugged sheepishly. "Sobriety

sucks."

Jon's harsh bark of laughter set Clint's teeth on edge. "Follow me back to my place," the dealer instructed.

Clint had counted on this. "See you there," he said with satisfaction. *What a dumb ass.* Clint wasn't much of an actor but the role of needy junkie, he could manage just fine. Jon wasn't that hard to fool, anyway.

Clint was reaching the boiling point but dialed his anger down to a simmer as he got in his jeep and tossed off a casual wave. *You have to show him first.*

He had some time to think as he listened to the radio and followed Jon's rusty Chevy Caprice. He waited for a whisper of doubt, some alarm bells in his head as he made the familiar turns to the broken-down trailer. When Clint saw the lopsided wooden sign for Pine Crest Trailer Court there were still no jitters.

Jon parked his battered car and had almost reached the door of his trailer when Clint flung his arm around Jon's shoulder, turned him around, and walked him toward the jeep.

"C'mon, buddy, let's you and me take a ride." Clint recalled the many months of practice he'd had forcibly getting Miranda out of places she shouldn't be, trying to keep her out of trouble. Same thing, except tonight he was going to walk Jon Tillman straight *into* trouble. He almost had Jon to the jeep before the man had time to process what was happening, react.

"Hey Clint, what the hell? I'm not going anywhere with you," Jon snapped.

"Oh yes you damn well will and here's why." He shoved Jon in the jeep and showed him the gun. A second later he peeled out of the trailer park. Jon's terrified eyes flitted toward the door, and Clint quickly pressed the automatic lock button so the jeep's locks went down on both doors with a decisive *click*.

"I don't think so.," Clint said, almost amused. "You're not going to bail and get out of this with a mere broken leg. There's something I want to show you, so you and I are taking this ride all the way to the end, Jonny-boy."

"Where the hell are you taking me?" Jon demanded, eyes growing ever wider.

"Just shut up. I don't want to listen to your voice anymore. We'll be there soon enough."

They drove the rest of the way in silence except for Jon's nervous breathing and the soft country music on the radio. When they reached the park, Clint shoved Jon out of the door and pressed the gun in his back.

"Walk," he told Jon simply.

No one was around, but Clint wouldn't have cared if they were. The soft breeze blew an abandoned Cheetos wrapper and a faded beer can across a patch of dead grass. To Clint it was a horrifying reminder, the moonlight a punctuation mark on what Miranda's bleak last view of the world had been. He was keenly aware of how Miranda had viewed this place, seen it as a metaphor for her life. Shelby had told him it was one of the last things Miranda had written about in her diary. Somehow it looked even worse tonight than the other times he'd been here.

He was tired of making this sad, sick pilgrimage to where Miranda had finally ruined herself for good. Tonight would be the last time. He yanked on Jon's arm when they reached the picnic bench with peeling green paint. "Stop right here. First of all, I want you to know that Miranda died, okay? She's gone."

"What? I thought she OD'd over a month ago," Jon muttered in surprise.

"She did. She's been in a coma all this time. Actually the term the doctors used was persistent vegetative state, but I'll try and keep the words small for you. She wasn't dead, you asshole. Well, maybe she was to you, since she wasn't bringing you money anymore. But she was alive to me."

Clint jabbed a finger at the picnic bench. "This is the spot where she overdosed on the drugs that you probably sold her. She didn't deserve to be found like a piece of trash left on this table. You do. She's dead and what do you have to show for it? A rusted out shitbox for a car and a crappy little trailer." He gestured toward Jon's Garth Brooks T-shirt. "What do you spend it on anyway, your wardrobe? I wish you had the brain power to think about whether or not it's worth it. Forget the affable buddy routine and your Eddie Haskell bullshit. You helped kill her."

"I told you before, I never forced anything on her. She always came to me," Jon insisted in a frightened whine.

"And I told you before to just walk away."

Now there was nothing more to lose and no reason to show the restraint he'd been forced to when he'd first issued the curt directive in the bar: *Just walk away.* This was the luxury of having nothing left. He punched Jon squarely in the stomach, was satisfied to hear the grunt of pain as the pudgy man dropped to his knees. Then he grabbed Jon's hair, yanked his head upwards, and sent his face smashing into the dirt.

"This is the last thing she saw! What you're looking at now! Dirt and dead grass and trash!" he screamed. *"How do you like the view?"* He ground Jon's face into the grass for good measure and pointed the gun at him as Jon wrenched free from his grip and attempted to do an awkward crab-walk away.

"Stop moving right now," Clint commanded.

"Look, I'm sorry about Miranda, but why is all of this my fault?" Jon demanded desperately, wiping the blood from his nose. His face was streaked with dirt and tears and he took a minute to spit out some of the earth that was jammed in his mouth. "Didn't you get her hooked in the first place? Why are you pointing the gun at *me*?"

"Fair question. And since I'm a fair guy I'll share some of the blame. We're going to be tomorrow's next big story, Jon. You and me, the sensational murder-suicide," Clint told him. He pictured Shelby Norris writing about it for *Atlanta Minute* in those stupid-looking horn-rimmed glasses, twirling on a pen with her head bobbing along to her iPod, and smiled at the perverse thought. He'd called her an hour ago, told her he'd give her a story. It was a hell of a time to wonder what music she listened to get her head bobbing and in the mood to write. Too bad he'd never get the chance to ask her.

"You're crazy," Jon whispered. Clint was startled when the man suddenly twisted, waved his arms wildly, and screamed, "Hey, you two! Help me! This asshole's crazy! He's going to *kill* me!"

Clint turned and saw Eileen and that damned Shelby Norris running toward them. "He's not crazy," Shelby gasped. "There's a difference between crazy and hurting. Give me the gun, Clint."

"Jesus, you two," Clint said with a start. "You're a little early, reporter. I'm not finished yet. Got my message, huh? Eileen, I'm disappointed she had to call you. You didn't get one of your 'feelings' or any bad vibes? Couldn't figure out that my planets aren't aligned for shit today and there's going to be big trouble? Your third eye's clouded these days."

"Maybe my third eye is clouded," Eileen told him quietly. "I'm sorry I haven't been able to see that you're hurting as much as I am. But this isn't going to make things right, it's just further waste," she said calmly.

"All of that new age spiritual crap you're into, and you can't come up with anything better than that? Next thing you're going to tell me it won't bring Miranda back, right?" Clint demanded.

"Listen to yourself, Clint. You're coming up with the answers all on your own," Eileen told him placidly. She seemed pleased with his response.

"He sold drugs to your daughter," Clint reminded her flatly.

"Let him go," Shelby commanded softly. "I don't blame you for the way you feel, but you don't want to kill yourself with the poison you've tried to give somebody else. I almost did that once, but it's not the way to go, Clint. You wouldn't have called me if you really wanted to go through with this."

"Listen to them," Jon interjected. His voice had an attempted note of authority to it that fell flat because it quavered instead. "Just do what they fucking say."

"Oh shut-the-fuck-up," Eileen snapped, the words

coming out in sharp staccato like the quick report of an automatic weapon. "We don't really care what happens to *you*."

Clint let out a startled yelp of laughter, still keeping the gun firmly trained on Jon. He noticed his hands were finally shaking. He was starting to sweat too. "We helped ruin her, and now we're going to pay," he said in a tremulous voice. It was a simple, childlike declaration.

"Clint, Miranda made her own decisions. You know that better than anyone," Eileen said quietly. "I've been wrong to hate you for making mistakes in the beginning instead of appreciating the way you tried to help Miranda the rest of the time. I should have thanked you for taking care of my daughter the way you did. Instead I tried to punish you by keeping you away from her because I needed someone to blame too."

Clint's face contorted. He took the shuddering breath of a person hanging on to the last shreds of self-control and said, "We were going to be parents. We had actually learned how to live with each other before it all happened." His free hand found its way to his side and dug in deeply, a habit he had developed to try and relieve the ache he felt every time he thought about Miranda and their brief days of baby books, prenatal vitamins, and hope. Sometimes when he dressed he would look down in alarm at the deep red scratches on his chest, forgetting how they'd gotten there. Along with the tattoos, they were more self-inflicted scars he'd carry around in the future.

Eileen nodded. "Yes. I'll never forget her telling me, 'Mom, I've got the best reason possible to change.' She was nervous about the responsibility, but she felt like she'd found a purpose."

"I thought we were going to make it. We would have if she hadn't lost the baby. We could have even though we did, if she wouldn't have taken off. I would've found a way to push, pull or drag us through," he said stubbornly.

"I know you would have, Clint. I can see that now. We never gave you credit for how much you loved her," Eileen admitted.

"You never gave me credit for a lot of things. I'm not stupid. Stop *patronizing* me, the both of you. Do I look like I'm in the mood to be placated? Get the hell out of here."

He said the words without conviction, uncertain now. Shelby stepped forward, visibly relieved, and took the gun out of his hands. The three barely bothered to watch as Jon Tillman heaved with the effort of getting to his feet and turned and ran as fast as his stubby legs would carry him into the humid Georgia night.

Shelby pulled a long look at Clint. "It's too late for Miranda, Clint, but not for you."

Clint collapsed on the ground. His sobs sounded as if someone were slowly tearing them one by one out of his chest. Eileen knelt down beside him and cradled his head in her lap, her own tears sliding silently down her face. The soft breeze rocked the rusted swing on the playground equipment back and forth while they sat there and listened to its gentle squeaking.

CHAPTER FORTY-SEVEN

By now everyone at Club 404, especially Jon's regulars, had heard the story. He told anyone who would listen how that crazy bastard, Clint Mullen, had kidnapped at gunpoint and threatened to shoot him. Most of his customers pretended to tune in until he gave them their drugs and they gave him his money. Then they walked away, silently cheering Clint.

They liked to take creative liberties and picture the part that wouldn't be told: Jon waddling away from the park, huffing and puffing, after Clint had showed him the gun. Maybe he had even wet himself and been forced to walk all of the way back to his trailer smelling like piss and feeling the moisture in his jeans turn cold. Had he cried when he made the call to the police and detailed what had happened? That delicious speculation made an even better chaser to the Jack's they drank than an ice-cold Corona.

They couldn't know for sure and he would certainly never admit it, but their guessed-at versions were close to the truth. Jon had walked halfway home before someone took pity on him and picked him up. The good Samaritan had almost regretted it when they smelled the stench of urine and noticed his wet pants. And Jon had most certainly cried in earnest when he babbled out his story to a 911 dispatcher.

Jon swaggered around 404 as if the story gave him some tough-guy credibility. *Yep, I've had a gun pulled on me.* He was plenty indignant too: *How dare he blame me? It's not my fault his junkie girlfriend took too much.* That was usually the point when his customers were ready to finish the deal and get away from him.

Now a woman who had frequented the bar for past few months approached Jon with an inward sigh. She knew him well enough and disliked him just as much, or more, than his other customers.

She was anxious to get the transaction over with but knew she would have to endure a series of pitiful come-ons before the deal was done. He didn't care or realize, even with all of her cool brush-offs and thinly veiled insults, that she was only interested in his drugs. She was all legs in thigh-high boots and a skirt that just barely satisfied the requirements for public decency. Her hair cascaded down to just above her waist, a nice shiny river of black. It was a pleasing contrast to her *Midnight Love*, the preferred shade of red her lips were always painted. A stunning face but one with a slightly hard edge to it. Brows that arched a little too sharply and a chin that was a little too pointed.

"Hello, beautiful," he greeted her magnanimously, attempting an inviting tone with just a hint of suggestion. He apparently had forgotten past insults and rebuffs she had doled out. "What can I do for you?"

Ugh, how about staying at least four feet away from me, but preferably farther than that. "I'd like some smack and some Oxy, Jon," she told him. "You can hook me up right now, can't you?" *And because I have to make physical contact when you give me what I need, I'll want to go home and douse myself in rubbing alcohol.*

Now he attempted a fatherly tone. "Hey, it's business hours doll. I'm prepared. But be careful how you mix those, okay? I don't want anybody else getting into trouble because they've taken too much or complaining about a bad trip because of the way they've mixed and matched."

Right, now you suddenly care about what happens to the people who buy your drugs. Because it came back to bite you.

The infamous story had come straight from Jon himself. She said good for Clint Mullen. *He should have shot you in the ass. Just give me the damn pills and the smack. I need it.* "I want three grams and twelve Oxy."

"Okay, how about eighty. A discount since you're so pretty. Let's go someplace a little more private." He tried to drop a hint of suggestion into these words as well, making the contents of her stomach further churn.

Okay, how about a black eye. Since you're so obnoxious. "Let's go outside. I need some air."

They moved outside of the bar and she waited while he went to his car. *Hurry up.* She mentally drummed her fingers a minute later as she thrust the money at him and held her hand out in anticipation.

The tiniest, imperceptible sigh escaped from her lips when he dropped the heroin and pills into her waiting hand. She was enormously happy that the encounter between herself and Jon Tillman was over but she did not walk away from him. She fought to keep a smile from spreading across her lips as the uniformed police officers came up and promptly began reading him his rights. She still had a part to play.

"Thanks a lot, asshole," she tossed in Jon's direction. "Great. Now I've got to spend the night in jail."

Jon, I'm afraid I have bad news, she thought to herself with an inward smile. *You're under arrest for the possession and sale and narcotics. And for being an all-around sleaze, if we could charge you for that.* She was an undercover officer. Uniformed police had actually also cuffed her for show, so no one in the bar would be tipped off that she was a DEA agent.

No doubt Jon could barely process what was happening: one minute he was selling the hot tamale he had been admiring in the bar drugs, the next he was under arrest. Jon tried to speak but nothing came out as the metal closed around his wrists.

Nothing to say? That's good, Jon. A nice change for you, she thought mirthfully.

At that moment her partner was ushered by. He was under fake arrest as well, part of the mini-sting operation. "Everything all right?" he asked in a low voice as he passed her. "I think we're all about ready to move out."

Six other agents had been milling around the bar

for the past three hours. Drugs were rampant at 404 and the department figured placing people undercover to find out who sold and who bought was worth their time.

If the bar's other patrons had been aware of the operation, they might have actually applauded the undercover agents. The tears they had speculated on when Jon had been taken by Clint were now welling up in the dealer's squinty blue eyes.

"We're all going to grab something to eat after," her partner whispered to her now. "You coming?"

"Maybe a quick bite," she conceded in a satisfied, languid tone. "Just a burger, because I want to get home and take a bath. In rubbing alcohol."

The drug task force that worked in conjunction with the police department relied heavily on tips. Though it was common knowledge that 404 was home to varying degrees of illegal behavior, a tip had provided her with the name Jon Tillman, a dealer with a lot of business. Interestingly enough, the name of the tipster was a well-known one at the bar too: Clint Mullen.

She sighed as she remembered the husky voice on the phone a few months ago.

"You're drug enforcement, right? Officer Dumfries told me I should get in touch with you," the voice had informed her in a flat, hesitant tone. "Well, I'm sure you guys know what Club 404 is like. There's this little stain there, Jon Tillman, and he sells a lot of drugs. Smack, pills. He's there pretty much every night of the week and usually comes in after ten. It would be nice if you'd bust him. Not that his buyers can't just go somewhere else but you guys are always aiming for one less on the street and shit like that, right? He sells for cheap. You can even tell him Clint Mullen said hey for all I care."

"Thank you, Mr. Mullen. We'll look into it."

"Please look into it quick. Even a day can make a difference to someone."

"You know, Mr. Mullen," she told him softly, "We'd have to bust whoever's buying from him too. If we were to go in, it could be at any time. We don't exactly announce ourselves before."

"Right," he answered in the same soft tone. They listened to each other's breathing through the telephone for a minute and understood each other perfectly. "I'll worry about the someone a day could make a difference to. I'm there to take care of them. That's my job. You do yours." The soft click as he put the receiver down had almost been a command.

If the kid had just waited a little while longer…They had to take their time to bust Jon and figure out who else was buying and selling so they could bring in as many people as possible.

But she knew only one of the customers there had really mattered to him: Miranda Linn.

Just a matter of days and Clint Mullen wouldn't have thrown his life away with Jon already in jail. She had seen worse outcomes in her job than a threat at gunpoint and someone smart doing a few years for an impulsive, stupid decision. At least Clint Mullen had pulled back at the crucial moment, but still…

CHAPTER FORTY-EIGHT

Anita was back on Jimmy's couch again, watching him flip through the channels. The constant flipping gave her a headache. Her eyes barely had time to adjust to what was on the screen and the image would disappear again, Jimmy in search of something better to watch.

Jimmy paused for a second on an infomercial for an abdominal machine, his finger hovering for a minute above the channel button. Apparently the ass of the woman working out on the machine was enough to hold his attention for more than half a second; he looked as if he was memorizing its outline before the image disappeared and was replaced by two men in a boat, one reeling in a large fish. Some sort of fishing tournament. That one disappeared almost before she made sense of it.

She wanted to take off with the remote as she and Miranda had done that day, make his new Braves cap casualty number two to the toilet. She thought about Miranda and a tear snaked down her cheek. Jimmy didn't notice and wouldn't have asked her about it if he did; neither would Anita have told him what was wrong if he had wanted to know. Jimmy didn't know yet that she'd died. Anita intended to keep that information to herself. She wouldn't be able to stand the callous comment that would come out of his mouth once he found out.

Anita imagined Miranda cursing her for coming back to Jimmy and his apartment, threatening to drag her out as many times as it took. She would come up with new ways to wreck Jimmy's little kingdom on each return visit.

The stab of anger and then guilt returned as she thought

about Miranda succumbing to the drugs that she'd been so adamant for Anita to leave behind. Miranda had all but kicked Jimmy's door in and been willing to face whatever was on the other side for the sake of a friend, even with a baby growing inside of her. *And where had she been when Miranda was suffering? All I had to do was put a hand out to her, at absolutely no risk to me. Just be there. Madre de Dios, if I had just found out in time…*

But there had been no outstretched hand for Anita to take, no opportunity to help pull her friend up from the depths. She cursed Miranda again for vanishing from the hospital without a word to anyone she cared about, then going on a final bender. *You had so many people who love you to lean on. I had only you, and Lindy.*

Everyone else on the planet had given up on her except for Miranda and Lindy. She'd been written off by her parents, who had thrown her out at sixteen in a string of Spanish curses when they caught her with a boyfriend. Her sister was embarrassed by the older sibling who was anything but a good example. Even cousins and a long line of *hombres malos* she had hooked up with during the hazy years had all disappeared.

Anita pictured Miranda blacking out Carmen's teeth and smiled. There had only been two people in the universe who believed in her even when she let them down. Knowing the count was down by one was perhaps the reason she had returned to Jimmy, to his couch, to the channels whizzing by.

She'd been surprised when he had just shrugged at the sight of her at his door again and stepped back to let her inside. He'd said nothing, just lit up a cigarette and went to the refrigerator to make himself a sandwich. Not even a vicious slap to serve as a reminder and warning. Possibly he was saving it to use against her at a future date of his choosing. Anita didn't bother to guess at his motivations.

"I'm going out to get something to eat," she told him.

"What for? Just eat something here."

"Jimmy, there's nothing in the refrigerator." Well, that wasn't entirely true. But she didn't feel like scraping mold off of what was there or having another beer.

"So just find something in the damn cabinet," he muttered crossly, as if she was incredibly stupid for not figuring this out.

There was nothing in the cabinet either, but Anita was not about to remind him. She didn't like where this was going. *I should have just slipped out and not said anything.* She hovered awkwardly between the door and the couch, uncertain of what to do now. The door or the couch?

Anita sat back down with a sigh and Jimmy resumed ignoring her. He watched thirty seconds of an old A-Team episode and then settled on a Pizza Shack commercial. Anita fixated on the pepperoni before the ad vanished and stood up again.

"Seriously, I haven't had anything to eat all day. You want me to get you anything?" She asked the question to avoid a complete meltdown on his part and possibly net a few extra bucks.

"Sit down," Jimmy told her, bored.

"I'll bring you something back if you want," she persisted. "I'm hungry." She was disgusted at the sound of her own voice, like a whiney child asking a parent for a snack.

"Sit down and shut up," he advised again in a casual tone.

"*Cerdo*," she muttered under her breath. "Pig."

"What?"

"Nothing, Jimmy. You just keep flipping your life away and I'm going out." Now she heard Miranda dare her. *Leave now, today. If you don't mean today, you don't mean it…*

"I don't think you heard me."

"I think I did but I'm just too hungry to care right now."

"Maybe if all the money I gave you didn't go up your nose and to shoot up, you'd have some left for food." His tone was still casual, still bored, but she saw a spark of malevolence in his eyes.

"Jimmy, have you seen me using? I haven't touched anything for the past six days."

Anita had been sick for the first two, sweating out a promise and resolving not to ever again touch the poison that had killed Miranda. For the last four she had slipped out to New Horizons when Jimmy was gone.

When she stepped back inside the white brick building she didn't know which was worse, feeling as if her insides were being rearranged from the constant vomiting or the jolt when she saw the site of so many memories made with her friend. Strange how a place that looked so unwelcoming on the outside could make her feel safer than anywhere else she had ever been. But it was different without Miranda. Anita had come undone when she stepped into Lindy's embrace.

"You do right by Miranda," Lindy had told her tearfully.

Anita hadn't been able to meet Mama Lindy's gaze when asked where she was staying, and Lindy hadn't pressed. Anita knew one of the nurse's many mottoes was "one battle at a time."

Jimmy sneered at her now. "Wow, almost a whole week. Is some kind of a record since you were thirteen?" He had taken awhile to respond, as if considering how best to insult her.

"It's not a record, but it's a start," Anita told him, her chin tilting up proudly. "My personal best is sixty-eight days."

Jimmy clapped his hands together derisively. "Well good for you, Anita. Maybe Miranda and the rest of your buddies at the clinic can throw you a party."

"Don't talk about her," Anita said, her voice an angry whisper. "Don't you even dare say her name."

"What are you going to do? Why can't I talk about Saint Miranda?" he taunted.

Anita swore in Spanish and reached back to strike him. He grabbed her hand, laughing, and kept her thin, bony wrist in a vise grip.

"Let go of me, Jimmy."

"Tell me, Anita," he insisted in a nasty tone. "Why am I

not supposed to talk about Miranda?"

Anita caught the malicious glint in his eye and realized fully that he must have heard from somewhere. When he had first brought up Miranda it was to bait Anita and make her hurt; that was just the kind of person Jimmy was.

"Bastard," she spit, wrenching her wrist free. She reached through a shimmering red curtain of rage to feel for the mace in the pocket of her frayed jean shorts. Good, it was still there. Just one more word, one more comment out of his sneering, ugly mouth...

"That's right," he told her. "I heard Miss High-and-Mighty got what she deserved. Guess the bitch should have practiced what she preached."

"*Callate!*" she screamed. "I'm warning you, Jimmy. Shut your mouth. *Cierre la boca.*"

Jimmy just laughed, a mean, ugly sound. That was enough for Anita. She whipped the can of mace out of her of pocket like an old western gun dueler, took aim, and shot its contents directly into his eyes. He screamed, his hands plucking at his eyes, and it was Anita's turn to laugh. He ran to the sink blindly and started splashing water frantically at his face.

"You'll never walk out for good on your own," he choked out, jumping around wildly and lunging for her.

"Who says I'm on my own, Jimmy?" Anita asked. She thought she could hear Miranda's throaty laughter join hers. "Isn't it funny? You gave me this mace and told me it was to keep me safe from all of the johns you sent me to. Lies! You wanted me to hurt them and steal their money. Instead I'll use it on you." She laughed harder, tried for his mean sound before she just let her natural but forgotten mirth take over. Then she turned serious.

"Jimmy, I'd like you to meet the new Anita. One that's officially done with this, with you. I feel like a new woman. I feel like celebrating. Maybe I'll celebrate by having a little cocktail. Then maybe, to cap off the evening. I'll find the biggest, meanest guy to come back here and move my stuff out for me. I'm done.

But I want you to know this, Jimmy: you will never hurt me again. If you do I will kill you, don't think I wouldn't do it. That's not a threat, Jimmy, it's a promise. And after I do I'll go out, have another cocktail, and howl at the moon. Believe it."

Anita threw back her head, laughed, and howled softly in Jimmy's direction. Before she shut the door on the apartment and his couch one last time, she whispered, "Believe it."

CHAPTER FORTY-NINE

The metal detector was silent as Shelby stepped through it. She waited patiently as an officer motioned her through, stopped her, and moved the wand up and down her body. The wand was silent too, with no telltale squealing sound to deem her unsafe. Lucky her, selected for random additional screening.

A minute later she pulled out her driver's license to show the front lobby officer, a solidly built woman with short hair that was brushed back from her face. The woman's alert eyes quickly scanned the inmate roster, then verified the information on the Notification to Visitor form Shelby had filled out. Shelby was escorted to the visiting room where Clint was waiting for her.

His lips tucked in and curled up in an almost sheepish smile when she sat down at one of the simple white tables. "First time inside a correctional facility?" he asked.

She noted that his healthy tan had faded some, making his intense brown eyes contrast more sharply with the paler skin. But his face was freshly scrubbed and shaved, his hair neatly combed back. Odd; he was sitting in prison but he appeared more young and innocent than she had ever seen him look. She wondered what he would look like when he emerged, whether he would retain this new, softer image or if he would have an even sharper, angrier edge than before.

"You know, in all the time I've known you, I don't think I've ever seen you smile," Shelby noted. "Now you're incarcerated and you're grinning."

"Funny thing, isn't it? Maybe it's 'cause I ended up in khaki instead of orange." He motioned to his prison-issued clothes. "Don't-pick-up-this-hitchhiker-beige looks good on me, doesn't it?"

"And joking. Self-deprecation looks good on you too. It's good to see you, Clint."

"So I didn't see any stories about my arrest and subsequent sentencing in *Atlanta Minute*," he said in an almost challenging tone.

"Nah, wasn't going to touch that one, Clint. I'd already stretched my reporter's limits and objectivity to bursting with Miranda's story."

She wouldn't have enjoyed writing about Jon Tillman pressing charges against Clint for aggravated assault and threatening him with a firearm. She would, however, have loved to do the story about Jon Tillman being convicted for illegal possession and sale of heroin and other narcotics. Jon's friendly neighborhood drug dealer persona hadn't gone over well with the undercover DEA officer he had attempted to sell drugs to. The bust at 404, ten arrests in all, was considered a fairly significant one by the city.

"One of the things I pictured that night with Jon was you writing about the whole thing, listening to that damn iPod of yours while you pounded out a story on your computer. I've been wanting to know ever since then…what the hell do you listen to when you're working on a story?" Clint asked.

Shelby cocked her head to one side and smiled thoughtfully. "Otis Redding, some country, the Beatles. Funny thing to wonder at a time like that," she pointed out.

"But I did. Maybe that's why I'm smiling. I'm around to ask you and find out the answer. That night I had made up my mind not to be. Probably a little hard to understand."

"Not hard to understand at all. You know I'd go in and talk to Miranda and I told her what I'll tell you now: I found out what hopelessness feels like. I thought about checking out. Having come close to that makes me appreciate the stupid little things. The other day I was grocery shopping and just grinning like an idiot in the frozen section when I was grabbing some Hot

Pockets. Hot pockets in the frozen section. The fact I was still around to notice something stupid and funny in the everyday, at least to me, well, it felt..."

"Yeah, I guess you do get it." Clint grabbed the left leg of his pants and started twisting at the material. "Funny, I never got that hopeless vibe from you. Even when you told me you knew what it was like to love someone you couldn't have a future with."

"Well, let's just say I still have my days but I'm working on getting a life as previously advised." Shelby smiled, then sighed. Both of them had been on the verge of self-destruct because they had known the pain and confusion of finding the centers of their world vanished. She had lived for Joe and he for Miranda, and they had walked around not knowing what to do after the two were gone.

"Clint, it's a childish thing for me to say, and God knows it's probably been said more times than a person could count in this room, but it's not fair," Shelby protested weakly. "You were never capable of taking anybody's life. They can't know that, but I do. You wouldn't have when you spent all of those months trying to fix things, save someone. That's why you called me. You weren't going to do it. You shouldn't be here."

"Yeah, I should," he told her matter-of-factly. "You were a little off the mark about something when you told Jon there was a difference between hurting and crazy. Maybe a little, but hurting as bad as I was can make a person crazy, and dangerous. I was an inch away from killing him and myself, and I still go back and forth about the exact thing that pulled me back. Maybe it was Miranda whispering in my ear, maybe it was cowardice or even a little bit of courage. It was you and even a little bit of crazy Eileen's telling me she forgave me. Ought to be clearer about what pulled me back before I'm unleashed on the public again. Got three years to figure it out."

He smiled his crooked smile again, then it faded. "I would have used again, too. It was only a matter of time. I wanted to, just like Miranda did, after we lost the baby. And when she died…"

"But you didn't," Shelby cut in. "You'd been tested in the worst way you could have, Clint. Twice. Losing your son and then losing Miranda. After all of that, you still didn't."

Shelby thought about the night in the café with Shane McCurty, how he'd shared the same thought with her. *Hurting can make you crazy.* She felt an almost physical blow, regret slamming into her chest. She'd realized then, when she'd looked into Shane's face and read the story about his brother's overdose, how alone and hurt could lead to this. The one teasing, cajoling voice that could have stopped Clint had been silenced, and there hadn't been another to take its place. She'd been too late in realizing that.

"Well I didn't go that far but I sure screwed things up royally, didn't I? Maybe I should have hired Graham Barrett to represent me. Probably would've argued extreme emotional distress or something," Clint said with humor. "Extreme emotional distress is exactly why I need to be in here."

"Don't suppose you have any idea what you'll do when you get out? Three years to figure it out, right? You'd make a great drug counselor."

"God, you and Miranda. She was so cynical in some ways but she still always wanted a Lifetime Movie ending to things. Wouldn't that be perfect, irony and redemption to wrap the whole thing up?" His face clouded over, as if his reality was dawning on him again.

"Shelby, I'm locked up. I've got three solid years to spend in here with nothing to do except read and think. That's one thousand and ninety-five days. My world's been chopped down to an eight by eight cell. Can't breathe when I think about it. And you want to cue the music at the end. 'After Clint was released…' I don't even know how I'm gonna make it through tomorrow. Jesus. What, are you picturing crying in therapy, having a 'breakthrough' and deciding that's how I want to spend the rest of my life after I'm out?"

"I still want you to consider it, Lifetime Movie or not.

A thousand and ninety five days gives you plenty of time to change your mind," Shelby persisted with a wan smile.

"I suppose I should thank you for stopping me," Clint conceded.

"Don't mention it."

She stood up and hugged Clint briefly, not too long or too fervently, under the watchful eye of the officers assigned to the visiting room. She was pleased when she felt the slight pressure of his arm around her, awkwardly returning the embrace. They broke contact just as one of the officers was getting ready to tell them touching wasn't allowed.

When she left she took care not to watch as he was escorted out of the room. She didn't want to see a slow shuffle instead of the determined, quick stride she was used to watching as he walked away. She hoped he could find something else to live for, a new sense of purpose besides the girl he would never stop missing.

*   *   *

Shelby opened Miranda's last diary later that night and skimmed the familiar words with admiration and sadness. She would return it to the Linns soon; it belonged to them, and she had all but memorized its contents anyway. She could almost feel some of the girl's energy vibrating beneath her fingers as she turned the pages to one of her favorite entries. It was the conviction behind the words, almost leaping off of the page, that struck her. Just a physical object left behind, but surely something of the girl's essence remained.

So, I've made a mess of things, and I suppose I should be ashamed of the way I treated those I loved. Most of the time I am, and that shame and worry consumes me. I can feel the regret constantly gnawing at me, and yet I am happy that I can regret. Too often I said and did the wrong thing, but maybe a little regret isn't uncalled for. It means you've learned something, at least. Taken a lesson away. If you're still around and have reflected on the situation enough to feel

shitty about it then that means you've still got a chance to change it,
or at the very least do better for yourself the next time.

Only twenty, but she had never gotten her next time. Shelby could sense Miranda Linn almost as intensely as she could Joe each time she read his goodbye note, in her ear, giving her unspoken directives the same way Joe had. There were lessons to be learned in the reading. She realized now that the most important one was to stop poring over scraps of paper and diaries rather than putting their simple wisdom to use. She'd been sidestepping Cole for weeks. It was time to stop.

Shelby left her apartment in a hurry, smiling at the propped-open door to Mona's apartment. "I hope I have something good to tell you when I get back," she called. The little woman would be waiting patiently with two cups of tea whenever she returned, hungry for details about Cole and whatever was on the menu for their next cooking lesson. She could already smell something unrecognizable emanating from behind the door, the beginnings of a dish they would finish making later.

"Don't come back til you have something real good. You bear in mind it takes a lot to impress old Mona. You go and get him, Shelby Norris," the old woman called back, then let out her trademark cackle.

Shelby let the blessed sound spur her on as she impatiently jabbed the "down" button on the elevator. Everything from the turn of the key in the ignition to the short drive to the medical center seemed to happen in frustrating slow motion. When she finally reached the hospital Shelby sprinted toward the emergency ward.

"I need," she gasped to the receptionist at the front desk, "to speak with Dr. Cole Michaels." She probably looked like a full-blown emergency case.

She'd become an expert in the past few months at charging ahead and doing things that seemed right until she was actually in the middle of doing them. At the moment she missed the days of approaching these situations like one of her stories, taking time to read and re-read the words in her head before she put it to bed. First drafts were crap and ninety-nine percent of writing a story was rewriting it before the final version went to print. But that life theory hadn't worked out for her so well.

"Miss, are you alright?" the receptionist asked calmly, but with a raised eyebrow. She looked prepared to hand her a patient intake form, probably suspecting shortness of breath was the reason for the visit.

"I'm fine, thanks. But could you please page Dr. Michaels immediately?"

The receptionist didn't question her any further. Shelby was mortified when the woman called Cole's name over the intercom in a silky, unruffled tone. There was no time to collect herself before Cole materialized at the front desk, his demeanor all business. When he spotted her his expression changed to one of concern. "Shelby, what are you doing here? Is everything okay?"

"Is this an emergency, dear?" the receptionist asked coyly.

"Marta!" Cole admonished the woman, embarrassed.

Shelby smiled, feeling the weight lift for a moment. Then she felt her brain do a slow rewind of the past few months and felt it return.

"I've been thinking about Miranda, and about you," she started uncertainly. "It sounds strange, but she was better to me than some friends I've had for years. She taught me things. In a way losing her has been like..."

She didn't finish the sentence, didn't need to. She was embarrassed when she felt her eyes start to burn and leak.

Cole said nothing, opted instead to be a steady silent weight she leaned against him. She took the tissue the receptionist handed her from behind the desk.

Now that she was here she was going to plow ahead, no matter what. "Two very wise people have been telling me for months to stop letting fear eat up precious time. They made mistakes but still did their best not to waste their minutes; unfortunately their time ran out. Joe did what he could to make sure mine didn't. I've been doing him, and Miranda, an injustice. I haven't taken care of myself in the past, Cole," she said with a sigh. "You know that better than most. I may pay for that later. No telling what I'm going to have to deal with in the future, and I'll have no one to blame but myself and my own carelessness. I'm not sure I'm a good bet."

"There are no guarantees for anyone, Shelby. You know that better than most. You're not time-stamped any more than the rest of us. Where did you get the idea you've got no future?"

"Maybe we should talk later," Shelby told him, suddenly feeling light but cognizant of the activity around her. A sense of responsibility hovered in the air. "Don't you get off soon? I'll wait for you. Seems like I'm making a habit of the whole snap decision thing. I didn't even stop to think. I could have waited just a few minutes more…" She trailed off and glanced around at the bustle of activity around her. Now she was professing her budding feelings in the middle of busy emergency wards?

She backed up and was almost ready to make a full retreat when Cole grabbed her wrist. "I think your snap decisions have turned out to be your best ones," Cole assured her, lowering her into a dip. His lips brushed hers lightly at first, then settled into the kiss firmly.

When Shelby's arms found their way around Cole's neck, the receptionist clapped her hands together. A gruff-looking man who had just arrived in the waiting area with a huge gash on his arm hooted his approval. "This is just like an episode of Grey's Anatomy!" he told his wife, who did not look amused at the display.

"Um," Shelby muttered as she collected herself, "I'll let you get back to work. I think our…talk has helped me sort out my latest… kerfuffle."

"I'm glad." Cole's melted-butter smile was in full effect now, but he hurried back to finish out the rest of his shift. Shelby bought a coffee from the hot drink dispenser and settled in. The man who had witnessed the moment between her and Cole had already been ushered back to a room for stitches from a doctor and more reprimands from his wife for being careless.

She sat among the rest of the waiting: a mother and a stoic little boy with badly scraped knees and arms, hopefully just experiencing the downside of an adventuresome spirit; an elderly woman whose breathing was ragged, her fingers laced with an old man's who wore a porkpie hat. The old man's eyes fixed on his wife's every breath, determined to stop his world from vanishing by keeping a watchful eye. Interestingly enough, it was he who breathed with the help of a portable oxygen tank. And finally, a lone man, crying softly in the far corner of the room. He held a forgotten, shredded tissue in his hand as he wiped his eyes on his shirtsleeve. Had he lost someone? Would he soon?

Shelby wondered at their stories, in no hurry. Cole had done his share of waiting on her, and she was happy to return the favor.

CHAPTER FIFTY

It was time for another party. The birthday party for Miranda should have been happy but wasn't. This party was something that was supposed to be sad but wouldn't be.

Shelby and Cole walked into the Atlanta History Center and caught up with Jim and Eileen. The place was awash in a sea of bright colors and smiling, painted skeletons. Sugar skulls smiled up from cookies and people sampled bread fashioned into crosses and bones. *Pan de muertos*, the bread of the dead. There was something eerily beautiful about the macabre but almost silly smiling faces of death all around the place. Here death was not something to be feared but accepted as the natural order of things.

El Dia De Los Muertos, the Day of the Dead, was a Mexican tradition but one readily accepted by the Linns as the proper way to honor their daughter. On October 31st the spirits of babies and children who had died, *angelitos*, would arrive at midnight to spend the day with their families. It was adults' turn the following day.

It was November 1 and surely Miranda would approve and happily return to a place like this, with color and music all around. A band was playing. No sad, plaintive hymns of longing here but instead triumphant notes that climbed above the shockingly bright skirts that flew and twisted as their owners danced traditional Mexican dances.

"Now this is a party," Eileen said with quiet approval as she took in the music, dancing, and cartoonish skeletons. Shelby admired the almost humorous grins on the skulls' faces and the flowers that decorated them. *See, this isn't scary*, they seemed to say. *We are your loved ones and we are fine. Live, because we're still living as long as you are. Celebrate and we will help you.*

All around elaborate altars were constructed to honor the dead. Flowers and other personal decorations were arranged around huge portraits of the departed. One display's picture was draped with a homemade ribbon that read *Tia Maria*. Someone's Aunt Maria looked like she had been a very cheerful woman in life, and the woman's round face reminded Shelby of Mona. *Tia Maria* was caught mid-chuckle in the portrait.

There were smiling faces and conversation as the relatives of the dead kept vigil, patiently waiting for the spirits of their loved ones to return. Clearly you had only to stop and ask and each vigil-keeper would be happy to share the story of their dead for as long as you might care to listen. The altars and the happy atmosphere made Shelby want to.

Not all of those who kept vigil were actual relatives. They stopped at a display with a picture of a beautiful, smiling girl. Red and white flowers around the altar were fashioned into the word "sister" but the face of the person beside it was very unlike the girl's. The vigil-keeper's face was much darker and her hair was black and straight in contrast to the wild blond hair in the portrait. Books and a dictionary were arranged by the photo, and a plate was piled high with oversized blueberry muffins. A Lord's Prayer necklace was draped over the portrait.

"Shelby and Cole, this is Anita Velasquez, a dear friend of Miranda's," Eileen said in introduction.

"Pleased to meet you," Anita told them, grabbing each of their hands simultaneously in a firm grip. "You were also a friend of Miranda's?" she asked Shelby curiously.

"Yes," Shelby said thoughtfully. "I was." She placed the journals of Miranda's to the right of the muffins, where they seemed to belong. The goodbye note Joe had written Shelby was folded and placed in the back. She knew Eileen would understand why it was there.

"You did a beautiful job with the display, Anita," Eileen told the woman. "I don't think I could have captured her essence better."

"One last addition, if you don't mind," Jim told Anita. He dug into his pocket, pulled out some pieces of Werther's, and dropped them in a random trail around the portrait and muffins. The candy wrappers punctuated the other bursts of color like gold coins and rounded out the memorial they wouldn't have thought was incomplete before then.

"You're great with color," Shelby complimented Anita honestly. "The display's incredible. One part understanding of the culture and one part talent, I'm sure."

"Little bit both," Anita agreed with a wide smile, her accent beautifully clipping off the words.

"This is definitely how you should spend your time, Anita," Jim told her, easily stepping into the role of lecturing father. "Using your creative talents…"

"Jim, just give the girl a compliment and leave it at that. It doesn't have to turn into a sermon about realizing her potential," Eileen told him, with no bite behind the words. Everyone in the group smiled.

"Is okay, Miss Linn. Girls like me need a *papa segundo*. Maybe even a third father to keep me in line. As a matter of fact I been talking to some of the people who organize the events here. They say maybe they could use me part-time."

The woman exuded good humor and cheer, something Shelby sensed was slowly being restored to her. Each time she made a joke a puzzled, slightly pleased look would spread across her face, as if to say, *I can't believe I still know how to do this. Just like riding a bike.*

Jim sent Eileen a comically exaggerated smirk and everyone laughed. When they finally moved away from the display to look at the other altars Eileen tipped her head towards Anita and announced, "That is part of my daughter's legacy."

Shelby started to answer Eileen when she heard the familiar voice behind her. "Are you writing you a story or just getting you some culture, re-por-ter?"

Shelby spun around, her smile widening. There was

Ernie, flanked by Lucinda, Bethie and Terrence. "Ernie! What are you doing here?" she exclaimed, and hastily made a round of introductions.

"I told you, we got culture. We also got neighbors in the hood. Miss Anita already knows us, she invited us down here."

Shelby smiled at this, then turned her attention to the children. "Have you caught a ride with those aliens yet?"

"We're still trying, miss," Bethie informed her.

"You be sure to send me a postcard from space when you get your ride, okay?"

"What kinda postcards they got in space?" Terrence wondered aloud.

"Oh, Lord," Lucinda sighed, and shook her head. She was clearly foreseeing months of "postcards from space" as a major topic of conversation at the dinner table.

"Don't know where we're going to yet, re-por-ter. We been talkin' about it, but ain't decided. Probably at least stay in Atlanta, though. That's about all I got to give you for your follow-up," Ernie said.

"I'll be by to check on you soon, Robin in the Hood. Lucinda, nice seeing you again. Kids, you make sure that he behaves," Shelby instructed sternly. Bethie and Terrence giggled. She wondered about the "we" in Ernie's statement, the way his hand had rested on Lucinda's shoulder when he talked about their plans. She didn't know if this was an old habit or a new one and stared curiously as they walked away with the children.

After some more sensory overload and a disastrous attempt by Cole to learn the steps to one of the traditional dances, Shelby told the Linns reluctantly, "Sorry to beg out. One of the best parties I've been to, but I've got to go. I haven't even started to pack."

"And where's our intrepid reporter going?" Eileen wanted to know.

"Home," Shelby told her.

CHAPTER FIFTY-ONE

Flight 1613, direct from Atlanta, touched down at Indianapolis International Airport on time. Shelby's hands had clenched during the musical ding of the seat belt sign coming on and were clenched still on the drive to Layton in the rental car. When she finally drove past the vibrant yellow and white Gingerbread Victorian, she thought about how well she knew the house, how she could easily walk through blindfolded. But then again, not these days. She'd be bumping into somebody else's furniture.

She smiled as she watched the young couple who had bought the house lazily pushing the front porch swing back and forth with their feet. They looked for all of the world like a Rockwell painting, the woman in a dress with her head on the man's shoulder. They were eating dinner on the porch, savoring the unseasonably warm November day. The requisite gray mutt lay to the side, fixated on whatever was on the man's plate, sad dog eyes uplifted. She could picture the next whimsical scene, the dog in mid-gallop with the food half in, half-out of his mouth, looking over his shoulder as his angry owner chased after him. There were some large blue urns on either side of the porch now; those were nice. Looked like they were taking care of the lawn.

She wondered if the couple had read her letter carefully detailing every plant and tree on the property, its proper care and feeding, and thought it strange. She had even told them what kind of fertilizer she used. Had they noticed it too the first time they walked in the house, the solid, satisfying *thunk* of the door when it closed behind them? Had it made them feel safe? Did they look up at the beams in the living room ceiling, the tin in the dining room, and appreciate Joe's handiwork? Shelby wondered if they would have children someday who would play safely behind the fence Joe had put up in the backyard.

She cruised past the little brick building next and thought about Leo and Jonah raising their Dixie cups to her. The office was closed up tight now. It was a Friday; this week's issue would be out tomorrow. Jonah was probably running the template up to the printer's right now, in a rush to get it there before they closed for the day.

In her first few weeks at *Atlanta Minute* she had felt like she was drowning and knew nothing about being a reporter, but Leo had taught her the most important skill: how to talk to people and really listen to what they were saying. She could hear his mantra in her head: *Every story is a human interest story.* Miranda had taught her that too.

Shelby was suddenly impatient as she turned onto Millstead.

When she pulled up to the green and white house with the messy front porch, Shelby's eager smile widened. The urns were still there but no longer nicely positioned. They were shoved off to the side and Shelby doubted any flowers had ever made it inside them. "Atta girl, Trish," she chuckled softly. "You're no good to anybody else if you can't be you." She bounded up the steps and was instantly engulfed in Trish's waiting arms.

"Trish, I'm turning blue..." Shelby gasped, holding on just as tight. Neither woman was willing to let go.

"You're too damn skinny," Trish sniffled. "You better hit the Diner for a fish plate tonight."

Shelby rolled her eyes. "Trish, the baby. Now. I can't wait any longer!" When they made their way inside, the messy theme continued. Boxes of pampers and baby wipes littered the room.

As if on cue, Adam made his way down the stairs. The sweats and stained T-shirt he wore were a far cry to the pressed jeans he'd had on the last time she'd seen him. His socks had holes in them; he was sporting at least three days' growth on his face and carrying a moving yellow bundle. Fatigued, but a satisfied kind of tired.

"This is more like it!" Shelby crowed happily, taking in the chaotic scene with pleasure.

"So we thought we had to have a perfect home to be good parents. We clearly got over that," Trish answered with a shrug.

"Shelby, meet Damon Joseph Norris," Adam said formally, his voice tinged with pride. "Came a little early but he's doing great. He was ready even if we weren't just yet."

Shelby stared in wonder as Adam handed her the bundle. "Lord, he's all hair and eyes," she laughed, stroking the dark tufts that were sprouting out of the baby's head in every direction. The electric pools of green calmly staring up at her were pure Norris, identical to Adam's and Joe's. He seemed to study her with the same intent wonder. His tiny fists and legs kept in constant motion as if he was rehearsing a silent cheer.

Shelby left three hours later. She wanted to stay in the messy house and thread her fingers through Damon's crazy hair forever, but there was another stop to make.

As she made her way down the blessedly dusty steps she thought about the thing that was developing between herself and Cole, the outline and shape of it still fuzzy and undefined. To allow herself to tell Trish and Adam about it and receive their silent blessing had helped fill in the edges. She'd also told them, "There's something in my Mom's basement for you. Rock Damon in it and when he gets older, tell him about his Uncle."

A few minutes later Shelby knelt at the grave that read, "*Joe Norris, 1972-2009. Died Loved, Died Famous.*" Just the kind of vague, irreverent inside joke Joe would have appreciated.

"You wouldn't believe the miles I put on the Toyota going back and forth to Atlanta, Joe," she said with a soft chuckle. "Nuts, when I could have just flown! But that's not the way it was supposed to happen, was it? You wouldn't believe a lot about my life now. But then again, I think you would. You've been with me all this time, nudging me along. I never could have done it without your help, but I never would have had to do it in the first place if it hadn't been for you. Strange how that works." She stopped to run her fingers along the marigolds she'd planted.

"I just read a book by a doctor. He talks about something called a compensatory pause. It's like a blip in the normal rhythm of the heart, as quick as the blink of an eye. It gives the heart a rest before the next beat. After the heart gets its rest it returns to the normal rhythm. You woke up my life while you were here, and you saved me from the same tired rhythm. At the same time you made it possible for me to go on to the next beat. You were my compensatory pause, Joe."

She lingered a few minutes more, considering the man who had, in a way, destroyed her life. But not without giving her the tools to build a new one.

The grass was freshly mown and the sinking sun was painting orange across the sky when she walked out of the cemetery. There was silence where a few weeks before locusts had taken up a loud, pervasive chant. Autumn had died. High schoolers who had made the cut to be a Layton Tiger would be nervously gearing up for their playoff game. They had a real shot this year after sweating through coach Dean's miserable two-a-days all summer. The Friday night dinner crowd would be trickling into the Diner for Trish's famous fish and slaw, the clink of the heavy, solid plates and the good-natured gossip never-changing. The smoke and insults would billow up from around the table in the back that was set up for the Friday night game of Texas Hold 'Em. The fliers stuck in the Diner's window would be different, advertising new upcoming festivals and school events.

There was new life, too. Trish would no doubt regularly show the baby off at the Diner, his car seat perched on top of one of the bright red tables so people could fuss and comment about how much he was growing. It was easy to flash forward to a child of six, with those shocking green eyes, importantly handing out menus to the diner's patrons.

After dinner she would make her way back to her mother's house. She might even do a few laps up and down the stairs--in the middle. Her Mom would return home the day after tomorrow. She was in the middle of the Atlantic at the moment, cruising the Caribbean--with Leo. Apparently the two had started reaching out to each other after Joe's death in grief and worry about Shelby. Satisfying, if a little strange, to think about her Mom and Leo as an item. As long as she didn't have to picture Leo sunning himself in floral swim trunks she could cope. After thirteen years alone, because of her son-in-law's death, Elise was discovering someone she had known for years. Her mother's discovery of Leo reminded Shelby of how Miranda had latched on to the dark side of beautiful places like Stone Mountain.

In return trips to the park Shelby had memorized the now-familiar plaque that had disturbed Miranda, the one that talked about the Klan's past at the mountain: "A Dark Side Of Our History."   But now Shelby preferred instead to notice the good things that could be born of grief and the unwanted.

She felt a sad indignation at the thought of the day-to-day here taking place without her. But there was another life waiting, or, Mona would correct, a different stage of the same one: Fighting the crowds at the Varsity after a Yellow Jackets game; trading insults with a domineering editor who had saved her life; A Robin in The Hood and his charges to check up on; a redecorating job to do on her apartment after a return visit to call-me-Gil for some lamps. Cole, most of all.

There was also another gravestone to visit. She knew this one would read, "*Miranda Linn, 1989-2009. A New England autumn in a hot Georgia summer, and beloved daughter and girlfriend who never walked on the left side of the stairs.*"

The Linns had asked Shelby to write an epitaph for their daughter's headstone, and Clint had agreed. Eileen had told her it seemed like the right thing to do since Shelby owed her life in part to Miranda. She was part of the girl's legacy and Joe's too.

Shelby had had no trouble deciding what to write. She meant for the carvings on the two stones to be understood only by those who knew and loved them best. It was the least she could do for these dead who had woken up the living.

LaVergne, TN USA
20 October 2010
201578LV00002B/5/P